THE NINETIES

The Nineties

Vinyl Tiger 2nd Edition

DAVE DI VITO

DDV

Disclaimer: The material in this book is for mature audiences only and contains graphic content.

It is intended only for those aged 18 and older.

The Nineties: Vinyl Tiger Second Edition is the updated version of *Vinyl Tiger,* originally published in 2015.

| 1 |

MEXICO CITY

Alex spent much of the spring of 1989 in a purgatory of his own making, unable to pinpoint why. His "comeback" album, *Without You I'm Nothing,* was a bona fide smash. Its second single, *Circumstances Unknown,* – one of his personal favourites – was now climbing the charts, and earning him yet more accolades. He'd even had a good time filming the video for it with Andres in Houston, in a range of locations around the downtown area.

Alex's modern "gypsy" look in the clip was even inspiring copycats, right down to the new accessory he'd added: a Star of David. It hadn't been intended as a religious or political statement, but once the video aired, stories of Alex's apparent conversion to Judaism began appearing in the media. Article after article quoted 'close sources' who claimed Alekzandr had long been in crisis, and that he had embraced the Jewish faith after meeting a charismatic rabbi.

Truth be told, the pendant was Ben's. It was among the trinkets in Ben's personal effects and Alex had begun wearing it in tribute without even thinking. Alex's new publicist, Kathy, was delighted by all the fuss. She was thankful that her star client was so hot, he was able to set tongues wagging by literally doing nothing.

But Alex *was* having a crisis. He had his friends, his wealth and a career that was once again soaring, but something seemed to be overshadowing it all.

He couldn't shake the feeling he was at a crossroads where so much of what had once fascinated or inspired him now seemed trivial. And though the talk of Judaism was unfounded, the reality was Alex *was* spending a lot of his free time looking into faith. He felt horribly fashionable for doing so, but after performing at a Tibetan benefit (his latest *cause célèbre*) he quietly began visiting a brownstone in Harlem, where, working with a monk he'd met at the benefit, he began a guided study of Buddhism.

It was only when working with Kathy and Kōji to promote the album that Alex noticed the intense glare of the press interest. Beyond their speculation about his faith, his HIV status and his love life, some in the media had also taken to referring to Alex as a *pop diva,* pitting him against the day's top female pop-stars.

Quips about how he, Paula Abdul and Janet Jackson stayed up all night, concocting ways to outfox each other with punchy dance moves and hot remixes, became a recurrent punchline on late night television.

Alex *knew* what the hosts were getting at. But he was confident no one in the mainstream media had the courage to openly discuss his sexual orientation. Doing so would undermine the unspoken agreement the entertainment press had with A list stars.

But the trashier news rags had their own rules of engagement. As *Circumstances Unknown* hit the top ten, some rent boys in New York and LA began making claims they'd been dating Alex, the tabloids swiftly running with the accusations.

"Half my luck," Alex muttered as Kathy's driver pulled up to the curb. Alex was standing at the newsstand near his apartment, perplexed to see it covered with images of his face and the headlines suggesting he had a thing for toy– boys. In the back of the town car, Kathy felt it necessary to remind him the tabloids were just part of the game, but Alex never found their claims as offensive as other, more litigious male stars of the time did. He couldn't bring himself to publicly comment on their accusations, knowing it would be disingenuous to deny his sexual orientation. If anything, the gay slurs and the press' weaponization of his sexuality only strengthened Alex's commitment to the GLBT cause.

In 1989 he hosted a number of benefits to raise money for GLBT charities in the tristate area and LA, and, appeared in two safe sex public service announcements. He was happy to lend his name and celebrity to all kinds of causes; to various environmental agencies, the UN; even to a gun control group in the US. But Ben's loss, above all, turned Alex into a warrior for the HIV/ AIDS cause.

It wasn't just Ben that haunted him. Alex's newfound activism was his way of shaking things up and doing something new. *There had to be more to fame than just success for the sake of it.* Alex felt it was time to use his voice and to take some chances.

To that end, he accepted roles in a range of movies, including the film that Max's company was filming in New York.

In between the shoots, he and Andres headed over to Monterrey with a small crew to film a video for his album's title track.

The heat was positively stifling, made worse by long hours under the lights and the scorching sun on location. Not even his hotel room offered him respite, its air conditioning unit just another victim of the lethargy of summer's peak.

Filming in Mexico did have its advantages though.

On his first day on set, Alex spotted a handsome production assistant who captured his attention. The guy was of a similar height and build. He was dark haired with a strong forehead and a chiselled jawline. When Alex got closer, he noticed the dimples and the grey eyes. Watching him throughout the day yielded other surprises; glimpses of tattoos, a touch of body hair under a white V–neck, and beautifully smooth skin which ran a range of russet tones depending on how the sun hit it.

But as a lowly assistant, the guy seemed so busy obliging his colleagues that Alex didn't have the heart to single him out or risk getting him into trouble with Andres.

The next day, filming a sequence on a steep road with astonishing views of the city and the Cerro de la Silla mountain range, Alex felt the heat. The assistant appeared shortly after eleven, explaining he'd been tasked with keeping Alex hydrated and shaded between takes.

"Adoro su canción,' the assistant said during a break, looking Alex in the eye.

Alex now knew what he sounded like and added the lovely timbre of the guy's voice to his lust list.

"Oh really? Thanks. I liked it too before I heard it for the fiftieth time today. ¿Cómo te llamas?" Alex asked, fanning himself with a piece of paper.

"Diego," the assistant replied, handing Alex a flask, which Alex accepted gratefully.

"Gracias Diego," Alex said, gulping down the cold water and handing the empty flask back. Diego put it away and then opened up an umbrella, enjoining Alex to stand under it. *Kōji was never anywhere to be found when it came to the heat.*

"So, you know some Spanish?" Diego noted, playfully nudging Alex in the rib with his elbow.

"Yeah," Alex said, "but if we go out for dinner tonight you could teach me something more useful."

"I don't know how appropriate that would be. You're the boss."

"Well, technically," Alex began, pointing to Andres. "He's the boss. I'm just the talent. So that means *we*," he added, conspiratorially, "are just colleagues. And free to see each other."

Over dinner, the conversation swung between English and Spanish, Alex learning that Diego was a film maker.

Diego explained he made documentaries, but took on any film-related work in between projects. He'd driven the almost twelve hours from Mexico City at a moment's notice, despite the pittance Andres' production team offered him and the fact he'd have to drive back home the minute the shoot wrapped.

"You can't stay? Not even an extra day?" Alex asked.

"I can't. I want to spend time relaxing before I go back to work. I'm working on a *telenovela* for the next few weeks. I need the money. Anyway, it's not such a bad job. I've worked with them before. I do a bit of field producing for them. I take care of some of the on– location segments and scenes."

"Sounds like fun," Alex said.

"It is actually," Diego replied. "It's a bit like doing music videos. Everything has to be done quickly, there's no time to mess around. It's good pressure to work under. And the soap isn't that junky. The writers are very topical… they're not afraid to talk about corruption or politics."

Staring at Diego, Alex sipped his vodka sour and lit a cigarette, unable to stop looking.

"Listen, I know why we're here," Diego said. "But I just came out of a relationship. A long one. Not an easy one either," he added, looking in Alex's direction but focusing elsewhere. "I don't think being someone else's good time is part of my plans right now."

Alex smiled. Diego's chutzpah was intoxicating. "That's mighty presumptuous of you."

"Sobre aviso no hay engaño," Diego said, smiling ruefully.

"Ah, like, *'don't say I haven't warned you?'*" Alex asked, nodding as he contemplated Diego's response. "Well, we're just having dinner. No need to jump to any conclusions."

Diego smiled again. "Famous last words."

By the time they'd left the restaurant a small crowd had formed outside. There were a couple dozen fans who were snapping away, the flashes on their long, horizontal 110 cameras flickering. The valet had brought Diego's car around for them, while two of the restaurant's security guards tried in vain to shepherd the fans away.

Once they managed to get into the car, Alex apologized.

Diego laughed. "You're in Mexico. You haven't seen anything yet. Lock your door."

Diego expertly steered the car down the sloping driveway through the swarm of fans, many still snapping away. When he finally reached the curb, he stopped for oncoming traffic. The mob descended onto the car again, screaming Alex's name and using their combined muscle to shake the car up and down. The impression Alex had that his fans were harmless evaporated. As the shaking got rougher, and the fans' screams louder, a surge of panic surged through Alex.

"Don't worry," Diego said calmly, briefly touching Alex's thigh.

Diego lurched the car forward to give the fans a bit of a shock, and when a few dispersed, he lightly applied the accelerator, pushing the car to the road's edge. The restaurant security finally intervened and waved Diego into the traffic. And with that, they were off.

Despite Diego's reluctance, they spent the night together in Alex's hotel room.

Alex struggled to get to sleep that night, his mind pulsating while Diego slept beside him. In the elevator on the way up, Diego had made it clear that sex wasn't on the cards, landing a light rebuttal to Alex's come- ons. But the following morning, waking up to Diego gave Alex a euphoria, reminding him of a type of intimacy he hadn't experienced in months.

On his next break between films, Alex headed straight to Mexico City. Putting his bags down, he surveyed the room before him, pleasantly surprised.

Diego's apartment was in the Roma Norte district, and when Diego disappeared down its corridor, Alex took it upon himself to have a look around. The apartment seemed like it had once been part of a grander space but had been subdivided in a way that created strange nooks. The original owners had however, annexed the terrace, it hemmed in by stuccoed white walls and lattice brickwork. Although it was a strangely laid out apartment, it was also clear that Diego had taken great care of it. The curved walls were a cool white and adorned with interesting images and fabrics, while the grey tint of the floorboards added an extra design touch to the place.

Though the kitchen was tiny, with a table that could only accommodate three at a push, it opened up onto the terrace which overlooked the street.

But it was the living room that Alex liked most. It was full of fifties styled furniture, artwork, and knickknacks. They all seemed to be considered, linked by colour or texture or by recurring motifs, no doubt acquired and curated from vintage stores and flea markets.

"I bought it last year," Diego called out from the laundry as Alex fingered a small black wooden statue of a bird, using it to try and get a clearer idea about its owner. "It was one of the lucky buildings that wasn't damaged by the earthquake."

"Earthquake?" Alex asked. "Right. The one from a couple of years' back?"

"Yes. I was away working at the time. But, yes, this is mine now. The bank's mostly, but mine, if you know what I mean," Diego added, stepping into the living room.

"I wasn't born rich you know," Alex said. "I haven't always had money."

"Sorry, that was stupid of me," Diego said, smiling. "Here, give me your bags, I'll put them away for you."

After a coffee in the kitchen, they ventured out for a walk to the local *mercado* to pick up some supplies. Diego picked up what Alex thought was enough food to feed a small army.

"There's a few more things I need to get around the corner from here, but you should keep an eye out for pickpockets," Diego explained. "Do you want to give me some of those bags?"

"No," Alex said, rolling his eyes. "Listen, I've seen and done it all. You don't have to worry about me. I know how to handle myself," he said, immediately regretting how sharply his reply landed.

Diego looked at him. "I'm sorry, I'm just feeling protective, maybe? I don't want you to have a bad experience."

Alex smiled. "That's sweet. And completely unnecessary. Unless the press finds out I'm here and then, well, it's all over."

***

They would go down as one of the biggest VMAs in MTV's history, with a stellar line up of talent.

Alex had been nominated for four awards and was due to perform *Without You I'm Nothing* live.

Backstage, he felt nervous. He mingled with the household names, some of them music's biggest and most controversial stars. Coming up in the early eighties he hadn't spent a lot of time playing the social game with his peers. The only time he saw many of them was at awards ceremonies or at promotional events. Things had changed when *Felicidad* went global, even if Alex had always felt like something of an imposter when surrounded by other A listers.

But at the VMAs, as he joked and drank with the other members of pop royalty, friends and acquaintances alike, he felt anxious. Not for himself, but for Diego. And to that end, he caught himself constantly checking that his *plus one* was okay, that Diego had everything he needed, and that Kōji was on hand to keep an eye on Diego when Alex was occupied.

Diego for his part wasn't star struck. It was true that some of his favourite bands were in attendance: The Cure, Guns N' Roses, even Def Leppard, and that waves of fandom momentarily overcame him. But he'd been part of the Mexican entertainment industry long enough to understand how the game was played, and by extension, how to deal with other creatives. He watched from the side of the stage as Alex began performing, before ducking out into the audience with Kōji for the last few minutes of the song. Being part of the audience as they sang along to the song that had brought Alex into his world gave Diego a sense of ownership over the moment.

For two months Alex and Diego spent as much time together as their commitments allowed, dividing their time between New York and Mexico City. But soon enough, Alex's management team insisted Alex head out on the road for a live tour to further promote the album. Alex capitulated, only agreeing to a mini tour with a handful of shows in the UK, Australia and Asia.

Alex insisted on a back to basics approach. A show without dancers or video backdrops that focused on the new material and aimed for intimacy. The lack of theatrics was welcomed by critics, and the final sold out dates in Osaka were even filmed for a home video release. Though not the financial boon his label could have expected from a full– scale tour, it nonetheless stoked album sales, which were now hovering around ten million.

At the end of the tour, Alex rang in Christmas and the new year in Mexico City along with Diego's friends. Diego's sister Yolanda and her husband José also joined them, coming in from Ixtapa where they ran a resort hotel.

Without much help from Alex, Diego decked his apartment out in the traditional festive colours and prepared a range of dishes for a Christmas lunch, repeating himself for a smorgasbord for New Year's Eve in time for Jasper's arrival.

"Do you think the two of them are going to fight?" Jasper asked, motioning towards Diego and Yolanda who stood at the terrace. "Diego looks really tense."

"I don't know. I hope not. She's very passive aggressive," Alex observed.

"Does she play the big sister because their parents aren't around anymore?"

"I think she's had to for a long time. Their parents died while they were still in school. That's when they moved to Ixtapa. Diego says she doesn't want him living in Mexico City. Plus, his ex was really abusive so I think she's protective."

"No way!" Jasper said, chewing on an olive.

"But get this, Yolanda's best friends with the ex! I hear Diego on the phone with her, and from what I understand, and it's hard to understand because they talk a million miles a minute, but the gist is, she wants him to go back to Rafael."

"So, she doesn't adore you?" Jasper asked, looking over at Yolanda. "That's gotta sting."

"We only met the other day but I can tell she doesn't like the idea of me. She must think I'm some rich gringo out to treat her brother like a plaything," Alex explained.

"Well you are the only white person in the room. Speaking of, I have a message for you. From Bono."

"Bono? What?" Alex asked.

"He wants to know when he can have his vest back. Do you realise they've become your new leggings? Seriously, a new decade starts in like, two hours. You need to make some changes. Cut that hair too, the gypsy look is dead and buried. And, I repeat, Bono wants his look back."

"Listen, I'm feeling fragile. Leave my hair and vests alone," Alex said.

"Why would you be feeling fragile? You've got that hot piece. I bet he's an animal in bed."

"We've never done it," Alex confessed.

Jasper looked at him and put his drink down on the coffee table. "Excuse me?"

"I mean, we've done everything else. Just not that."

"Why not? And why are you still with him?"

Alex looked at Diego and then back at Jasper. "Actually, I'm just having a lend. He's brilliant in that department."

"Oh, thank god," Jasper said. "I was worried you were taking that Buddhism stuff too seriously."

"But do you know what? We didn't have sex for the first month we were together."

"Why on earth did you wait so long?" Jasper asked, picking up his drink and scoffing it down.

"At first he didn't want to, and then I didn't. It was like starting afresh."

"Oh, so you both played the virgin card? What then? Did you do the bridal waltz? Did you carry him over the threshold?"

Alex laughed. "How's Scott the Scotsman? Are you still dating him?"

"Yes and he's in Glasgow. Family. Cold weather, rubbish food. I wasn't going to put myself through that again. I wanted something warm. And since you weren't going to Australia, Mexico seemed like a good enough compromise."

"Why haven't you got any films lined up this year?" Alex asked.

"I don't know. I think I want to take it easy. I want some shorter projects."

"I have two more music videos to do," Alex added.

"No, no, no, no, no, no, no."

"Please? Andres is all funny with me. I think maybe because I hooked up with Diego on his set."

"No, it's not about you," Jasper snapped. "Andres landed a feature for Paramount."

"Oh. Well good for him," Alex replied, annoyed. "Come on, they're great songs. And I have ideas."

Jasper looked at Alex resentfully. "LA. Only in LA. I don't want to do it here. I want my crew, my guys. And my team. And

I only want to deal with Celia, not Kōji. So you'll have to find him something else to do," Jasper warned.

"Oh, stop it, Kōji is coming, but, yes, you can play with Celia."

Jasper smiled. "And no vests," he added.

Though the party was tame by Alex and Jasper's standards, they nonetheless embraced gratefully when midnight arrived.

"I guess we managed to survive the eighties after all," Jasper noted, giving Alex a kiss.

| 2 |

OBITUARY 1981–1990

Alex was in a jovial mood when he began promoting the greatest hits collection, *Obituary 1981–1990,* the first of his career, which featured fifteen of his singles and two new tracks.

"I'm in a good space so I wanted to write something a bit upbeat and fun," he cooed, when a journalist asked about the inspiration behind the new songs.

The promotion had come as an afterthought. *Without You I'm Nothing* was still selling. One of its last two singles, aided largely by Jasper's incredible video, had peaked briefly at No.1 on the US charts. This had led to the decision to put the compilation out without any fanfare. But as his studio album finally lost its steam in the summer of 1990, Alex was finally put back through the promotional paces.

Alex wasn't sure what putting out a *greatest hits* signified. Was it that he'd nothing new left to say? The end of a chapter?

Or simply a decade of work that needed to be documented, repackaged and resold to capitalise on all his efforts?

In any case, its release fulfilled Alex's contractual obligations with his parent label. For the first time since his early years in New York, he was technically out of a recording contract and a free agent. Representatives from all the major labels had come knocking and Celia was keen to sit down with him to go over the options. Equally keen to do so was Michael, whose hot streak with Epic was coming to an end, in more ways than one. But Alex wasn't ready to voluntarily sign his life away again, no matter how lucrative it could be.

Instead, he was happy to divide his time between New York, LA and Mexico City, the chaotic, crazy, capital getting under his skin more and more.

Alex had also taken a rental in LA, spending much of 1990 there while working on films. As an interloper in the film industry, he worked to union rates, arriving on set each day with a humility that would never serve him in the music industry. And though people were curious about how he'd fare on the big screen, they were more interested in the greatest hits album which was shaping up to be a smash.

Although Alex appreciated the renewed interest in his music, he couldn't understand why there was so much nostalgia for his past releases. Especially when he felt his two new songs were so progressive by pop music standards.

But throughout the interviews he gave in LA, he was asked to talk about his old music and answered the questions without investing himself too deeply. To him, the 1980s weren't represented by his radio hits, but rather, the extraordinary relationships he'd forged while hitting the pavements on almost every continent on earth trying to prove himself. Even now there were times when he wondered how he'd ever found the energy to do what he had.

The true legacy of that decade for Alex was in its friendships. He would've been happier talking about who'd survived the Reagan era: who had or hadn't succumbed to big illnesses with small names and who'd walked away from the trail of heartbreak the eighties had left in their wake.

"It's another smash for you, this album," the journalist noted. "They're estimating something like seven or eight million copies already. Did you ever imagine you'd find yourself in this position when you started out? That people would be so loyal to your music? To your ideas?"

Alex despised these kinds of questions, even today when they came from his old friend Richard, a popular Australian television journalist. But Alex knew Richard was just warming up. Richard always bided his time on his way to the jugular.

"I don't think I ever imagined I'd be releasing a greatest hits album," Alex said. "But it's the kind of thing that my fans have been asking for and that the record company wanted, to kind of commemorate all these years. I guess it's also a good entry point for a lot of people who haven't followed my career very closely, to get an idea of what I'm about."

"Do you think it sums you up, musically?"

"They're snippets of what I've done," Alex said. "I think when I started out doing live shows, I wanted more songs of my own, you know? When you do a gig with just some singles or an EP to fall back on, you really struggle to fill out a set. I'm proud of what I've done so far, but I'm sure if I go back into the studio, I'll make music that's better than anything I've done before."

"Do you feel that? More confident each time?"

"Well, the more you do something, the more you commit to it, the better you get. When I first started, I was quick to come up with ideas. But I don't write and record like that anymore. I put a lot more thought into it these days."

After some questions about the movies Alex was working on, his inability to do a full scale tour due to his film commitments, and the vaguest of plans for the future, Richard finally got to where he was heading.

"Can we talk about Athena for a minute?" Richard asked.

Alex bristled. "Sure."

"You were married?" Richard asked, a look of surprise occupying his face.

"We were."

"But you decided to keep that from the public? From your families?"

"I think everyone is entitled to some privacy. Even people that are famous."

"Isn't it odd to keep that kind of news from your loved ones?"

"Not in this day and age, no, I don't think so," Alex replied, shaking his head.

"Was there a reason for it? I mean one could argue you were both teen idols and that it would've hurt your appeal if your fans knew. But that wouldn't account for why you wouldn't tell the people in your life, surely?"

Alex cleared his throat and sat silent for a few moments. "We made a decision. We decided it would be better to keep things in a cone of silence. Not just for us, but also for our family and friends. We didn't want to put them in a difficult position."

"The two of you divorced in the end after, what, four years?"

"Give or take," Alex said.

"Was it acrimonious?"

"I think separating is difficult for everyone, no matter who you are. We're still friends," Alex added. "It didn't work out between us, but I want the best for her. Just like I'm sure she does for me."

"Have you heard her new album?" Richard asked, his left eyebrow arching.

"Of course."

"She seems to have some things to say," Richard said, smiling mischievously.

"That's okay. Divorce is complicated. Even among friends."

"You're not offended by any of her lyrics? I mean there's some damning stuff in there."

"You'd have to ask her if they refer to me. I can't speak for her," Alex said, smiling icily. "If you want to know what she's singing about, maybe you should interview *her*."

Richard smiled. "Nothing you want to add? No right of reply?"

"No, I don't have anything to say about her. She's a great person. I've always admired her and I always will. That's what I have to say about that," Alex said, adjusting his shirt cuff.

Once the film crew turned out the lights and began to pack up the equipment, Alex cordially thanked Richard.

"You held back," Alex said. "I was expecting more."

"They warned me not to cross the line," Richard admitted, folding away his clip- on mic.

"Who? My team?" Alex asked.

"No. Mine. They wanted a *feel good* with just enough juice to sell it to other markets. Apparently, it's the only full sit- down interview you're doing, so we're going to milk it."

"Oh, I see," Alex said.

"No plans to sign another deal?" Richard asked. "There's some big numbers being bantered around."

"No plans. I'm thinking of doing a Momoe Yamaguchi," Alex said.

"What?" Richard asked.

"*Who*. She was a Japanese singer. My favourite one I think, of that era. But she just gave it all up. Said she wanted to get married and focus on her private life."

"And that's what you plan to do? Settle down? Get serious with Diego?"

"No. But I like the idea of really stepping away from music. Just living without a bounty over my head for a bit. What are they saying in Australia about Diego by the way?"

"Nothing. Like here, I guess. I guess they just think he's part of your posse."

"That word doesn't sound right when you say it," Alex said, wincing.

"All the kids are saying it," Richard replied, smiling.

"Come on," Alex said. "I'll take you out to lunch and widen your vocabulary a bit."

***

Although Alex liked having the freedom of driving in LA, he didn't like LA all that much. He'd come to think of it as Athena's city. Spending too much time there drove him crazy, especially now with the messy public aftermath of their divorce.

When Athena released her own album earlier in the year much of its publicity campaign centred around the breakdown of their marriage. Alex felt like Athena had betrayed him, especially when she publicly painted him a career and publicity fiend. Around the same time "reliable sources close to Athena" publicly revealed that Alex and Athena had indeed been married, but that Alex's ongoing infidelity had doomed the union.

The talk in the press undoubtedly benefitted Athena's album promotion, but it also sparked renewed interest in *Without You I'm Nothing,* whose lyrics were being dissected again with the new facts at hand.

Furious with Athena for reneging on their pact, Alex found himself in damage control mode with his family, Diego and other friends for not having fully disclosed his past. Why hadn't he trusted them with it? Why the big secret?

In her songs she sang of a man who couldn't be trusted. A man who hid from the truth. A man who didn't acknowledge her power or listen to what she had to say. A man who had manipulated her.

He decided to never dignify her accusations, publicly attributing them to creative license anytime anyone had the courage to ask. But when he eventually ran into Athena at an event in LA, he was livid.

"Everything I've said is true, Alex," she'd said the minute she saw him.

"I didn't think you'd throw me under the bus," Alex said, skipping the pleasantries. "Not for the sake of selling a few more records."

"We didn't have an NDA Alex. I reconsidered my options once I had time to think about it. There was no point in me keeping mum about things."

"I guess that in your books it's fine to stab a friend in the back for some publicity."

"Alex," she said, forcing a smile as she cosied up to the man who sidled up next to her, "this is Matthew, my fiancé."

"Pleasure," Alex mumbled, shaking Matthew's outstretched hand.

"Oh, we've met before," Matthew said, "at the rainforest benefit."

"Have we? I have the memory of a sieve," Alex said. "Congratulations. When's the big day?"

"Next weekend," Athena gushed. "We're doing it in Sydney! At Whale Beach. Our families are going to be there," she said, beaming at Matthew and then at Alex.

"Great," Alex said, "all of Sydney must be buzzing with excitement."

"Oh no, it's going to be a private thing," Matthew said.

"Of course," Alex concurred, furrowing his brow. "Well, again, congratulations."

Almost twenty years after she and Alex divorced, and after over a decade out of the spotlight, Athena published her memoirs, clarifying some of her views on Alex.

"We were both too young to know better. We had this deep bond because we'd both come from the same place and been on similar jour-

neys. We went from unknown to infamous together. We were best friends and that was everything. I know we both prized our friendship. But we didn't prioritise our marriage in the same way. It was a by–product of our friendship. We were just kids who began to think of our marriage license as a piece of paper.

"When I got remarried in Sydney I was furious with Alex. I literally cursed his name when the paparazzi were taking our photos on the beach. I was sure it was him that had tipped them off. And so for years I despised him. But time has a way pushing the truth to the surface. Turns out it was one of my cousins who'd tipped off the media. Alex had nothing to do with it.

"For years his affair with Michael really hurt me, but I made my piece with it in the end. For all his faults, Alex never once said a negative word about me publicly. I think I represented the last trace of the straight world for him and I think he, in his own way, treated that memory sacredly, never speaking poorly of me or the time we had together.

"In hindsight, I shouldn't have fallen for someone who had been ambiguous about things from the start. And Alex should've walked away. But everything connected to our time together was disproportionate; the scrutiny, the secrecy, the end. We were two kids who wanted to keep an eye out for each other, but we were also two professionals, busy living our own lives at two separate ends of the continent. And soon enough we were in two completely different worlds.

"We email from time to time. I like to think that he still has a soft spot for me because I certainly do for him. We were each other's firsts in a way. That kind of thing never leaves you."

***

When Alex wrapped up his work in LA, he was only too happy to give Kōji the order to pack up the most important of his belongings and send them on home. Rather than follow them on to New York, he headed down to Mexico. In addition to spending time with Diego, part of the attraction of heading there was knowing he could simply disappear into its crowds, the city affording him a level of anonymity he hadn't experienced in years.

He and Diego had been discreet over the year and a half they'd been together, aided by Mexico City's urban sprawl and their lowkey existence there. It was one of the biggest cities in the world, but one of the last places people might assume Alex was hiding out in.

He'd come to regard Diego's cosy apartment as a home away from home, and, letting himself in, quickly scanned the place to see if he could detect any new flea market acquisitions. He almost felt he needed to sit Diego down and have 'the talk'. Diego's addiction to knickknacks was getting out of hand.

Inspection done, Alex made himself a cup of coffee, and sat down on the couch with the intention of reading the trade magazines he'd picked up at the airport. He and Diego had been playing phone tag for days, Diego away on location in the south of Mexico. Alex was excited and hopeful that Diego would make it back that night, but gave in to his fatigue, falling asleep on the couch. When he came to, it was already evening. Realising

Diego wouldn't be getting home that night, he ventured downstairs to pick up a few things for breakfast and some take away from one of the local joints he and Diego frequented. It was the closest he'd gotten to doing anything remotely normal since he'd last seen Diego.

Back at the apartment he opened the shutters in the kitchen so that he could at least peek out at the world outside as he nibbled away at his dinner, mulling over the notes Celia had attached to the three scripts he'd also brought with him. Only one of them piqued his interest, that about a traveling group of carnival performers clinging to their traditions despite the world changing around them. Celia noted that he'd been offered the main supporting role by Max's company and that there would be no need to audition.

He liked the script. Found the dialogue believable and the story intriguing. There were of course some glaringly, off kilter ideas that made him worry, but overall, it was far better than anything he'd worked on over the last year.

The more he read, the more he liked it, but alarm bells sounded in his mind, warning him not to get too attached. Max's film projects always had an air of uncertainty to them and, Alex had never even heard of the director. To cap it all off, there was the issue that Alex's role was that of a trapezist, and that Alex had a deeply ingrained fear of heights.

But the script was better than anything he'd ever been offered before.

By the time he was ready for bed, he'd read two thirds of the script. He cursorily brushed his teeth, stripped and pulled up the blanket, unable to think of anything but the film project until sleep got the better of him again.

The next morning he awoke to the sound of the front door, and as it opened, he excitedly called out from the bed. "Estoy aquí!"

He rubbed his fingers along his teeth and gums, sniffing them to check if his breath stank, and gave his morning hard on a little nudge as the footsteps approached the bedroom. As the bedroom light came on, Alex threw off the blankets, proudly revealing his naked self. But looking up, his euphoria morphed to shock. It was Angel, Diego's best friend, who, granted, didn't waste the opportunity to soak up the view. His embarrassment fading, Alex smiled sweetly and decided there was no point now in covering himself up again.

"Qué onda?" Alex asked.

Angel held up the two bags of groceries in explanation. "I thought you and Diego were arriving today," he said, pursing his lips.

"No, the plan was always to get here last night. I did. I thought Diego would too," Alex said, gesturing towards the underwear on the floor. Angel obliged and threw it over.

"I'll make you a coffee," Alex said, jumping out of the bed and putting on the underwear, kissing Angel on the cheek on his way out. "Thanks for the groceries," Alex added, from halfway down the corridor.

Over breakfast Alex and Angel caught up, and with Diego's arrival later in the morning, Alex largely forgot about the script. Angel excused himself shortly after lunch, leaving the two of them to lounge around all day, catching up.

"Yolanda is pregnant," Diego said, snuggling under a throw blanket on the couch.

"Oh wow, that's great news," Alex said, easing himself under the blanket. "You're going to be an uncle! Why the face?"

"She's having complications. She wants me to go and stay with her for a bit."

"And are you going to?" Alex asked.

"I don't know," Diego said. "I had planned on beginning the interviews."

"For your documentary?" Alex asked, excitedly.

"Yeah. But she says it's really bad. The doctor wants her to rest and there's a lot to do at the hotel now that the season's over. Maintenance."

"Can't she hire someone?" Alex asked, perplexed.

"José doesn't trust anyone. Thinks they should save the money for the baby."

"And you're prepared to go there and work? For free?"

"She's family."

"How long would it be for?"

"A month or two," Diego said, tucking his feet under himself.

Alex looked at him for a moment. "Don't take this the wrong way, but I don't think it's a good idea."

"Why not?" Diego asked.

"Well, it's one thing if you want to go and spend some time with her… to be of help. But I don't think the solution is for you to put everything on hold and go and work there."

"I don't care about the money. I mean, if I'm working on the documentary or if I'm working at the hotel, it's not going to make any difference. I'm not being paid for it," Diego said.

"I can give you the money," Alex said. "That way they can pay someone that knows what they're doing."

"But I don't want your money," Diego said.

"It's just money," Alex said. "I'm not saying don't go. I'm saying go, and spend the time that you want to with Yolanda, but don't get stuck in a situation that'll put the rest of your plans on the backfoot."

"You wouldn't understand," Diego said, sighing.

"Why? Because I'm rich? Because I've never had to work for anything?"

"No, because family means something very different to you," Diego said.

"I come from an Italian family," Alex said. "I think I know what you're referring to."

"You don't. You don't know what it means," Diego said, emphatically.

"I do. I know what it means. I just don't buy into it. That's a decision," Alex said, straightening himself up on the couch.

"Yolanda is my only family Alex. You can't understand what that's like."

"Yet you're letting José make the decisions for you both?"

"It's not like that," Diego said, dismissively.

"Seems like that to me," Alex said. "Seems like José is putting Yolanda in a spot and she's putting you in another. If that's what family is about, then, maybe you're right. Maybe I don't understand what family is."

"I didn't mean it that way," Diego said. "I'm just saying it's different for me."

"Well, ultimately you need to make your own decision. If you think you need to go and be there for Yolanda, who am I to stop you?"

"Come on Alex," Diego said, sighing. "Don't be offended."

"I'm not, honestly," Alex said. "And you know what, maybe you should go. Maybe it will be good for you to spend some time with her. You haven't been to Ixtapa for a long time."

"Maybe you could come with me for a couple of days?" Diego asked, twirling and cracking his wrist.

"I don't think so," Alex said. "Yolanda doesn't really like me, and if she's already having a difficult pregnancy, the last thing she needs is me underfoot."

"You know, you should let me make some decisions sometimes too," Diego said. "For the two of us."

Alex decided to bite his tongue. He didn't want to spend his first day with Diego arguing.

An air of tension settled over them for a few days, but they nonetheless carried out their routine activities together, visiting up and coming art galleries, going for runs at the Bosque de Chapultepec, and having dinner parties with Diego's closest friends.

With Diego deciding to depart for Ixtapa earlier than planned, Alex decided to return to New York, having been away for the best part of the year. There, he fell into his own routine and resumed reading the script he'd put down in Mexico, instructing Celia to set up a meeting with his film agent, Tyler, at the first possible opportunity.

As negotiations for the project began, Alex was summoned to LA, where, along with Tyler, he visited the offices of the German film director Uli.

Uli and the film's executive producer, Serge, went to great lengths to complement Alex's acting, doing their best to convince Alex that it was not a form of stunt casting on their part that led them to considering him for the role.

Once Tyler brokered an in principle agreement, negotiations began between Kēvala and Max's company, Lightning, who were keen to have Alex supply a soundtrack for the movie.

Reasonably confident a deal would be struck, Alex began his research, having Kēvala staff supply him with a box load of Balkan music. He also reached out to friends in London, explaining that he was on the lookout to work with someone new and interesting.

He wanted to work with someone other than Ian this time around.

| 3 |

CARNIVAL

[MUSIC FROM AND INSPIRED BY THE FILM]

For almost two weeks Alex immersed himself in the sounds of Balkan folk and pop music, marvelling at the horns, the percussion and the rousing vocals and choruses. He didn't understand a single word of what he was listening to, but when one of the Kēvala staff put him in contact with the director of New York's Balkan music festival, Alex booked an appointment as part of his research.

As negotiations for the film and soundtrack progressed, Alex organised for an up and coming London based songwriter/producer, Paulina Milak, to be flown over for an exploratory meeting. Alerted to her existence by his London contacts, Alex wanted to be the first to take advantage of the growing interest in her hybrid pop/folk sound.

Due to begin filming in LA for another project, *Outing,* a socio–political thriller exposing forced coming outs and blackmail,

Alex would also have to juggle commitments for the *Carnival* project. There would be little time between *Outing* wrapping up in LA and Alex arriving in Hungary for the start of filming in June.

Somehow, he'd have to lay the groundwork for the soundtrack and begin trapeze and tightrope training in LA in his downtime. He would of course have a double for the new film but needed to be able to pull of at least some of the basics.

Back in his LA rental, Alex wrote the skeletal outlines for three songs; inspired by his *Carnival* film character; *Best Foot Forward, Hang Me From The Stars* and *Tightrope*. The demos were rough and raw, and once he had time to think about them, he worried Paulina would dismiss them for being too basic.

Between rehearsals and pre-production obligations, Alex meticulously studied Milak's music, and began meeting three times a week with his new Russian circus coach, Stefan, an ex-gymnast who, even now in his early fifties, still had what Alex regarded as the best physique he'd ever seen on a man. Stefan created an intensive training program for him, training Alex in an old high school gymnasium and at Will Rogers State beach.

Stefan was a hard sell from the beginning. Serge, the film's producer, had introduced them at an informal brunch, and Stefan had instantly been sceptical of Alex. After the first few sessions in which Alex obediently followed Stefan's instructions, despite his fear of heights, the Russian lightened up. Stefan's authoritative stance quickly morphed into a more supportive kind of coaching, and Alex relaxed, gradually managing his inhibition and fear better. The gripping panic he had of hurting or making a fool of himself, was writ large over his face during the first few sessions, but in time it was replaced by a steely determination that made the Russian proud.

One morning when Alex wasn't required on set for *Outing*, he drove to Stefan's apartment on the other side of the city to pick him up, as Stefan was having car troubles.

In the car on their way out to Rogers, they had their first proper conversation, Stefan finally breaking the ice.

"You're planning on training in those tight jeans today?"

Alex looked down at his lap and then across at his silver haired coach, whose red track suit with a blue three stripe, barely concealed the meshy singlet that he wore beneath.

"No, I have a change of clothes in the trunk," Alex said, "I had some meetings this morning. I couldn't go in a tracksuit."

"But this is LA. Of course you can."

Alex was adamant. "I can. But I won't."

"I listened to one of your records last night. I asked my daughter for it," Stefan said, gruffly.

"Oh no," Alex said, checking his mirrors, and then glancing over to the top of the singlet, where Stefan's skin cells seemed to sit, tightly knit under a sleek silver necklace and a spattering of light chest hair. "You didn't like it. Which one was it by the way?"

"The one with your hair long on the cover. My daughter told me it was your last one."

"My *latest* one? Yes. But you didn't like it."

"I was curious," Stefan deflected. "But I want to know something."

"What?" Alex asked.

"The way you breathe. Did somebody teach you? When we're together you don't breathe properly. When you sing you don't breathe properly. You sound desperate for air. Why?"

"I've never really thought about it."

"You must have. You panic so quickly. It's connected to your breathing. When you're on stage or you're dancing or you're acting, do you think a lot about breathing?" Stefan asked, looking out the passenger window.

"No," Alex said, "not unless I'm dancing and its really complicated."

"So, you breathe suddenly, like in two or three puffs, no?"

As Alex began to think about it, Stefan put his hand down on Alex's lower abdomen, startling him.

"You don't breathe from down here," Stefan rasped, slowly sliding his palm up Alex's stomach, "you breathe too much from here," he said, reaching Alex's chest, "and here," he concluded, a little sadly as he reached Alex's temple.

"You need to learn how to breathe all over again. I want to teach you. You could have a very nice voice if you knew how to *respire*. Do you know, sometimes I've worked with musicians? Not to teach them how to walk the rope or to jump into a hoop, but just to breathe, so that they can understand rhythm better. I know you're a good dancer. I know you move well. I watch you when I make you do the exercises. But you can do so much better. You're like the jeans that you wear you know? You're a little bit tight. I can see everything underneath," Stefan said, smiling.

Alex felt his face redden.

"It's so transparent," Stefan said, looking beyond the windscreen, "your way of doing. But if you were more like me and my big pants, you'd conceal a lot of the details. When you watch me, you don't see me concentrating or thinking much. It's hidden. And this is what an artist should do. Athlete, musician, actor, dancer, anybody. That is what separates us. And you need to be more fluid because, like I said, you can be much better than now. You just need to learn how to take the air in better and to control it."

Alex let out a slight breath as he pulled into the lot in front of Rogers.

"So how long will it take you to teach me then?" he asked.

"Oh, it won't take long. But then after I teach you to breathe again, you have to start to learn to do all the things you do in a different way. You have to learn how to exercise differently, how to treat your body more like a good machine, more like a temple as they say here."

"And how much is this going to cost me?" Alex asked.

"Oh it's not about the money. For you it's a pittance. We're already together for the next two months, and the film company is paying me already. To focus on your specific needs it will just be my usual rate. I will begin un–teaching you and reteaching you while I also make you an expert of the big tent. If after that you want me to continue working for you, I will. You'll never need to go to the gymnasium again after working with me. I'll give you a body just like mine," Stefan promised. "I see the way you look at it. You can have it too. I'll be your personal trainer."

"I don't spend much time here in LA, Stefan. I don't know how we could make it work even if I considered it," Alex said, getting out of the car and heading to the trunk.

"I can come with you when you want me to. I have my other clients here in LA but we can do a week or two together when you have the time," Stefan said, holding Alex's gym bag open as Alex changed into his sweats. "Once we get the basics done, it'll just be like coming in for maintenance. You'll be able to work out on your own mostly."

Alex placed his jeans into the bag and Stefan pulled the heavy equipment out of the trunk with no exertion whatsoever. They walked together and as they put their things down onto the crisp white sand, Alex spoke.

"I guess it can't hurt to try. But I won't be back in LA again until September after I've finished filming and maybe recording too. After Hungary, I'm probably going to London to make my next record."

"We'll begin today. And we have some time here before you leave. Then, if you bring me for two weeks before you start recording, or if you come back here, I guarantee you'll already have results in time for the next record. The way that you force the air in as you sing, it will disappear. With me, you'll hold it. And you'll feel better, more relaxed."

"Okay, we'll work out the details."

✳✳✳

That night, Alex took Paulina out for dinner at an elegant Japanese restaurant and turned on his charm. He discovered they had a mutual friend; a documentary maker in Paris, as well as a mutual love for the work of Marina Abramović.

They talked about Milak's recent work and Alex's film projects as well as how, to his mind, a soundtrack project would be a great step for her. He explained the soundtrack could be an exciting collaboration for them both, and that together, they could make a truly "progressive" record that would have people talking.

Paulina seemed impressed by him. Alex listened intently when she spoke, asking all kinds of questions even if he knew they were earnest.

She'd been prepared for this, having taken the liberty of calling Francois, their friend in Paris, who'd assured her Alex would quickly disarm her if she let him.

"Be careful with him," Francois had warned, "he has a way of thinking his projects are 'revolutionary'. That he's not just a pop-star."

Prior to speaking to Francois, Alex had barely made it into Paulina's thoughts, other than at moments like at dinner parties where talk inevitably shifted to celebrities. But after speaking to Francois – whose documentary on beekeeping Alex had financed – Paulina thought Alex might not be such a corporate puppet after all. Enquiring further, Paulina discovered Alex had also funded two documentaries by an Italian couple she knew of, and of course, Diego's controversial new investigation into HIV in Latin America, which was now making waves across Europe.

As she sat and listened to Alex speak, she realised that Alex's main artistic talent wasn't his voice or his song writing. It was that he had his ear to the ground. He wasn't the poet or the spokesperson of his generation. He clearly wasn't Bob Dylan. Hell, he wasn't even Prince, but she found him both candid and down to earth, and wiser than her misgivings had painted him to be. Sure, the scale of his project and the severe time constraints worried her, but she liked the spirit with which he was approaching things… how he seemed prepared to put in the work.

She finished her dessert and finally spoke. "So, when do we start?" she asked, wiping her mouth with the napkin.

***

Paulina returned to London with copies of the tapes Alex had made, along with a copy of the script and some additional background information about treatments, the landscape, and the ethos behind the project. None of it was especially new to her, but on the plane, reading the script, she saw that there were a few new ideas to make the film seem vaguely worthwhile. But the script didn't matter so much. She'd agreed to the project because Alex was making an accompanying piece, not an official soundtrack, so she wouldn't have to be a slave to a narrative.

***

As time on the *Outing* set began to wind up, Alex made arrangements for Diego to fly into LA to save him from another trip down to Mexico and give him a chance to squeeze in some more lessons with Stefan. When not working on set, training with Stefan or making peace with Diego, Alex devoted his time to Paulina and the phone calls and courier packages they exchanged, discussing their DAT tapes at length.

Paulina had done a good job in fleshing out his demos, rearranging the music so that it seemed a little chopped up and layered rather than traditional.

She also forwarded him leftover music from some pieces she'd scored for an indie film but later abandoned, and he began to work on those pieces, making notes about the music, writing pages and pages of lyrics which he hoped to later cull from.

Arriving in Hungary, Alex and Diego had an idyllic first couple of days, exploring Budapest in the company of a friendly, if bashful security guard/driver, István, that the film's producers insisted Alex always be accompanied by. István eventually was tasked with driving the boys up to Lake Balaton and around the outskirts of Sopron where filming would take place.

Once filming was underway, Paulina also arrived and with István's help, set up jamming sessions with various troupes of local musicians; sometimes in Alex's presence, sometimes not. She recorded the sessions, adding them to a bank of stems she was creating for the album. With Alex constantly required on set, Paulina and Diego traipsed around the countryside, forging a friendship in the process.

It was an arduous shoot for Alex, as Uli favoured doing numerous takes and using natural light. It was already hot in Hungary, and even if it wasn't always obvious, it was apparent the country was undergoing immense change after the withdrawal of the Soviets. Filming had been halted numerous times, resuming only after payments were made to the local authorities, the petty theft of equipment only adding more pressure to Uli's already complex schedule.

While covering Hungary's shifting political dynamic, the international press occasionally made visits to the set, images of a heavily made up, almost unrecognisable Alex filtering out into the media.

Despite the pressures on set, Alex nonetheless enjoyed working in a foreign country. His occasional escapes out of Sopron with Diego and Paulina in the hunt for authentic local folk musicians made up for the long, hot days filming.

Interest from the outside was mounting once again, buoyed by talk of *Outing's* late autumn premiere and the brewing media frenzy over Alex's new deal with Max's label.

It was a complicated deal, designed to give Lightning an *Alekzandr* album, but a one off deal, which would keep Alex a free agent until he decided how he wanted to proceed musically.

Despite Alex's friendship with Max, he instructed his team to well and truly make Lightning come to the party. After months of negotiations, Alex was offered a six million dollar non–refundable advance. In return, he would provide Lightning with a "soundtrack" album for the film. In addition to his huge advance, Alex would also be given an eyewatering 22% of royalties if the album sales exceeded five million. Observers noted that Alex stood to walk away with a cool ten million, a figure many decried as exorbitant.

Paulina for her part came into negotiations without a clear idea of the figures being vaunted for the project. Her agent had secured her a very respectable 3.5% royalty in addition to generous *masters* and *overages* that had been negotiated for her. But the leap she had to make to actually pull off a high profile project like this one was huge.

When Alex's filming wrapped and they moved on to London to concentrate exclusively on the soundtrack, Paulina often found herself immobilised. She worried that the stems she'd recorded in Hungary might later expose her to copyright claims and that there wasn't enough time to meticulously cut and slice up the recordings in the way she wanted.

With Diego back in Mexico, Alex only had two things on his mind, and both made him anxious. The first was the soundtrack's looming deadline. The second only reared its head when, in London, he finally began to catch up on things in the world of pop. Doing so had caused his other obsession to materialise; he'd discovered the existence of pop's latest sensation; Seal.

Seal's husky voice, his incredible look, better than average lyrics and his debut album's masterful production had Alex incensed. Unwilling to head straight home after a long day in the studio, Alex drove around London late one night, listening to *Crazy* and *Killer* on repeat until he couldn't handle hearing them any longer.

By the end of September, still without much to show from his collaboration with Paulina, the very thought of his own album began to give him heartburn. With the November deadline looming, Alex and Paulina both began to feel the pressure, worried they'd have to start cutting corners to get things done. The idea that their project could end up being a patchy affair created great tension in the studio.

One morning, they'd been shouting at each other for nearly half an hour when Celia arrived. She'd walked into the studio mid argument and had to raise her voice to get the two of them to stop.

"Alex, go and get a cup of coffee or something, I need to talk to Paulina," Celia said, primly.

Alex glared at Celia for a moment, but not in anger. The look was quizzical in nature. *How in the hell was Celia going to resolve things?*

Celia had proved one of his greatest acquisitions. The Hong Kong born, Canadian raised girl was part ingénue, part living stubborn streak. She had many strengths, but her mediation skills were unmatched. Since taking on the role as Alex's manager, she'd brokered a peace between Alex and Michael and also smoothed out hostilities with Alex's record company when his expensive dalliance with Max's label threatened to derail their own negotiations.

So as Alex disappeared as ordered, Celia carefully prompted Paulina, waiting patiently as Paulina did her best to explain where the problems laid. And as she listened, Celia read between the lines; Paulina was feeling the pressure and there was some resentment that the label and perhaps Alex didn't trust her.

"It's like his attitude has changed since we got to London," Paulina said, "and he's not as open to my ideas anymore."

"Putting yourself through this kind of torture is pointless Paulina," Celia said. "Alex has a lot riding on this. Perhaps more than you do. He's used to seeing things done in a certain way and by a certain time. When he doesn't see that, he gets panicky," Celia said, throwing her bag onto the couch and taking a seat at the control panel.

"What we're doing is really complicated," Paulina said. "It requires time, but then he changes his mind about things and we have to start again almost from scratch. It's taking much longer than it should."

"I think you know by now how hands on he is," Celia said. "But I think you could delegate a lot of technical work to someone else. An engineer or an assistant could be doing a lot of the detailed stuff for you."

"I'm not sure how that would work," Paulina said.

"For projects of this scale it's par for the course. We'll whiteboard everything… make up a plan for each of the songs and the tasks. You'll assign them as necessary," Celia said. "You can't do it all on your own. And don't write Alex off. You can push back on his ideas if you don't like them, but if you treat him like he doesn't know what he's doing, it's at your own peril."

"I think he hates me right now," Paulina said, sadly. "It's very difficult to work in these circumstances."

"Listen sweetie, you have no idea of what he can put people through in the studio," Celia admitted. "You're getting the best of him. He adores you. And by his standards he's in a good working space."

| 4 |

THE HELLFIRE CLUB

Carnival, the movie, opened to mixed reviews in early 1992. It did reasonably well at the box office, even if the film was considered uneven and the acting shaky (particularly Alekzandr's).

Alex's soundtrack had become a hit, if a moderate one by his standards. Sales kept it firmly lodged at No.2 in the US, Alekzandr unable to topple Garth Brooks from the top. But the lead single, *Tightrope*, became his fifth US number one, succeeding number ones from Michael Jackson and George Michael. *Tightrope* earned Alex career-best sales of over five million copies, almost outselling the album. But, unlike his previous records, the soundtrack had a relatively short chart run. Once the dust settled, *Variety*, Hollywood's trade bible, suggested that Lightning had considerably overpaid Alex in relation to the album's performance. They wondered aloud whether it was because much of Alex's fan base had moved on, or if the Balkan sound was simply too niche for the mainstream market.

In addition to securing Alex the soundtrack deal, his management team finally pulled off a new, long term contract with his old record company. The new deal was one of many super deals that swept the industry at the time. It would allow worldwide distribution for Kēvala, this time as a fifty–fifty venture. This, the most lucrative deal of Alex's career, which would reportedly see him pocket $50 million, would allow him to release his own music, sign other artists and develop films and other projects.

Although many in the industry had dismissed Alex's Balkan soundtrack as a vanity project and a failure for Lightning, Alex's music had already generated incredible revenue for his label. With his career sales estimated at well over 100 million by that stage, Alekzandr was as sure a thing as the industry could offer. In endorsing him for a new, six album deal, there was great faith that Alekzandr would prevail over the changing public tastes that some naysayers believed he was already on the receiving end of.

A deal of that magnitude was the major label's only way of maintaining their grip on one of their biggest ever cash cows.

The first new album for the deal had already been given the green light, with a tentative release date of October 1992. With more creative freedom than ever before, Alex envisaged an urban, industrial sounding album that would be partly produced in Australia.

Recording in Australia was a decision partly motivated by his desire to be nearer to his family, but also a result of Alex having been turned down by Seal's producer, who refused every lucrative offer Alex's management team threw his way.

Instead, Alex had to go scouting for "fresh" talent. He wound up choosing an Australian singer songwriter named Stuart Carp, who'd ridden high in the charts during the 1970s and 1980s with an intellectual–pop group. Carp was now writing and producing electronica for a range of artists and Alex had discovered his music by chance, on a mix tape an Australian friend had sent him. Partnering with Carp could give Alex an edge; an unexpected sound that none of his peers were making.

The remainder of the album would be recorded in LA with another Australian producer, Paul Hirst, who'd ridden the wave of the No–Wave and New–Wave movements in the 1980s, and who'd also moved towards writing and producing for others. In the mid–eighties his and Alex's singles had competed in the Australian charts, but since then Paul had produced an underground dance album by an LA act which had been one of Alex's favourite releases of 1991.

Arriving in Melbourne without any fanfare or attendants, Alex felt motivated and inspired, excited to see family and friends, desperate to return to the studio with so many ideas for his new record.

Arriving at the suburban home his parents still called home, Alex overcame the initial trepidation of ringing the buzzer at the gates, and was greeted warmly by his mother Eleni. They hugged for an interminable time.

"I haven't seen you since you brought Diego," she murmured.

She was referring to the week Alex and Diego had snuck over to Australia to ostensibly out themselves to Alex's parents. But the trip had been all for nought. Alex's sister Sofia, had apparently broken the news to his parents almost a year earlier and his parents had played mum until the visit, waiting to hear from the horse's mouth.

"Where is Diego?" Eleni asked, ushering Alex inside.

"He's working in Los Angeles. He's finishing up on his new documentary. He said he'll come down later."

Truth was, Diego had made it clear that he was tired of following Alex around on his projects, of the speculation in the press about their relationship and of the constant interruptions to his own burgeoning career.

"Is everything okay with the two of you?" she asked.

"Fine," Alex said, putting his bag down.

"I expected to see a few pictures of him at the premiere."

"He didn't want to attend," Alex said.

"I see," Eleni responded. "Darling, I saw the movie. I thought it was beautiful. Your father fell asleep during it, though. Don't ask him about it."

"Oh, you know I gave up on those kinds of conversations years ago."

"Oh, but he loves the CD. He's always listening to it. I think it's the first time he's ever really bothered. He says it reminds him of your grandfather's music."

"Mum, that's possibly the worst thing I've ever heard anyone say about my work."

"Oh," she said dismissively, "take it as a compliment. I think he meant it sounds authentic."

Together they gossiped and talked about their latest news, including Alex's disappointment at the repeated postponement of *Outing's* release. The film company had decided to shelve the film, concerned about the wave of censorship sweeping the

States at the time. There had already been threats of a boycott across the US, due to the controversial nature of the film, seen by some segments as pushing a *gay agenda*.

When his father returned home, they dined together, and it was Oliviero who resumed the inquisition into Diego's whereabouts, Alex feeling like he had to deflect, careful to remain diplomatic. But even he was worried about Diego's resistance.

After a nap on the couch, Alex woke, made his apologies and headed to his apartment. An assistant had already organised for it to be prepared for him. His staff had been provided with laminated sets of the rules that applied to Alex's gamut of properties.

1. *Properties have to be cleaned and aired in the week before arrival.*

2. *Linens and any clothes in the wardrobe have to be laundered in the days leading up to my arrival.*

3. *Fresh flowers that are not too fragrant are to be placed in the living areas.*

4. *The kitchen needs to be stocked with my favourite brands and things (see the attached lists for each home).*

5. *Fresh, market bought fruit and vegetables are to be put in the kitchen.*

6. *Cleaning rosters need to be printed and left in a visible area so I know when to expect things will be done.*

As was now usual, he'd travelled with his special overnight bag, laden with his lyric books and demo tapes.

Since the spectacular falling out with Paulina one month out from the soundtrack deadline, which resulted in an extra engineer having to be brought in to help them complete the album, Alex was now approaching collaborations differently. His collaborators would have to now work with an album coordinator who would be responsible for managing timelines and workloads.

The late delivery of the *Carnival* soundtrack had cost him tens of thousands of dollars and destroyed what was left of his relationship with Paulina, who'd been noticeably absent from the album's London launch party.

Alex wasn't prepared to miss a deadline again. So, in addition to the tracks couriered between he and Stuart from LA to Melbourne, Alex already had a schedule for the new album's recording ready.

From the outset, Stuart was proving to be combative, even if he had excellent ideas and a meticulous skill set. Stuart wasn't afraid to berate Alex, whether by fax or phone, when he disagreed or disapproved of something. On the last fax Alex had received before arriving in Melbourne, Stuart had signed off by scribbling; *if you're going to insist on so many loops, I have to insist you find someone else to work with.*

Alex was excited by the lobbing of ideas and not in the least bit perturbed by Stuart's terse missives. He was curious to see if Stuart would be as grouchy in person as he was on paper.

In any case, Alex was approaching the new project as a challenge.

Recording in Australia was already going to be a test. His professional standing there was murky. Throughout his career,

Australian radio had all but ignored him, his music receiving less airplay there than in any of his major markets. The relatively late to life Australian music association only begrudgingly acknowledged him. Their award nights routinely overlooked his work in all but the commercial categories.

Alex wanted to throw down the gauntlet to the Australian recording industry and, more widely, to the country's obsession with masculinity. He wanted to make something that pushed him artistically in a way nothing else had before.

Taking a long morning walk around the inner city the next day, Alex found himself revisiting memories of his younger self. He saw a couple of the places he used to wait tables in, their names and facades now different. He watched the old trams shunt by, remembering how he used to hop on and off them in the prime of his youth, zipping from university, to work, and to the leafy suburbs of his professor, Angus, who later provided the catalyst for Alex's nomadic wanderings.

Alex felt his old world was like a quaint Lego set. He marvelled at how such a tiny pocket of the city had seemed like his entire world back then. Moving in and out of stores he noticed the music on the radio. Hated what he heard: the staple Aussie rock in the fruit shop, some insipid R&B in the sportswear store, and cloying indie covers in the grog shop. So many samples. So many covers. No inspiration, daring or innovation.

At that stage of his career Alex knew he could've pretty much released anything he wanted and be guaranteed a respectable response and flutter on the charts. He was, as Neil Tennant of the Pet Shop Boys later coined, in the middle of his *imperial phase.*

But walking home, he was convinced. If his new deal was to be a success, he had to be prepared to be bold. To do something unexpected. To be prepared to fight and not look for an easy set of hits.

By the time he let himself into his apartment, he was resolute. After the seismic artistic growth he'd felt with *Carnival* and *Without You I'm Nothing*, he knew he had a responsibility to take yet more risks and be more truthful than ever.

The following morning, his walk led him to a slightly dishevelled doorway in Fitzroy, less than a kilometre from his own apartment. Alex knocked on the door, and while he waited, looked around the front yard, noting that a couple of cats were having a field day near the garbage cans. He heard an unsteady gait of boots on floorboards and someone grizzling *'Who the hell is it at this ungodly hour?'* before the front door suddenly opened.

"Hi," Alex said, nervously. At which point Stuart's demeanour shifted from cranky to surprise.

"Oh! Come in. Come in," Stuart said after awkwardly hugging Alex. "Oh gosh, you found it okay?"

"Yeah, no problems," Alex said, following Stuart down the dim corridor and pushing his sunglasses up to the top of his head so that they acted like a headband. His hair was now as long as it had been when he'd released his first album, but jet black and wavy.

Stuart sat at the coffee table with a cup of coffee and a lit cigarette and invited Alex to take a seat on the sofa. Stuart poured him a coffee and offered him a fag, which Alex accepted to help put the producer at ease. This was the first time they'd met in person.

"Have you lived here long?" Alex asked absently, taking in the eclectically furnished room.

"Yes, years, but I only bothered to do some renovating last year. We used to do live gigs around here all the time. In fact, I still do some acoustic shows now and then with some of the boys, or by myself. You're familiar with the area?"

Alex explained he'd lived nearby during his brief time at university.

"I'm sure you can see how much it's changed then. It seems to be becoming the *it* strip."

"Yeah, it doesn't look much like I remembered it, at least not Brunswick Street. Looks like it's been cleaned up," Alex said, exhaling.

"Yeah. The oldies are moving out so rapidly, and lots of yuppies are moving in." Stuart sighed, looking ruefully at Alex for a moment. "I have to say, I was kind of surprised that you, *the music video idol,* wanted to work with me. You know you're an idol now, right? *The music video idol* as they say on the news. I heard them talking about putting your face on a postage stamp the other week."

Alex, more than anything, wanted to quash the awkwardness between them, and deflate the inference that he was just another yuppie encroaching on Stuart's bohemian territory. He wanted to be direct and tell the man in front of him that he'd worked for what he'd achieved, that he had a past just as remarkable and edgy as the life Stuart was carving out for himself. But things were already awkward, so he shrugged off Stuart's insinuations.

"I thought you and me working together might be one of the more inspired combinations," Alex said. "I figured that we'd probably do something together that no one else would be capable of. And also, I've heard some of the things you've been working on lately. They're remarkable and the kind of songs no one else seems capable of making. I want that tension, that abrasiveness on my record."

Stuart smiled in acknowledgement, studying Alex for a moment. "I have some of your singles. I loved your early Bollywood stuff, especially the first album. I think I even have some of the twelve inches!" Stuart said. "And that *Circumstances* song… *killer*! I absolutely love that. I think I have the album," he said, pointing to the wall that was brimming with LPs and singles, crammed into the floor to ceiling shelves. "I'm a big collector," Stuart explained, butting out his cigarette. "I collect everything."

They talked some more about the kind of music that dominated their collections, and how Stuart was resolutely sticking to vinyl, even though it was getting harder to find. "It's disgraceful this push towards CDs."

Beneath his steely gaze, the beanie and the industrial knit jumper, and those old, old jeans, there was something incredibly alluring about Stuart. Alex saw that time hadn't been kind to him, but Stuart was still a handsome man. After doing some research, Alex found that throughout his career, Stuart had not only scoffed at the idea that he was a sex symbol but had literally reprimanded people anytime they mentioned his looks. Alex recalled reading at least a couple of interviews that documented the great pains Stuart went to in quashing the idea that he was merely a singing heartthrob.

Alex admired Stuart's antagonism. He'd put Alex's management team through the hoops before agreeing to work with

Alex, not even entertaining the idea of the collaboration until he'd directly spoken at length with Alex about the project.

***

Stuart didn't eventually agree so much for the financial returns, which would come in perpetuity with an artist as big as Alex, as he did for the challenge of doing something subversive with a real pop star. Something *'fucked up and twisted'* as Stuart had put it to Alex during the telephone call that had sealed Stuart's commitment.

Though in demand in Australia, Stuart was now languishing with run of the mill pop singers. He was working with soap stars who needed credibility and legacy acts who needed younger audiences. After first seriously considering the proposal, Stuart had sat down with Alex's entire catalogue and spent a week listening to it. Song after song, he scoured the lyric sheets, interviews in the magazines in the State Library collection, and watched old VHS footage, trying to locate the essence of the *postage stamp music video idol.*

Having been a performer and a chart act himself, Stuart knew how to distinguish pop confection from the real deal. He thought about each article and interview in its context, devouring the fawning teen music magazines and the more critical industry press alike. He felt like he was some kind of investigative reporter by the end of that week. And he'd decided that even with a decade long career, comprising six albums, Alekzandr's level of artistry had been pretty weak up until that point. And this was where the charm and opportunity lay. Stuart wanted to bring his own intellectualism and depth to someone who, although an undisputed idol, could not be easily categorised as either a mere pop act or an underground act with a huge following. In his eyes, Alekzandr was more like an interloper; a cultural phenomenon who just happened to make music.

In Stuart's estimation, Alekzandr was a mass media performance artist. The interviews, the photos, the films and above all, the videos, were as important as the songs. As long as he could reign in Alex's pop tendencies, there was a real opportunity to produce something interesting. The difficulty would be in convincing Alex that he had to make concessions. It would be the only way to ensure longevity in this, the second phase of the idol's career.

****

When Stuart finally turned on the equipment, it was only after they'd spent a few days in each other's company, discussing their ideas and music. Alex had forced himself to resist the temptation to go straight into studio mode that first day in Fitzroy. Sensing that Stuart needed one final prompt to understand his current frame of mind better, he organised a late night excursion to the recently opened Hellfire Club, an S&M nightclub located in walking distance.

"Look beyond the obvious," Alex said, clutching Stuart's elbow as they entered the premises. "Don't get distracted by the exhibitionism."

"I can't see much beyond all the leather," Stuart said.

"You have to suspend your thinking a bit," Alex said. "The leather isn't just leather. It's a symbol. Of constraint and consent and resistance," Alex said in his ear, as they watched a guy in leather chaps receiving a paddling on stage. The guy's pale skin reddened with each blow, his face broadcasting his discomfort.

He only managed to endure the pain for a few minutes before the host dismissed him from the stage, unimpressed with his constant squirming.

"That's not sexy," Stuart noted as the MC called for another volunteer to step on stage.

"It doesn't have to be, not visually anyway," Alex said, taking off his top and handing it to Stuart, walking up to the stage and dutifully following the MC's instructions.

Stuart watched as Alex stretched his arms above his head, the host cuffing them at the wrist to the room's applause.

"We want to see more!" the host yelled into the microphone, taking it upon himself to unbuckle Alex's jeans and pulling them down to his knees.

"Nice jocks," the host said, spinning the podium made of steel carrier pipes around and lifting Alex's underwear at his buttocks.

The host then cuffed each of Alex's ankles, asking Alex to demonstrate how he was now locked into place. Alex pulled at his wrists and feet and was unable to tease much movement from the chains he was clipped to.

Two people joined them on stage, each clad in leather. The first, a guy, held a leather and wooden flay in his hand, the other, a woman, a cane rod in hers.

"You ready?" the host asked, and the room responded for Alex, the flay crashing down on the side of his thigh, the rod on his buttocks.

Alex grimaced at Stuart as he endured the strikes, smiling and gasping in turn as the guy shifted his attention to Alex's bare chest.

"Let's give him a twirl," the MC growled over the din of industrial house music, spinning the podium around so that the audience could only see Alex's back, buttocks and legs.

"Harder," the MC commanded, the two attendants striking Alex now more forcefully and quickly than before.

Alex felt his eyes watering, the cold air making his skin hard and more susceptible to the stinging pain. Spun around again to face the audience, Alex locked eyes with a guy who stared at him intently. With each landing blow, Alex maintained eye contact, wondering whether the tall redhead would come to his aid and take away some of the sting.

The spectator winked at him, blowing him a kiss as Alex endured another round of blows. The stage attendants increased the force and speed with which they 'punished' Alex, hitting and whipping him for five continuous minutes before Alex finally signalled he'd had enough.

"Oh, what a good sport this one's been," the MC said as the music was turned up. The attendants uncuffed Alex and helped him get dressed, Stuart clambering up to the stage and handing Alex his top as the crowd politely clapped.

"Did you plan that?" Stuart asked.

"No, it just looked like fun," Alex said.

"You're shaking," Stuart noted.

"Just the cold air," Alex said dismissively, looking around. "I need a stiff drink."

"I'll go, just wait here," Stuart said.

As Alex reassembled his outfit and watched Stuart join the line at the bar, the redheaded spectator re-emerged.

"That looked like a lot of fun," he said.

"It was," Alex replied.

"I don't know if I could do it. Stand up in front of everyone like that."

"The trick is finding a friendly face to focus on," Alex said.

"Yeah, I saw you staring at me. I'm Jack," he said. "I couldn't do it though. Too intimate."

"It was just a bit of fun," Alex said. "It wasn't really very intimate."

"I don't know," Jack replied. "There were a few moments there where it looked pretty intimate to me."

Alex smiled.

"If you're up for something a little more private," Jack said, "my place is just around the corner."

Stuart returned with the drinks and without missing a beat handed Alex a scotch.

"How's your arse babe?" Stuart asked, turning to stare at Jack, who looked at Alex for a moment before scurrying off.

"Incredible, I leave you alone for five minutes," Stuart said, "and you're already picking up."

"You cock blocked me," Alex said, sipping his scotch. "Unforgiveable."

"You'll thank me tomorrow morning. You're already gonna have a hard enough time sitting tonight."

| 5 |

ANDROGYNOUS

"We need a new bridge. Those lyrics don't work there," Stuart said.

Lyrics belonged to Alex; Alex thought he had made that clear from day one.

"Play it again," Alex barked, pen and paper at the ready. He listened and reluctantly agreed; the tempo was not a good fit. He scribbled down a couple of things while Stuart re–cued the song and retooled the mixing board. As Stuart tinkered with the settings, Alex asked him to isolate the bass track, singing the song to himself as it played back.

When the bridge arrived, Alex looked down at his new notes and sang them out, staring out at the glass bricks, where the room's only natural light seemed to enter in from. He concentrated on his breathing like Stefan had taught him, and when he stopped singing, Stuart looked at him impassively.

"Better," Stuart said, re–cueing the tracks. "Let's do it again and this time hold the last note a little longer."

With the advent of their visits to Hellfire and other clubs, where they convinced the DJs to test out some of their in-strumentals, their demos had changed considerably. The beats had become more industrial, but Stuart and Alex found ways to add flourishes to the mix. The songs variously included hooky basslines, percussion from *djembe* drums, and even wailing vo-cals recorded from the kitchen. With time Alex also detected other embellishments in the tracks; among them a passing refer-ence to a middle–eight he'd originally written way back in 1987. It was an arrangement which had been buried deep into the cho-rus he had written for *Feel.* The moment he heard it resurface, he looked up and saw Stuart smiling back.

'Glad you noticed', Stuart's face seemed to be saying. When he wasn't busy being stern, Stuart had a face like Morrissey's. The kind with the piercing blue eyes that Alex almost always went weak for.

They recorded and improvised all around the house. When the microphone cords weren't long enough, Alex would make do, diving down onto the grubby floors or leaning against the walls to coax out his vocals.

While his vocals were smoother than ever, his lyrics were bittersweet and caustic. His experiences with Ferris and Diego were on his mind and had come to the fore. As he later pointed out in an interview, the songs "differ in tone. Some are about the buzz of exploring the physical sides of love and infatuation. How it's like a rollercoaster you can never predict. But there are also songs about the emotional side, where there is less of that freedom. Because so many men look at their partners as adversaries because that's the way we're brought up to look at other men. So, when they find themselves in a relationship together, many choose either to mimic straight couples or, go to the other extreme, where they consider sex the be all and end all. Some couples struggle to find more nuance than that."

Alex and Stuart's working relationship proved a mostly healthy one. Neither seemed to need much from the other, and they rarely bothered to speak too personally about their life experiences. It was the proverbial meeting of two planets with a huge black hole floating somewhere between. Each was a guest in the other's world, and neither was sufficiently fluent in the other's language to build anything more than a working relationship.

Stuart needed the work, and enjoyed the challenge, but he knew they could never really be friends. They argued constantly over tiny details but never to the point of being volatile. Both were wise enough to value the other's strengths, and as the weeks progressed, they worked hard to remain open to each other's suggestions.

It became apparent that although the soul of the album was in Stuart's hands, the more uplifting tracks were being saved for Paul in LA, where Alex hoped the studio would be drenched with natural light.

Alex's aim for the album was now to juxtapose romanticism with cynicism. The Melbourne songs were turning out to be darker and more biting than anything he'd done before.

When one of the visiting American VPs of the record label, Simon Levy, came to listen to the album tracks, Alex insisted that the meeting not take place at Stuart's home. Knowing the ropes, Alex already knew this was going to be a project he'd have to fight for, creative freedoms or not. He wasn't convinced Stuart needed to be part of the deconstruction of the songs. Record company analysis was about deducing how marketable songs were, and that, in Alex's eyes, could not be Stuart's concern.

Celia had also flown into Melbourne, a few days before Simon's arrival. She'd been so busy working on re–establishing Alex's boutique label with Kōji and some of the ex–staff who were brought back on board, that she hadn't been following the progress of the album as closely as she might've normally.

Truth be told, on the first playback, the songs made her nervous. Very nervous. It was not only quite unlike anything Alex had recorded before, but also quite unlike anything else that was in the marketplace. Commercially, it was very risky. The backbone of the album was definitely dance music, and that gave her some faith. But the divide between these songs and what the label were probably hoping for was, well, wide by her estimation.

Alex did his best to convince Celia that this album was going to set a new standard in dance pop. Yes, it was darker and harder than anything else he'd done, but it was also fresh and edgy. There were hooks, bridges and choruses that reasserted the melody for anyone who cared to look for them, but *accessibility* was not a priority for him. Celia wasn't entirely convinced, suggesting that at least three or four of the songs would ostensibly be album tracks, unable to be considered as singles.

"I love it. But it's going to be a hard sell," Simon said curtly, after the demos had been played in a Melbourne boardroom. He'd madly scribbled his notes about each individual song.

"It's either going to explode or bomb spectacularly. Nothing in between," he affirmed, to a few nodding heads in the room.

"The problem is, how do we position it Celia? It's not going to go to radio well. It will go well to the clubs. But perhaps it's an idea to rethink some of these songs." He began to sound exasperated as he continued. "I mean, give them a minimum of a pop edge. It's already going to be tough getting this into stores without an advisory sticker, and if we do have to put a sticker on it, then, we're going to lose a lot of the chain stores."

Alex had waited impatiently for his own turn to speak and interjected as Celia went to reply.

"Simon," Alex said coolly, "firstly, the sticker is a non–issue. Way more explicit things have come out this year and not been slapped with a sticker. There's no profanity on my album.

"What you've heard today is the darker aspect of the album, but I've got another five or six songs that I'll be working on in LA which are going to balance these ones out. I do think at least two of these ones could be singles. You know that I've never let the label down before. In a year's time, everyone's records are going to sound like mine. This isn't an easy album, but I never promised you easy. I said I'd give you a *great* album, and I think you have to admit that these songs are the bomb. They're hard but they're the kind of songs that people are going to want to hear when they go out, to really pound it out and dance to. But I need you to get behind me on them. To trust me."

Simon and Alex had a long professional relationship and usually managed to see eye to eye. Simon had been in A&R back in Alex's early days at the label and had graduated to junior VP around the time of *Felicidad*. Simon had been one of the few who had seen the potential in it, even if, only three years later, he'd initially suggested *Without You I'm Nothing* wasn't commercial enough, especially after such a long hiatus from the market.

Although he wasn't always right, Simon's track record in steering artists to huge success had earned him the nickname *The Green Lantern.* Without his okay, a pop release at the label was unlikely to be given a green light. While Simon's approval was not vital to Alex, having it would secure the label's full promotional resources, which Alex knew was going to be essential. A lot was at stake; Alex's reign as a tastemaker in pop among them. Pop was already losing its edge, and baying at its heels were the new bands coming out of Seattle as well as an army of contemporary R&B artists. And in America at least, a new wave of country music was also capturing the attention of the masses (and had kept Alex from the top spot last time around). Together, these new, opposing trends in music had swiftly rendered dance–pop passé in America.

Simon asked the assistant to replay the third and fourth tracks, and, referring to his notes as the songs played back, he asked Alex to consider changes; the removal of strings, the adding of harmonies and backing vocals, an additional key change here and there. In two listens he'd nailed the songs. He'd understood them and set about casting just the necessary amount of doubt in Alex's mind, knowing Alex *would* go back into the studio thinking about the suggestions. He'd always had the knack of making Alex's mind tick.

In the end harmonies were added but the strings stayed. The strings didn't just stay... Alex organised for a quartet to come in and re-record them live, partly to spite Simon, and partly because Alex conceded they weren't quite right in their original synthesised form.

Stuart, knowing how things worked, realised that Alex must've been battered by the studio execs at the meeting, so he played nice for the remainder of their time together.

After a relatively quick and painless time in the LA studios with Paul working on the album's upbeat dance anthems, Alex's record neared completion by September.

While the album was being mixed and mastered, Alex 'unintentionally' kicked off its promotional campaign.

Arriving with a couple of friends and Diego, who'd finally resurfaced, Alex and his crew partied into the night with hundreds of other ravers in an old LA warehouse. Dressed in a sheer top, which was ripped midway through the night by an overly enthusiastic raver, Alex and his crew formed their own posse, dancing and writhing the night away together. At one point, amidst the scene they were creating on the dance floor, Alex leant in and passionately kissed Diego. Though they'd had the good sense not to step beyond the line of decency, no one in the group seemed aware of the two *scene* photographers who had their SLRs trained on the group's every move. Trained professionals, neither missed the opportunity to capture the very public kiss before quickly leaving the premises. It was only in their dark rooms that the explosive nature of the images revealed themselves.

In the space of a week, Alex was bearing the brunt of their publication, the grainy photos making it into almost every major tabloid around the world. The pictures left very little to the imagination, and it was clear, even to outsiders, that there *was* something between him and Diego, even after years of no comment. The irony was that things between the two of them had substantially cooled by then.

Kathy, Alex's publicist, was inundated with calls, the photos spurring global interest. Amidst the furore, Kathy insisted Alex release a statement to stem the controversy erupting in the press.

I really enjoyed my night out. I've been working so hard on my new album for so long that I needed a night to let off some steam with my friends. That seems to have gotten a whole lot of people worked up over nothing. If the idea of two men being together or kissing is as frightening as everyone is making it out to be, I think we, as a society, have major problems. We should be championing people who express affection for one another: not demonising them. Get a grip. Work hard, play hard, but lighten up. That's what I'll be doing as I get ready for my new record to drop.

Alex and Kathy's refusal to issue a denial incensed Diego. It all but confirmed in Diego's mind that it was Alex who had orchestrated the photos all along.

Alex pulled a few last minute changes to take advantage of the swirling controversy. He dropped the working title for the album *Hard Up* in favour of *Androgynous,* renaming its first single *Velvet* (originally *The Velvet Glove). Velvet,* an electronic ballad brought to life in Stuart's studio, was given a slight redo by Paul in LA, who added a cinematic touch to the song, softening its sparse, electronic sound.

Alex chose it as the album's lead single as he felt it bridged his more familiar sound with his new one. Crashing into the top ten around the world (landing inside the top five in the triumvirate of the UK, US and his home country), it became a hit, even if it was to be eclipsed by what was quickly shaping up to be something of a backlash.

The album launch in LA got the ball rolling, bringing out the press and some of Hollywood's biggest stars, who wanted in on the year's most tantalising scandal. But as the album hit stores, the media was awash in debate about Alex and his sexuality. His outing landed him his first ever *Time* magazine cover. In the accompanying article, just one of many that examined the cultural significance of the moment, Alex's new lyrics were dissected.

Diego had been conspicuously absent in all of this. He'd refused to attend the album launch or to be photographed with Alex who had taken on a decidedly glam, androgynous look when in public. Busy with back to back interviews and unable to head to Mexico, Alex tried instead to reach Diego by phone, days passing until he finally made it through.

"You only wanted me there to promote your album," Diego snapped. "I know you won't ever admit it, but you've compromised what we have for your career."

"I swear I had nothing to do with it," Alex declared. "I have always respected your position on things."

"Alex, I didn't want to be outed. Not in that way. We've been together all this time, but it seems more than a little coincidental that our relationship makes front page news now that you've got a new record to promote."

"That's bull Diego. It was just a spur of the moment kiss. And you kissed me back by the way."

"I've told you all along that I wasn't prepared to be under the microscope any more than I already was," Diego said, the line crackling, "and now you're even denying it."

"You honestly believe I planned all this?" Alex asked. "That I would orchestrate outing us for publicity?"

"I think you didn't think it through. But yeah, I do think that you planned it. You thought I'd let you get away with it. Do you know how hard these last few days have been for me? My phone never stops ringing. My sister is getting threats in Ixtapa. I swear people are looking at me differently."

"Oh, Diego I'm sorry. But I'm sure it will all blow over."

"You can't begin to understand the hysteria here over all of this. I don't think this can be fixed."

"It will blow over. I can organise for an escort for you if you need it. Or you can come here until things cool down. People will find something else to obsess about soon enough."

"Will they? I don't think they will Alex. Worse still, I'm furious. I feel like you've ruined my life. I can't see how I am ever going to recover from this. I'm one step away from being lynched, thanks to you," Diego said dramatically, hanging up the phone.

When Alex couldn't get back through to him, he realised Diego had probably disconnected the phone from the wall.

Androgynous hit the stores alongside two equally divisive releases from Prince and Madonna who were courting their own socio/sexual controversies at the time. *Androgynous*, debuted strongly, shifting more than a million copies worldwide in its first week.

The album received mostly glowing reviews in the music press. *Rolling Stone* labelled it Alex's first true *masterpiece*, lauding it for its fresh take on dance music and electronica, and Alex's handling of the themes of sex and masculinity in the safe sex era. But in the wider press, the controversy about Alex's sexual orientation and the highly sexualised work of three of pop's biggest superstars all but drowned out the music. All three were accused of finally having pushed the envelope too far. *'The (p)opportunist's luck has run out'*, one headline screamed just as *Outing* finally hit cinemas, the distributor capitalizing on Alex's white hot media presence. Much like the album, the film enthralled critics but enraged the mainstream press. Film critics saw it as a searing portrayal of gay life in modern America, drawing the obvious parallels between the film and Alex's own life, as well as the controversy surrounding the activist group ACTUP, who were waging public outing campaigns at the time.

As a second single, *Warmth of Your Touch,* hit the market in time for Christmas, the media's vilification of Alex went into top gear, a British tabloid landing a sensational coup in tracking down the only two surviving artists Alex modelled for in his pre–fame days. For a purported £25K a piece, they laid out just how far Alex used to go in order to earn his payments.

Times had clearly changed and the tabloid scoop was damning. If Alex had been courting the establishment's ire with his work and the unveiling of his sexual orientation, then the tabloid confessions, some thirteen years after the fact, seemed like the final nails in Alekzandr's coffin.

Warmth of Your Touch achieved the unfortunate distinction of being the single that ended Alekzandr's record breaking run of US top twenty hits, becoming his first since 1983 to not reach the top forty. It was the same across many of Alekzandr's tried and tested markets; aside from in Europe, the single bombed everywhere.

Despite their critical acclaim and initial commercial flourishes, by late January the commercial trajectories of *Androgynous* and *Outing* abruptly ended.

A campaign to have Alex blacklisted from radio stations took hold in the US and later in South America, with some stations even encouraging listeners to come and dump their old Alekzandr records outside their offices for mass bonfires.

In damage control mode, Alex's label opted for radio friendly remixes of three more singles, but without sufficient airplay, none of them reached the top forty.

The swift and forceful backlash, rooted in homophobia and an outright rejection of the themes of his work, instilled incredible anger in Alex.

In public, he was unrepentant, using what little airtime he was afforded to criticise the hypocrisy he felt subjected to. Alex spent much of the first half of 1993 waging a personal war against homophobia and censorship in the press, but this did little to dent the public's indifference to him. Crowing at his demise, the press began to demonise him, many suggesting he'd well and truly worn out his welcome.

Though Alex maintained a brave public face, 1993 represented a turning point for him. Being at the centre of a media hurricane that hadn't blown in his favour had destroyed his confidence. He'd thought he'd become accustomed to experiencing doubt and character assassination, but the scale on which he'd been brought down surprised even him. After years of playing with sexual, religious and political imagery, and being celebrated for doing so, it seemed he'd lost his magic touch, and, in the process, also Diego, who had all but disappeared from his life, moving to Spain but refusing to say where.

For the first time in years, Alex felt like a true outsider again, branded with his own scarlet letter. He was seething that Diego had left him so abruptly, and cringed when people began referring to him as the world's most famous queer.

So, Alex largely headed back underground, spending the second half of 1993 shuttling between LA and NYC, working away at new music and planning his next venture; a world tour.

There were days he didn't want to get up, didn't want to go to the studio. *What's the point in making something else that will be ripped to shreds?* Didn't have the energy to fight for or defend his ideas. *No one listens anyway.* Didn't want to see his name being bandied about in the press, tarnished by untruths and ridiculous speculation. *Haven't they got someone else they need to hobble?* Wasn't interested in the cultural studies courses at universities re–examining his entire career with a queer eye. Couldn't see the point in taking part in the uncomfortable discussions in his management offices and at his record label. Didn't want to think about how they were ever going to recoup their investment now. Didn't know how he should feel after so triumphantly signing to the label only to have the first album on the deal flop so badly. Had no idea how he could ever climb back on top while radio and retail chains were actively boycotting him. Couldn't fathom how so much of his audience had turned away from him in droves.

His management team was sure a tour would help Alekzandr find his footing again, along with a new market of fans. But Alex wasn't so sure. He could sense there'd been a fundamental shift away from him.

Invited to perform at the VMAs, he heard the booing the minute he hit the stage. Though he still had allies in the entertainment industry, some of whom publicly championed him for his bravery, he found himself the punchline of all kinds of homophobic jokes that night. This after months of being ridiculed in rap verses and snubbed by Hollywood's casting directors and producers.

With the bulk of his new record completed, Alex picked up sticks, taking a brief holiday before returning to work on the new album. He took up residence in a rental near the recording studio in West London while he waited out the completion of renovations to his London house.

Back in London, the city he loved and hated, the entire experience of the past twelve months led Alex to believe he might have to be prepared to step away from the US more permanently if he wanted to have a chance at a normal life.

And if he chose to do it in London, it wouldn't be like starting over, but it wouldn't be all that different from it either.

| 6 |

OUTING

Androgynous divided Alekzandr's fans into two camps: the first camp considering the album a watershed moment; the second, a needlessly controversial release which sullied Alex's pop pedigree and marked the end of any relevance he held for them.

A year after the album's release, Alex sat down for an interview with *The Advocate,* the gay monthly. The two–part interview, syndicated across the world, resonated with diehard fans. Years later, when his fan community moved online, they took to labelling the interview as one of the key artefacts of Alekzandr's nineties era.

Gary Soto, the journalist who conducted the interview with Alex later recalled; "He was in good spirits the two times that I saw him. We'd spoken off the record beforehand a few times, and he was adamant that he wanted to use the interview to clear the air. He'd told me his management team had warned him against sitting down with me, but he wanted to speak without interruption. There was a sense of conviction in him. He didn't mince words, but at the same time he chose them carefully. I could sense a lot of anger from him. There was a lot at stake for him and there was talk that he was at risk of being released from his contract. His label was already under immense pressure with some other controversial releases at the time, and people were saying he was going to be the first to be shown the door."

The temptation to believe we know someone better than we think we do is sometimes irresistible. When we've grown up alongside somebody and watched them scale their heights and scrape their lows, we often feel we were part of their journey... part of their evolution.

The eighties gave the gay community a lot of goodtime idols and a handful of icons. Each has played their part in our lives and we all have our own favourites.

Some of these pop culture stars actively sought us out, taking their part in the war against homophobia. Some used their spotlight to bring attention to AIDS awareness and prevention. Others simply gave us chugging tunes and edgy videos which nodded at our culture. And we co-opted them the way they did us.

We choose our icons carefully. Not everyone makes it onto that heady list. More often than not we identify with the most tenacious stars who have had dramas to overcome. It's what separates an icon from the pack.

Alekzandr has long been one of our staunchest icons. He surfaced from the London and New York undergrounds in the early eighties, part of that fabulous mix of high and low art. As one of a pioneering group of artists who queered things up, he has consistently used his mu-

sic and videos to get the mainstream talking about sexual and identity politics.

Like other alumni of the downtown scene, Alekzandr's influence on youth culture became global. Droves of fans around the world dressed like him and worshipped him, even as he increasingly dared audiences to keep up.

As recent events have proven, Alekzandr has never been one to shy away from controversy. The storylines that fuel his pop hits, videos and movies often get critics hot under the collar. His has been a career in which his every move attracts the kind of attention some artists can only dream of.

Constantly an underdog, with critics always ready to take him down, Alekzandr has recently pulled off an arc of albums that have exceeded expectations. The latest, 'Androgynous', which capitalizes on the new 'sleaze' underground dance movement, is a collection of songs that go back to his dance roots. Its lyrics explore the intersection between sex, romance and community in the GLBT world. The songs are fascinating and have acted as a war cry to the queer community. On 'Sanctimony', a typically dirty house anthem, he practically growls "get up/ own up/ be who you are/ others' good graces can only carry you so far."

His forays into film have proven equally prescient. His recent movie, 'Outing', inspired by the ACTUP coalition, is one of Hollywood's first queer blockbusters. In it he plays a prominent politico – Andrew Ellis – who is the target of an outing campaign. We watch as the care-

fully orchestrated house of cards he has built to protect his secret spectacularly collapses around him.

It was not a movie inspired by his own life, but Alekzandr's own house of cards burned down similarly this last year. Pinned down by a press that once openly championed him, speculation about his personal life has now become a staple on the talk show circuit.

I thought I knew him better than I actually did, because even on this chilly day in New York, I found him full of surprises. We'd spoken on the phone a few times earlier in the week before the photographer and I arrived at his sprawling NYC apartment. The apartment? It's expensive but understated. That dizzying kind of eclectic style that can only be pulled off with money, good taste and a dedicated interior designer.

When Alekzandr opens his front door I realise he's taller than I imagined. His caramel eyes shine and his hair, long at the front and short everywhere else is dark henna red with lots of regrowth. He's wearing jeans and a very European looking cardigan. When he sees the photographer sneak a look at his exposed chest, he doesn't miss a beat. "It's Italian. I picked it up in Rome," he says, buttoning the knit up to cover up his chest.

He pours me and the photographer green tea. We're staying in the kitchen it seems, and while the two of them debate the details of what they want to do, I look around the room, noticing that there's mismatched chairs at the long table and French doors that open onto his balcony. Though currently sodden, its green and generously sized by NYC standards. I imagine how he and his famous troupe of friends get down on it when the weather allows. Back inside, there's an expensive sound system above the fridge, and lots of framed photographs around the walls and on the surfaces. But the one object that commands my attention is a huge Spanish propaganda print of a topless iron smith 'forging' a new Spain. My eyes dart from the illustration to Alekzandr and back.

When he dispatches the photographer, he comes and sits at the table with me, apologising and musing about why photographers always want to change things at the last minute.

GS: "Are you in New York for work?"

A: "Kind of. I'm filming some videos. I plan on using them for a project I'm working on. I'm only here for another week and then it's back to Europe to keep working on some new material."

GS: "Before we talk about the new material, can we talk about 'Androgynous'?"

A: "I think we have to, seeing as I don't have anything to say about the new stuff yet."

GS: "'Androgynous' didn't quite land the way a lot of people expected it would."

A: "No it didn't. But I knew that was always going to be a possibility."

GS: "Why? You've had a great track record so far."

A: "I guess. But we're in the middle of a very conservative phase at the moment. You know when I put that Balkan record out people were like, 'why is he doing that?' It's the idea that we're all supposed to stay in our lanes. Not rock the boat. Bullshit basically. People don't want me talking about things that should be swept under the rug."

GS: "The reaction to 'Androgynous' has been unparalleled, hasn't it?"

A: "Well yes. It all feels a bit taboo. Heaven forbid a pop star crosses the line and asks people to think. They'll make you pay for it."

GS: "It's your job to toe the line to a certain extent though, isn't it? Even if that doesn't fit in with the global imagination of what a rock star should be."

A: "Probably. But I've never toed the line. I think I'm just finally paying the price for it now."

GS: "'Androgynous' has been described both as one of the year's best and one of the year's worst albums."

A: "I know," Alekzandr replied, adjusting the cuff on his knit. "But I think that's a good thing," he says coldly.

GS: "How so?"

A: "First of all you can't please everybody. As an artist you shouldn't even try. I'm not saying my record is perfect, but I think a lot of the people who reviewed it weren't talking about the music. They were referring to me or to the videos or the film. I think a lot of the negative reviews were just poorly written, really."

GS: "But you don't expect them to tell you that, I don't know, 'your chorus is problematic or that your bridge doesn't work', do you?"

He seems to reflect a moment while he pours himself some tea.

A: "No. But to describe it as porn makes me wonder if they even bothered to listen to it."

GS: "Are you happy with the record?"

A: *"Absolutely. I think it's really good. But as always, my music gets lost in the larger conversation. Now that they identify me as being the world's biggest queer, the message I get is 'Sorry the inn's full', you know? It's odd. I mean it's not like people haven't always been obsessed with my sexual orientation. They're acting like it's a new thing."*

GS: *"Can you say something about why you didn't say something about your sexuality earlier? Was it a professional decision?"*

A: *"It's a layered thing. Since day one, people have had an opinion about my sexuality. I never wanted to dignify the question. Everyone wanted to talk about it, but not with the view of accepting it. I've always considered myself queer, but at the same time, I refuse to be defined by any label."*

GS: *"Why come out now then? Some people might think it's to sell more records."*

A: *"On what planet? The press came out for me. They made the decision. When I made this record I made the mistake of thinking people would be adults about the themes of the record. I'm proud to be queer but in outing me, the press has outed the people around me. And on the whole, in this society, being queer is synonymous with being punished. I've been crucified, I've received death threats. It destroyed my relationship... I've been blacklisted by radio... been completely villainised. And yet what alternative is there? Don't ask, don't tell? It's a no win situation."*

GS: *"You've mentioned the pressure. How are you handling it?"*

A: *"I'm resilient. I won't let them destroy me. I won't be silenced. What upsets me is when I think about what this means for any kid looking for the courage to come out. What will they be walking into? We have to grow up as a society."*

GS: "Let's go back to the album for a minute, because we've been side tracked by everything else. In your own words can you explain how you see it?"

Here Alekzandr searches for his words for what seems like an eternity.

A: "I started writing it after I went to Philadelphia for the march in April. It was inspired by some conversations I had there and the feelings that it brought out of me. That day I talked to people who'd travelled thousands of kilometres to be there. It got me thinking about how we compartmentalise. GLBT people have a lot on their plate. They work hard to create new families for themselves and to be activists for their community. And yet a lot of gay men have a hard time integrating sex into their lives in a healthy way. They're often reduced to fleeting encounters. To me, that march... those stories I heard, just seemed to scream to me, 'this is what you have to write about!' You know, the dichotomy of the two lives so many of us live."

GS: "Do you think your message got lost somewhere? The album comes across as a bit schizophrenic. You go from depression and anger to euphoria in the space of a few songs."

A: "I think people think the songs are completely autobiographical. They're not. They're about different characters in my mind. Men who are at different stages."

GS: "Is that the biggest misconception about the album then? That it's autobiographical?"

A: "That, and the idea that it's some kind of sex crazed record. People have jumped to the conclusion that everything is about sex on this album."

GS: "It's not? Not even on something like 'Uncontrollable Urges'?"

A: "Not at all! None of the songs are about sexual acts. That's the irony of it all."

GS: "Really? Then what are they about? That one in particular?"

A: "They're about the politics behind the sex. 'Uncontrollable Urges' is about this idea of 'Yes, I'll fuck you, but I don't want any of our friends thinking we're together'. That to me is far more interesting than singing about sex."

GS: "So it's about one night stands?"

A: "Not even one night stands. I think we are compartmentalising more than that. We demand the complete solidarity of our friends, but at the same time we encourage each other to be emotionally distant with sexual partners. There are lots of guys having sex but so few who are connecting while they do it. You know, 'come to bed with me but I don't want you in my house the next day?' I mean it's depressing!"

GS: "But doesn't that run contradictory to the idea of sexual freedom that you, among others, have been championing all these years?"

A: "I don't think sexual freedom exists when you treat someone else like a piece of meat. That isn't sexual freedom to me. It's oppression. The gap between what we're prepared to touch and what we allow ourselves to feel is scary."

GS: "But isn't that a form of freedom for some people? Don't you think that you're just making a distinction between romance and lust?

For someone who's always encouraged experimentation and empowerment it seems contradictory."

A: "No. Not at all. Be experimental, be empowered! And doing that in this climate takes real balls. But don't for a minute equate sex with real, human interaction. This is what I'm saying. Some people's idea of sex begins and ends in a dark room at a club every week. If you do that, you're just fetishizing. You get off, but you can never get the same kind of rush in other areas of your life. I've seen it happen to people I know. That's what I'm exploring on some of the songs."

GS: "Can we talk about 'Hard Up'? What's that about?"

A: "Longing. Yearning. Unrequited love."

GS: "It's a love song?"

A: "Erm, I guess so. A love song for the modern age. It's about when something's right under your nose but out of your reach. How you have to take things into your own hands."

GS: "So it's about masturbation?"

A: "The stages leading up to it, yes. The romanticism of wanting someone that doesn't want you back and a way you can deal with it."

GS: "One of the sadder moments on the album is the song 'Decision Never Made'. Can you explain how that came about?"

A: "It came from a moment in the studio when Stuart and I were talking about my old New York days. About watching some of my friends and one person in particular who I loved, die. How their families had abandoned them and how their disease labelled them as people to be afraid of. So, fear robbed these wonderful people, that wonderful man, of the love they deserved in their final days."

Alekzandr pauses for a moment, and seems to collect himself from more introspection, always touching those cuffs.

A: "When I think of how amazing those people were, the lengths they went to because they wanted to be true to themselves, it just makes me angry. Those lyrics came from that. And Stuart, who's a genius, said, 'let's just strip it back to the basics because it's already so power-ful'. So it's just my vocal and a synth. We didn't polish it up. It was all done in one take."

The album proved too edgy for mainstream audiences, as did 'Outing', which, nonetheless earned Alekzandr his first ever Golden Globe nomination for his portrayal of Andrew. The film, inspired by real life events and the current GLBT climate, triggered debates about privacy and the obligations of public figures. It seems an obvious match to some of the themes on his album.

GS: "What drew you to the film?"

A: "I felt I had a responsibility to do it. I thought it was a great part. I trusted the director. I knew that if it was done well, it would get people talking. I think it's the best film I've worked on so far."

GS: "Has your opinion about outing changed in light of recent events? Before the film came out you said you were a little ambivalent about it."

A: "I'm still fascinated by groups like ACT UP. I don't always agree with their tactics but I think they're about exposing hypocrisy. I think they're trying to speak truth to power, especially when they target politicians. But ultimately, I wonder if they are simply contributing to *a climate of fear instead of creating the conditions to make coming out easier."*

GS: "What would you say to someone who has been outed? Or is worried about being outed?"

A: "I think ultimately, you need to focus on living your life on your own terms. It's important to surround yourself with supportive people and live as openly with them as you can. I don't know how I could've gotten through this past year without my friends and family's support. I have some difficult days every now and then. But the people who insist on giving me hell don't realise that I will overcome. Their attacks only make me more committed."

Alekzandr's GLBT fans are equally divided about the scorn that's been reserved for him this last year. At this year's pride marches, his face and music were everywhere and his mantle as the world's most high profile queer artist had people talking, for better or for worse.

GS: "I think you've still got huge support in the community, but a lot of people resent the fact that you've suddenly become the movement's public face by default."

A: "I can appreciate that."

GS: "I think some people think you've taken a lot of gay culture to the masses. But that you've profited from borrowing from the subculture when it has suited you. What do you say to that?"

A: "It might piss people off but I don't think anyone should tie their entire existence to their sexuality. My work isn't limited to gay themes. I get inspired by a lot of things and I try to put my own spin on things so that I'm adding something to the conversation you know? Everyone has to do their part to end discrimination. I think that's been central to a lot of my work. I feel like I've been chipping away at things. If homophobia or discrimination could just be resolved in one blow, someone would've done it by now."

GS: "And the idea that you're the poster child of the movement?"

A: "I personally don't see myself as that. I may be one of the first, but I won't be the last. Hopefully it'll be a bit easier on whoever it happens to next because it will happen again. In the meantime, I just say that it's a bad idea to turn your back on any ally, even if they don't think in the exact same way you do."

GS: "Do you want to clarify that any further?"

Alekzandr chuckles. "Not really. I just think you have to choose your battles wisely."

GS: "Can I ask, I noticed on this album that you basically took a step back from talking about religion, where in the past you have often really grappled with the idea of religion in your work. Why not this time?""

A: "I don't think I've ever been against religion. I'm against oppression and I think sometimes organised religions repress some groups. I wasn't interested in attacking the church even if it contributes to the current climate. For me, this was an album about emotions and feelings. I wanted to write about the truth of what it means to be queer today. The idea of religion didn't really enter into my mind much on this album. I was more interested in delving into relationships."

GS: "Are you looking for love?"

Alekzandr laughs. "Not actively, no."

GS: *"Can I ask you what your experiences have been? I mean, as someone in a gay relationship."*

A: *"The ones I have been in are probably pretty similar to everyone else's... maybe just subject to way more scrutiny."*

GS: *"Aside from the media interest, I'm keen to know how being queer has been for you. People have this idea that you live a pretty wild life."*

A: *"Well, you'd be surprised, but I don't really have an over the top lifestyle. I've had my moments, like anyone, but I think that because I'm Australian, the idea of living ostentatiously is a bit off for me. I work hard. I play hard. I love hard. If anything, being queer has added a lot of nuance to my life. I get to see things from different angles compared to other people I know."*

GS: *"What do you have to say about the general climate of fear? I know a lot of gay people face discrimination on a daily basis. Have you?"*

A: *"Well, derr. I mean, it can be harrowing. I remember being in Europe last year, walking late at night with my ex. I always thought things were better in Europe than they are here in the States. I'm not sure they are. Anyway, we were holding hands, and it was summer and we were just chatting after a great night. God knows what we were talking about. We'd been out for some drinks with friends, and as we were walking back to our car, we heard someone shouting from the other side of the road. The local word for 'faggot'. We looked around and realised it was coming from some guy in a car. We just kept walk-ing, hand in hand and ignored it, and then this guy, does a U—turn, drives right up to us and throws a bottle at us. It missed, but whatever it was went everywhere, and he drove off, and I was so furious. I wanted to chase the car and pull the guy out of his car and give him a good seeing to. But after the adrenaline wore off it just left me feeling really bummed for days."*

GS: "So even you can understand what so many people have to go through every day?"

A: "Well of course I can. I've been plagued by it forever. Since high school people would call me a fag or a homo every day. The absurd thing was I wasn't even aware of it; I mean my sexuality. I was just different. I was creative and arty and the idea that I might be gay didn't bother me. I wasn't even thinking about love or sex or anything back then. I was just different. I wasn't sporty, I was ethnic, and I was more interested in learning than being popular. So I wore those insults like amulets over the years, not because I was afraid I had to ward anything off, but because I felt like I had to own them. Not be owned by them."

GS: "A lot of people think that homophobia stems from people who are in fact also gay."

A: "I don't think so... not always anyway. I think they [homophobes] think of me as an object and not as a person. The guy with the bottle... there were times I wondered if he would have done the same if he had a gay brother or gay friend. It left me with a bad taste of the place, even though it's a place I absolutely love. But as a queer, you're supposed to just accept violence as a part of your life, and I refuse to. Whether it's physical or mental. Why should I have to take the high ground? It's ridiculous. I think an out and proud gay man is more of a man than a homophobe will ever be. Because some days it takes balls just to walk out on the street."

GS: "What is the world's highest profile queer looking for in his partner?"

Alekzandr laughs again. "If I was looking for someone, probably the first thing right now would be to find someone who has the balls to be with me. Someone that's prepared to be followed by paparazzi everywhere. Someone that won't care that they'll write horrible lies about him and probably call up every one of the people from his past looking for an angle.

"I don't know what I'm looking for right now, or if I'm even looking. I have a feeling it will be someone strong and compassionate when the timing's right. But right now, I've got other things I have to focus on. I'm writing and recording and I'm developing ideas for a tour."

He returned to that cold voice again, this time tucking a few stray locks behind his ear, as if they'd been annoying him all this time and he only now had the chance, the time, to put them back in order. "Work comes first."

The unwritten rule that you don't talk about these things in public led to many heated discussions between our editors and Alekzandr's management. There seemed to be some dissent in his camp about this interview, but Alekzandr made good on his promise to see things through.

GS: "How do you think you're going to feel once this issue is published?"

A: "Hopefully like I've been heard. That people start thinking about why they weaponize sexual orientation. I'm not interested in selling records to bigots or being made to feel inferior. But if people could understand me a little more than they have this last year, I'll be happy."

The tea has well and truly gotten cold by the time he gets up and boils some more water, but I can see that he's over talking. He's wary, and after having bared his soul to me, I feel like I'm the trade from the night before that he wants to leave. He has no energy left to give me. I can feel it.

When I next see Alekzandr, it's after our plans to meet again have changed twice. I had the feeling that his label was stonewalling, but, when we meet, I see that he is working on the set of the videos he mentioned, and doing so with a pretty nasty flu. It's a closed set, and I sit at a distance being very quiet, watching as he and his troupe of androgynous dancers run through their routines time and again for the director.

Alekzandr's in a jovial mood when they break, even though he looks tired. He's wearing a platinum wig and an outfit that can be described only as Elegant Goth; lots of black and grey layers, so thin that his co-manager Kōji arrives with a big fake fur to cover him with.

GS: "Are the videos going well?"

A: "Yeah. Jasper's a perfectionist and he's making us do take after take, but I don't mind. It keeps me warm and it lets me sweat out this fever. I've been sick all week."

GS: "It's a bit of a departure from your usual stuff."

A: "It's actually a video backdrop. For the tour. We were kind of inspired by Jean Eustache. Well, actually, I wish I could say we were inspired by Jean Eustache. We were watching his film at my place last night, me and the dancers. Today we've been reciting lines between takes. The video has nothing to do with it though. We just wanted something exciting and striking, so we have to pretend there are references to other things to make it sound more arty."

GS: "Do you spend a lot of time with your dancers?"

A: "These guys? Yeah, when I'm in New York. We go out sometimes, or they come over and we watch things together. I think some of them are coming on the road with me. But I still have to finish the album."

GS: "Will it follow in the spirit of 'Androgynous'?"

A: "No."

GS: "Why not?"

A: "Because I'm not interested in making the same album twice. The songs keep changing. And I'm about to spend two weeks in India, so who knows what effect that'll have on me. Things always work out differently to how you first imagine them."

GS: "They do. What does someone like you do in India?"

A: "What anyone else does. I travel. I make my peace with the place. It's a place where a lot went down for me. I think it was where I became who I am today."

GS: "And who's that?"

A: "A fighter. A risk taker, despite my snotty nose," he said, dabbing his nose on his sleeve.

GS: "Who are you listening to these days?"

A: *"Everything. I mean these days I listen to things that I collect from around the world. Nothing that you'll hear on the radio. Nobody is taking risks anymore. It's all fake Prozac. I refuse to buy into a lot of the music that you hear today. It's like manufactured anger. And musically, everyone is so unwilling to take a chance."*

GS: *"Who would you work with if you could choose anybody?"*

A: *"Hmm. Well I'm not feeling that inspired by others in this period. If I could go back in time I would have a wish list that would never end."* He pauses for what seems an eternity. *"I'll tell you what, I absolutely loved Neneh Cherry's last album even though it wasn't as big as her first one. I thought it was cool. I have no idea what mine will end up like. Whatever I do, it probably won't be very close to anything that's on the charts at the moment. I'm still in a risk taking mood."*

GS: *"So it seems. Can you afford to be?"*

A: *"Well, I always believe in following your heart. That's always been my motto, from day one. If I followed my heart right now the music would be really varied. I can tell you for sure that you won't be hearing people rapping on my album, or me making a bunch of covers like they want me to. I mean, what's the point? I get that a lot of the kids haven't heard these songs before, but it's not really very useful to put someone else's song on a loop and say that it's yours."*

GS: *"Do you think you'll ever settle down? A partner, two dogs. Summer in the Hamptons?"*

A: *"Not if I have anything to do with it. I like to move around, be inspired, stimulated."*

GS: *"Any dates lined up?"*

A: *"I have a few more video nights and then India on the horizon. I don't have a dance card at the moment, but I'm quite happy about that."*

And with that he's gone. He's ushered back onto the soundstage and as the song pipes back up for the millionth time, he's going back through the motions.

Nothing has changed, he's still doing what he has always done, but my perception of him is somehow different. He's still that stratospheric star, whose career has made its way into many of our lives, but he's full of surprises. Maybe in a few months' time he'll come back singing the virtues of new age mysticism. A few weeks later I receive a phone call from Varanasi.

"You know, I was thinking after I meditated this morning. There's a flipside to everything. If I'm honest with myself, I think a part of me wanted the fortress to burn. Is it weird to say I feel free despite all the consequences? It's just been one of those moments in life when I've had to decide whether to give up or make something new from what I've been left with."

And with that, he's gone again.

| 7 |

HELSINKI

In 1994, after more than a year in the proverbial sin bin, Helsinki seemed as good a place as any to launch a world tour. It was time to visit places Alekzandr had previously neglected for his first full blown concert tour in seven years. Alex had never been a huge fan of touring, but even he had to concede one was long overdue.

The fallout from his last album was ongoing and tensions were high at Alex's labels. Many of the staff were nervous, especially once threatening letters and suspicious packages addressed to Alex began arriving at their offices. The boycott at US radio was still firmly in place and journalists and columnists continued to skin Alex alive in the press, now decrying his move to Europe.

Androgynous had been a bust, not even selling a quarter of what had been projected. Millions of copies that had been shipped to stores were now being shipped back to warehouses, awaiting an unpleasant and combustible fate. But a split boardroom vote resulted in a decision to honour Alex's contract for the time being. He was sent back into the studio only after making assurances that he would *tone things down.* The decision to send Alex back out on the road was partly to allow the label to recoup some of its investment.

Because the reception for *Androgynous* had been better in Europe than elsewhere, it'd been decided that the tour would kick off there. Dates were set before the competitive summer concert season to maximise ticket sales. Max's touring company and Alex's management agreed to a long list of dates, scheduled in broad geographical sweeps that would see Alex performing in a number of new markets along the way.

Planning a tour on the eve of a new release was a tricky proposition. Alex's market stocks were at the lowest point they'd ever been, and there was no way of knowing how audiences would react to the new material. But a tour was the best way of shoring up support for him while refilling the coffers with ticket sales and merchandising, especially after such an unprofitable period.

Securing dates in medium and large arenas according to demand, the European leg would include shows in Israel and Turkey before moving across the Asia Pacific, stopping en route in Hawaii before a handful of dates in North America. From there, the tour would climax with a final leg of stadium shows in Central and South America. In total 72 shows were booked over five months. There were only a few week–long breaks scheduled to make the itinerary feasible, but even then, they were kept to a minimum so as not to eat away at profits.

By late March 1994, preliminary rehearsals had come to an end in outer London, after months of simultaneous work on the new album *Mantra* and the complex show. Paul Hirst, who'd produced the bulk of *Mantra* with Alex, was appointed the tour's musical director. Together with the band, they combed through Alex's catalogue to come up with a setlist. Though Alex wanted to focus exclusively on material from his last three albums, Paul convinced him to include some earlier hits, either as standalone songs or instrumental interludes.

The setlist changed repeatedly as they adapted the music to suit the show, which rather than being a straightforward rock concert was planned as a theatrical interpretation of Alex's music; the kind of show that Michael Jackson, Madonna and U2 were already receiving accolades for. Having been off the touring landscape for so long, this was Alex's first real hyper sensory show, designed to help him "catch up" to his peers who had long embraced technology.

In Finland, in April, to officially launch the new album and announce the world tour to the international press, Alex reflected on how he would be embarking on another career chapter in such a far-flung place. Despite events of the last year, he still had some clout. But now more than ever, smaller markets, like Scandinavia, were just as important to him as his more robust ones.

In Helsinki he cut a striking form. His hair was now shoulder length and red, a nose stud completing his new look. Edginess was again everything in music and Alex was swiftly accused of jumping onto the indie bandwagon. It was probably a fair observation given his creative confidence was now at an all-time low.

Pure mainstream pop was well and truly on life support, its giants increasingly bowing to a troop of grunge and hip hop acts who were now the taste makers.

Alex wasn't the only pop giant who'd fallen on hard times. Many of his 1980s superstar peers seemed to be on the backfoot, locked in contractual battles against the labels they'd made millions for, or, struggling to remain relevant in a market that was now only interested in *unplugged* sets from them.

As was noted by the press, Alex was thinner than he'd been in years; speculation attributing it to career pressures, depression and even illness. Though the stress accounted for some of the weight loss, Alex's new shape was more the result of a regimented approach to eating and exercise. Stefan, his trusted personal trainer, devised a program to give Alex the stamina he'd need for the long world tour.

Alex turned to those close to him to help guide him through his latest comeback. More than ever before, he canvassed opinions on his new music, no longer willing to trust his own instincts. For the first time, he actually welcomed the chance to sit down with label executives to whittle down the numerous songs he'd recorded for *Mantra* into a tight, cohesive track list.

Though he felt weakened by his new outsider status in pop culture, he wasn't ready to completely relinquish control over his career. To regain some of his confidence, he decided he needed to be more heavily involved in the tour's planning. Promotional schedules, backdrops, lighting, merchandising… he had a hand in everything. He loved Celia and Kōji, but he wondered whether he would have been better off begging Michael to help him out this time around.

When Alex woke up in his hotel room in Vironniemi on his second day in Helsinki, his first thought was on breakfast, but the minute he headed out of the hotel with his bulging tour diary, his thoughts returned to the huge tasks at hand. He made his way on foot to the café the local record label rep had told him about. He planted himself on a chair outside, in the cordoned off space on the footpath. The enclosure was warm just as the rep had promised, despite the chilly April weather. *Amazing what passes for normal in different parts of the world*, Alex mused.

Dressed in black, his hair slicked with a side parting, Alex felt good, ordering breakfast and flicking through his tour diary. Shortly after his coffee arrived, he pulled out the Polaroids of the costumes studying them in the day light. He felt his stomach rumble and felt immense relief that the waiter was now crossing the footpath with his breakfast on a tray, Alex tucking the photos away and making space on the table in anticipation. But as he did so, a jogger rounded the corner and crashed straight into the waiter, sending the tray and all its contents all over Alex's back and shoulders.

Both Alex and the waiter let out piercing wails, the commotion bringing staff and customers out from the café and onto the frosty pavement. The jogger, who'd been sent to the ground in the confusion, staggered back onto his feet, apologising effusively in rapid Finnish before barking instructions at the shocked waiting staff.

"Olen pahoillani," said the jogger, oblivious to the blood gushing out of his knees.

"I don't speak Finnish," Alex said, struggling to pull off his soaking wet jacket.

"I was saying *'I'm so sorry'*," the jogger said. "I wasn't watching where I was going, and now I've ruined your day and your clothes," he said, grabbing a pile of napkins with which he tried to blot the liquid from the jacket.

Alex bit his tongue. "It's not the end of the world. I'll just have to go back to my hotel and change and try all over again, I guess."

"Try what again?" the jogger asked, handing over a large banknote to the waiter.

"To have breakfast," Alex said, annoyed as he gathered his wet sweater and jacket, feeling the cold pierce through his thin, black top.

"Well, the least I can do is pay for your clothes to be cleaned. And take you for a breakfast that you can actually eat."

"Oh, really, it's not necessary," Alex said, standing and checking he had everything.

"No, I must insist. Where are you staying?" the jogger asked.

"No, really, I don't have the time. I'll just get something at my hotel."

"Please don't!" the jogger persisted. "I'm Tomas," he added, holding out his hand. "Come on, you can't be too busy to spare an hour. I'll take you to breakfast at a place much better than this one," Tomas said, nodding his head.

"I'm Alex," he said, shaking Tomas' outstretched hand.

"Come on, you're completely wet."

"And you're in shorts and you're bleeding," Alex noted.

"Yes, but I'm Scandinavian. I'm used to the cold. And I'll clean myself up. Maybe at your hotel."

Tomas put an arm around Alex, who was shivering, and steered him down the street, dismissively waving at the café staff.

"Where are you from Alex?"

"Australia." It was pointless going into any detail.

"Yes, you don't look at all Finnish," Tomas said, the organisation of his words ringing in Alex's ears.

"I didn't realise it was a requisite."

"A *requisite?* I'm not sure what that means," Tomas said, confused, "but I'm not Finnish either. I'm Swedish."

"So why are you running around like a madman in Helsinki?"

"Oh, there's a sports game tonight."

"What? And there are no buses? You have to run there?" Alex's terrible joke brought out a smile from Tomas, but clearly one of pity. "You came here to watch a game?" Alex asked, recovering from his own embarrassment.

"Kind of," Tomas laughed. "I'm a journalist. I'm here to cover the game."

A journalist.

"I see," Alex said, mentally devising an exit strategy. *A journalist? For god's sake!*

They walked into the hotel and Tomas made his way towards the armchairs in the foyer, before abruptly turning towards the reception desk, as if he suddenly remembered he had something he had to do.

"I won't be long," Alex promised.

"Don't worry. I'm not the one in a hurry," Tomas said, accepting some bandages from the concierge.

Over breakfast they talked awkwardly, searching for common ground. Alex took great pains to speak figuratively about his work, explaining he was merely in Helsinki on business, but soon enough Tomas put two and two together.

"I thought you were familiar!" Tomas chirped. "The minute I saw your face I thought I'd met you before. At first, I was trying to understand if it was in Hamburg or Stockholm that we'd met, but now I realise."

Alex bristled again, his thoughts returning to exit strategies. "You're *that* singer."

Alex felt his face burn a little. How could he get up and leave without leaving the impression that he was either a rude foreigner or a *diva*? Diva, the pejorative word that seemed to have crept back into the public's fascination was a label that the press now seemed fond of using for every female artist. And Alex.

"Yes, I'm *that singer*," Alex said, "but no one seems to have recognised me yet. And I'd like to keep it that way."

"Oh, don't worry, the city is on alert for all the hockey players that have flown in from Copenhagen. I think they've got everyone's attention."

"That's going to piss my managers off. We have a press conference to get through this week," Alex said, his irritation surprising even him.

"Are you touring? People only do press conferences here if they plan on doing a show. Or if they're doing an endorsement."

"Yeah. I'll be doing a show. And I'm launching my album too. If I can get everything organised."

"Don't you have staff to do that kind of thing for you?"

"Kind of," Alex said. "Do you live in Stockholm?"

"Mostly. Sometimes Germany, depends on the time of the year and the sports calendar. I'm away for work a lot."

Alex sipped his coffee. "Do you love your job?"

"Yes," Tomas said without hesitation. "You?"

Alex thought for a moment. "Sometimes. Some parts of it, at least."

"I don't really listen to pop music," Tomas smiled.

Apparently no one does.

"I prefer hard rock or classical music," Tomas added, helpfully.

"That's extreme," Alex said, softening and finding himself marginally intrigued.

"I've always loved heavy metal. But my ex–wife was a classical musician. She taught me to appreciate the classics." Tomas said, biting down on his croissant.

"I see," Alex said, suddenly disinterested in continuing the conversation any further.

The two of them politely ate in silence, Alex occasionally looking over in Tomas' direction.

"Hey, are you busy tonight?" Tomas asked when their eyes finally met again.

"I'm always busy."

Tomas flashed him a megawatt smile. "*Really* busy?" Tomas asked.

Alex smiled. "It depends. I mean I *am* busy, but it's nothing that I can't get out of."

"You're the boss after all," Tomas said. "I want you to come to the game with me. To make up for everything. It'll be wild and we can have some dinner after. I know a great place."

"Oh I don't want to intrude," Alex replied. "Plus you'll be working. Won't be much fun."

"No, it will be! And you can stay in the booth with me!" Tomas said.

"And your crew? I'm sure they won't appreciate me being there."

"Oh no, they are off to Tampere tonight right after the game. The network is doing a story on some of the up and coming talents."

"And you don't have to go?"

"No, the producer will do the interviews. Besides, it's so boring being in another city on your own. So, what do you say? I can pick you up at the hotel. I think I have another press pass."

"Sure, why not?" Alex said.

Tomas beamed. "Great!"

True to Tomas' word, the match was electrifying. Alex was spellbound by the aggression on the rink that echoed throughout the packed stadium. He'd never seen a hockey game in his life, but sat wide-eyed in the commentary box, watching Tomas narrate the game with an enthusiasm that made everyone in the booth occasionally jolt, Tomas included. Alex watched as the Swede's angular features contracted and released with his excitement for the match's unfolding events. Tomas' complexion was darker than his colleagues', but still fair, his goatee and its silver flecks the only hints that he was at least in his mid-thirties. His nose looked like it had been broken at some point; broad at the top, crooked in the middle and clumsy and bulbous at its tip. But overall, his shorn, sandy hair and blue eyes lent him the kind of

Nordic handsomeness that Alex usually only appreciated from afar.

At the interval, after the crew stepped out for refreshments, Tomas lent in and kissed Alex, who was initially startled, but then kissed him back with aplomb.

"I hope you're enjoying the game," Tomas smiled, touching Alex's cheek and then repositioning himself as he heard someone at the door.

Alex flashed his trademark grin, "I am… it's a very enlightening evening," he said, gratefully accepting the beer one of Tomas' colleagues handed him. When the game resumed, Alex found himself acknowledging how surprising Tomas was proving to be.

After the game, Tomas completed his on camera round up, and after seeing to some work formalities, led Alex out of the stadium and into the car park, saying his goodbyes to everyone they passed. Alex enjoyed the novelty of being in Tomas' shadow.

Tomas didn't once second guess himself as they drove out of the city. Alex guessed they were heading north, but only because the waterfront was behind them. He chastised himself for having no in built compass. He relaxed as Tomas expertly managed the tight curves and the increasingly steep roads. In the mirror he saw the distant flickering of the city lights. Tomas turned again, driving onto an almost pitch– black road, switching to the high beams and proceeding cautiously until they reached a tiny car park. There was very little Alex could make out. It was as if they were in the middle of nowhere. He wiped the condensation off the window and wondered if he was imagining things when he spied a lamp post and the hint of a gravelly path in the distance.

"Where are we?" Alex asked.

"Oh, we're here for dinner. Quite amazing place, great food. I come here as often as I can. Some of the best food in the city, according to the Michelin guide."

"You're a man of many surprises," Alex said, turning to face him.

"Were you expecting a burger in a roadhouse?" Tomas quipped.

"I don't know what to expect with you," Alex said, feeling a lump in his throat.

"You know, a little bit of mystery is a good thing," Tomas said, turning off the headlights.

Alex looked down for a moment, his eyes adjusting to the dashboard light.

"You're right. Thanks for the game tonight. I'm just feeling a bit overwhelmed."

"I don't know what that means," Tomas said. "But I hope it is a good thing."

Alex smiled, taking a deep breath before he kissed Tomas. It was a long and expressive kiss, but he was sure to keep his hand on Tomas' knee and not to let it wander further.

"Come on, let's go eat," Tomas said, smiling and touching Alex's cheek. "If we don't do it now, we never will."

Opening the car door, Alex felt assailed by the bitter, cold air. He zipped up his parka and clenched his fists, pulling his sleeves down over his hands, as he shuffled to catch up to Tomas who was gliding across the sodden gravel. Alex smelt something in the air, and assumed it was pine. As they walked further along the path, an old building came into view, bathed in orange light. Close up it looked like a simple, squarish building, its style suggesting some British colonial had left it behind on his way out of Finland.

Tomas held the door open for Alex who gratefully slid into the warm air.

"They say that the upstairs was once a ballroom," Tomas said, in between an exchange in Finnish with the cloak check. "Seems a long way to come to dance," he said looking at Alex, absently handing his coat over to the staff member.

Over a quite remarkable meal and equally good wine, Tomas opened up, his backstory proving fascinating.

Alex learned that Tomas had been a professional ice hockey player who'd competed at the Winter Olympics in Sarajevo and Calgary. Injury had forced him to make an early retirement from the sport without being able to realise his dream of attending a third games. By the time the Albertville games rolled around, he was working for the national Swedish broadcaster as a sports journalist and commentator, and thus was sent to France as a correspondent. He still didn't know whether being sent to cover them had been a consolation or just bittersweet torture.

Alex listened with a flicker of recognition as Tomas also explained his marriage of four years to a Norwegian cellist had already begun to sour with their endless work commitments years before his sexual orientation had finally driven a wedge between them.

Tomas also went on to talk about his early life, explaining that he'd grown up in Haparanda, a small town near the Finnish border. He'd moved to Umeå when he was eight or nine with his family, where he was discovered by a talent scout and, at age sixteen, was sent to Stockholm to train and work full time as a professional athlete.

"I know I have been talking a lot," Tomas said, "But I felt like I had to make things even."

"Why?"

"Because I read about you in one of the encyclopaedias in the book shop this afternoon," Tomas said, smiling shyly. "So I know that you were born in Australia, you began your career in London and moved to New York where you became famous. Um, you married another pop singer… they say you had all kinds of lovers, really. And that you had lots of successful albums and tours. And one of the longest runs of hits in history. Unfortunately the book was published in 1991, so I couldn't find any other information."

"That's probably more than you need to know. Remember, mystery is a good thing," Alex winked. "Besides, you know how shallow those things are."

"Shallow?"

"Yes, um, superficial. I'm sure there are millions of things written about you if I start to look."

"Don't look. Ask me. I will tell you," Tomas said, seriously.

"Same for me then," Alex replied.

"Are you dating someone now?" Tomas asked.

"No," Alex said.

"Do you miss your family?" Tomas asked.

No one had ever really asked Alex that question. But in doing so, Tomas had gleaned something like guilt out of Alex. Alex knew the last year or so had been particularly difficult for his family who, despite the distance, were bearing some of the brunt of the public's condemnation of him.

"Sometimes. I'm so used to being far away from them that it seems normal. But I love seeing them when I can," Alex finally answered.

"When was the last time you saw them?"

"Oh, I think maybe three or four months ago. But I call them. And sometimes I send them letters or cards or whatever. I have a brother and a sister who are both married. And I have two nephews and a niece, who I adore. I sometimes think I should go back to Australia and be closer to them, but I don't think that's my destiny. I always have friends around me. As for my family, I don't know, I help them out financially but I think they resent it sometimes. Like, you're so far away, a cheque is not going to make a difference."

"I have two sisters," Tomas volunteered. "They're married too. I like one of my brothers in law. We were friends in Haparanda when I was a kid. The other one, I don't like him so much. But I have nieces too. My sister is pregnant again and I think she is hoping for a boy this time."

"The one married to your friend or to the arsehole?"

"Oh, he's not an arsehole. He's just... not so friendly with me. Anyway, everybody lives in Umeå, and because they're so busy with their lives, I only see them on birthdays or Christmas or if I have time to visit. You know it's not really a problem. I only live a couple of hundred kilometres away, so it's not like the end of the earth. I could be there in a couple of hours, you know?"

"Mmm hmm," Alex replied. "Are you dating?"

"No. I thought I didn't have the time to."

"Oh, I've used that excuse a lot too," Alex said, smiling.

For a few moments Tomas watched Alex carefully. "You know, I have seen lots of your photographs today, and you always look... cool. But I must say in front of me, you are extraordinary... *vacker man.*"

"I'm not really sure what that means."

"Beautiful! Handsome!" Tomas said, enthusiastically.

"Thank you," Alex said liltingly. "Coming from you that is quite a compliment. I mean, you are so good looking that you've made me nervous from this morning when you were acting like you were in the middle of a hockey game."

"No, no, no! I'm not violent at all! I was just running. I'm competitive, it's true... but I can see you are too. And you are only nervous because I think you have an idea of what I would like to do to you tonight."

Alex laughed nervously. He could feel himself blushing.

"Oh, look at you. You're all red!" Tomas said, chuckling.

"I'm just shy. And I always forget how you Europeans love to get to the point."

"Well let's be practical," Tomas said, taking his glass of red in his hand. "We are both in a foreign city. If I don't take you home with me tonight, I might not ever get the chance again."

Their heavy petting in the car fogged up the windows such that Tomas instructed Alex to open the door to clear the condensation. The drive back into the city didn't seem at all familiar. Nervousness descended over Alex, his mind racing into the realm of possibilities. Only the distraction of another set of headlights pulled him out of his thoughts. By the time Alex realised they were back in the city, Tomas explained he was taking Alex to the apartment the television channel kept for visiting journalists.

The apartment was pretty basic; IKEA furnished with a couple of more tasteful pieces littered around. But what saved it from being anonymous were the spectacular views of the water and the Senaatintori, the senate square. There was also a remarkable, top of the range sound system which Tomas wasted no time in firing up. He went with a classical option, choosing a modern interpretation of a piece that Alex couldn't name.

Everything felt *different*. Alex had been living in London again for some time but had not yet embraced European living. His heart and mind were still in New York, but his body was unsure of where it was.

Tomas set a bottle of wine and two glasses down on the coffee table, and Alex obliged, opening the bottle as Tomas fidgeted around with the lighting to try and create a bit of ambience. Tomas' noisy pissing with the bathroom door open probably didn't help the atmosphere cause, but Alex found it to be somewhat stirring. Tomas was turning out to be a one of a kind.

As they intermittently downed the wine between exploratory kisses and caresses, Alex found himself relaxing. Shoes were slipped off and outer layers of clothing shed, until they were both lounging in their underwear.

Alex looked over Tomas' body. It still more or less bore the trademarks of an athlete's training. Certain parts and angles of his body were honed and exaggerated, others sinewy and polished, the dim light cascading over them and rendering them silver. Tomas' complexion was noticeably fairer from the neck down, the smattering of body hair running from his chest and towards his abdomen in a diamond form, replicated by a similar formation at his navel. As Tomas lifted his arm behind his head to prop up a cushion, another diamond like crop of body hair revealed itself. Alex moved in closer and kissed it, running his nose and tongue all along it, enjoying its faint dampness.

Alex had spent decades avoiding intimacy with blonds or the fair haired on account of always feeling insecure about his own colour palette. If he completely avoided the sun, his skin could be alabaster white, but usually it was deep olive in colour, and year– round he found himself plagued and embarrassed by his stubbornly dark body hair and nipples. Even now as an adult, he still felt the sting of having grown up in an Anglo–Saxon environment, where he'd been made to feel that he'd been overcooked in comparison to everyone else. Whether by insinuation, innocuous banter or outright racist remarks, it was a feeling he'd only begun to shake in New York, where the melting pot was more pronounced than in Australia. And he'd only done it by conditioning himself to seek out darker featured lovers, as if their appearance would offer him respite from his insecurities.

***

Tomas was not immune to Alex's exotic charms; the almost naked body in front of him lithe, its unusual tones exciting him superficially. But caressing Alex's body with his fingers and mouth, he was struck by something else. A feeling. That Alex was someone that he already *really* liked. And he hadn't been with anyone he *really* liked since, well, not since the earlier part of his marriage all those years ago. And it was hard because that left him feeling like he was inexperienced when it came to other men. No one ever lived up to that feeling, yet here he was with a complete stranger who was ticking every box. Problem was, Tomas wasn't sure what he needed to do to satisfy him.

***

As they kissed each other, Alex pulled down Tomas' underpants, and began to fellate him. Though Tomas was clearly enjoying the moment, Alex felt panicked. When Tomas reached into Alex's pouch and noticed things weren't reciprocal, he tried to knead a reaction out of Alex with a range of hand movements. Alex felt Tomas pulling himself out of his mouth and knew that the intensity of the moment was evaporating.

"Are you okay?" Tomas asked, "did I do something wrong?"

"No, you're perfect. I'm fine, I'm just... I don't know. This doesn't really happen to me," Alex said, putting his t–shirt back on.

"Is it something I'm doing? Maybe I did something wrong?"

"You? No, you're perfect. I'm sorry," Alex said sheepishly, sitting up, and burying himself under the plaid throw.

"Shall I try again?" Tomas asked, reaching for Alex's groin.

"No, don't... it doesn't look like it's going to happen. Oh my god, this is a nightmare! I'm sorry. I can help you get off if you want though," he offered, mortified.

"No, no. No need," Tomas said, now sitting up and smiling.

"Maybe I should go," Alex said, standing up and reaching for his slacks.

"What? Are you mad? Where are you going? Come here," Tomas growled, pulling Alex back onto the couch. Tomas hugged him, burrowing Alex's head into his chest. "You're not going anywhere. These things happen."

Alex made no response. *Not to me they don't.*

"Come on, it's nothing. We can try again later. Or another time," Tomas said.

"Yeah, but when? We're in a foreign city, remember?" Alex said.

"Come on, we are having a great time. Don't ruin it."

"I think I already have," Alex said, smiling bitterly. He struggled against Tomas' force, desperate to stand up. "I'm just… I just want to go to the bathroom. Don't worry, I'm not going anywhere," Alex said.

***

Tomas watched Alex walk towards the bathroom and then raised himself up and killed the lights. He took the wine bottle and the glasses into the kitchen and left them on the bench, and when Alex came out of the bathroom, led him through to the generic looking bedroom. Embarrassed by how it looked like student housing, Tomas spoke.

"Do you know what my favourite word is in English?" Tomas asked, fluffing the pillow.

"No idea," Alex replied, icily.

"*Cuddle.* I am obsessed with that word," Tomas said, slipping off his underwear and then Alex's, pulling back the sheets and patting the mattress. "Come on. I want to *cuddle* with you."

***

Although he was dying to smoke – *anything* – Alex got into the bed and obliged as Tomas moved into a big spoon position. It felt nice to be held. It'd been more than a year now. *Diego.*

"I think you're adorable," Tomas whispered, his voice throaty. "You're sexy. Smart. Funny. And you have an amazing body. I want to get to know you."

Alex smiled and he knew he was thawing. Not like a glacier, but at least a layer of ice had just shed itself under Tomas' warmth.

"Don't make a big deal about tonight," Tomas added, Alex lost in the intoxicating warmth of his embrace. "We just met. We've been drinking. Our bodies have to get to know each other. I just couldn't wait to see yours. To taste it. I'm sorry if I rushed things," he said, kissing the nape of Alex's neck and deeply inhaling Alex's scent.

Alex felt like he was in a cocoon, or immersed in some protective field. It took him ages to remember how to speak. "Tomas, don't apologise. It was all me. I was just nervous. Embarrassed. I think you're *amazing*."

"Well why don't we get a little sleep and then see if you still think I'm amazing in the morning?"

The following morning Tomas woke Alex, nudging him suggestively from behind.

"Good morning," Alex said in the happiest tone he was capable of.

"*Hejsan*," Tomas said instructively until Alex repeated it correctly.

Although Alex seemed to be having a recurrence of the issue from the night before, he shook it off, descending to take Tomas in his mouth, relying on all the tricks in his arsenal to please him. Afterwards they lay in bed for a half hour or so chatting, until

Alex realised he had to be at a meeting and be in a presentable state for it.

The two exchanged a series of phone numbers. Tomas was heading back to Stockholm that afternoon, Alex reminding him that he would be busy in meetings with sponsors for the first of two official press engagements.

At the door, they kissed lingeringly.

"You're sure you don't want me to drive you?"

"I'm sure," Alex said. "I'll find a cab."

"You'll call me tonight? To make sure I got home alright?" Tomas asked, smiling cheekily.

"Sure. I wish you could stay a few more days."

"Me too. But we all have to work, don't we? Call me tonight. I will stay at home."

| 8 |

MANTRA

Throughout the day's meetings, it took all Alex's strength to continually bring his attention back to the matters at hand. There were three principal tie–ins for the show. A Swedish alcohol brand and a Finnish mobile phone manufacturer were the commercial sponsors of the tour, Alex signing on for a year-long promotional deal with them. Both were pushing for a greater market share outside of Scandinavia. Alex agreed to appear in worldwide print campaigns in exchange for their multimillion dollar endorsements of the tour, whose production and operating costs were reported to be at almost $20M.

The third tie in was with an assortment of AIDS and HIV charities, who Alex authorised to distribute promotional literature, condoms and promotional merchandising at almost all the venues on the tour.

As the deals were already in place, the Helsinki meetings were more to give executives and the press sufficient face time with Alex and to bring attention to the endorsements. Alex hoped the endorsements would also convey the message that someone still had faith in his commercial appeal.

After filming a few tète-à-tètes with regional marketing heads for the brands in the early part of the afternoon, the corporate crowd was joined by representatives of some of the HIV/AIDS groups who were also in town for a European WHO conference.

Alex pressed the flesh with some familiar and new faces, his mind constantly drifting to the events of the morning and the night before. He glanced around the room, imagining it was filled with Tomas and his clones, constantly forcing himself to crash back down to reality and the responsibilities of networking.

"Ladies and gentleman, can I have your attention please?" Dylan, Alex's new European publicist said over the microphone. "Alekzandr has a couple of final words to say before we move on to the cocktail lounge. Alekzandr?"

A round of applause erupted as Alex took to the podium. He took a few deep breaths, surveying the room. Glancing beyond all the cameras and lights, he felt his brow furrow. It *was* him. Tomas *was* in fact present, in a suit jacket, a bright blue press pass hanging around his neck.

Though he felt poised in his tight black suit and a striped sailor tee, knowing he looked every inch a popstar, Alex melted as Tomas locked eyes with him. Tomas seemed to be pointing at Celia, Kōji and Dylan whom Alex had vividly described over dinner the night before. Alex nodded as if to say *'yes that's them'* and once again did his best to focus.

"Thank you everybody. I wanted to thank you all for being here. I know you have more important things to do in your week than rub shoulders with me... but seriously, I feel great about our partnerships. I wanted to take this opportunity to personally acknowledge you and your work, and to apologise in advance because I know that once the tour starts I'm going to be missing in action. We shouldn't make any mistake about this. We have a war to win. And it's a long one."

He looked away from his notes for a moment. "I know there are a lot more important things in life than pop music. I've meditated on that fact a lot recently. But we're here because art, in some form, has brought us together, and art is going to help us reach out and heal so many people. I'm not speaking scientifically. I'm talking about the work we have ahead of us in combatting the illness we have as a society. I'm talking about the discrimination so many people face on a daily basis. Discrimination and isolation that arises, like it always does, from a lack of understanding and knowing the facts. When we're uninformed, it's that much easier to strike out at somebody rather than offer them compassion. Like so many, I too have faced some of the discrimination and violence that seems to accompany any discussion on HIV. I too have been scapegoated. We live in a world where diseases are less scary than people's reaction to them. To the stigma they come with. But we can cure the stigma even if we haven't got a cure for the disease yet. One of our biggest challenges is to educate people. To encourage them to be more compassionate in the face of HIV and AIDS. We already know much about how the disease destroys our bodies, but we don't always focus enough on how it ravages our minds. It doesn't matter who you are; gay, straight, an adult… a child. Positive or negative. We are all at the mercy of this cruel, unforgiving disease.

"Each and every one of you here is doing work that is very dear to my heart. Or supporting it in your own way. I would like to think that together, we can take on the lack of tolerance and compassion that, to me, is the real plague. I'd like to think that together, we'll be able to bring more light into this dark, dark time. And what better way to do that than by turning to the power of art, to go hand in hand with the power of science?"

A round of applause chimed around the room.

"I'm dreaming of a future free of this disease. One where people aren't made to feel like lepers. One where we work together to end the suffering. Where people talk and learn and listen and destroy the stigma."

A few supportive howls came up from the charity contingent.

"I want to take this opportunity to thank my tour sponsors for their support. To acknowledge how they are making all of this possible and to thank them for having the courage to put their money where their mouths are."

Another polite round of applause rang out.

"Yes, it's great, right? *See*, we're all friends already! Alright then, that wraps things up for me, so, thank you, and please enjoy the hospitality and I hope to see you all again on the road."

Dylan helped Alex down from the podium as the applause rang through the hall. Alex signalled to security to let Tomas through the throng of people that had pushed forward.

"Shouldn't you be at the airport?" Alex asked, caressing Tomas' forearm.

"I told my boss I could stay and do a couple of interviews for a human interest story. Some background preparation," Tomas smiled. "But he told me to relax and have a couple of days off."

"How long will you stay?"

"I guess I can stay a couple of days. But can I come and stay at your hotel? I had to leave the apartment because it's already booked for another journalist. My things are in the lobby. I hope that's okay?"

"Sure," Alex said, grinning at yet another of Tomas' surprises. "I have to be here for another half hour at least. I'm meeting some great people who're doing some great work here."

"Well, I might stay. Why is there so much vodka around?"

"It's to help everybody relax," Alex said.

"Ah, and you made fun of me when I said people only come here when they have an endorsement."

Soon enough there was a beeline of people waiting to speak with Alex. Alex excused himself and began to speak one by one with the assembled people. Dylan took over the microphone again as Tomas watched as Alex's team worked the room.

***

"I felt like I had to stay," Tomas explained in the car. "I thought a few days at least. Before we become a pair of voices on the telephone or a smile and a memory."

"I'm really glad you did," Alex said, fatigue in his voice. "Listen, Tomas, do you mind if we just hang at the hotel for a while? I need some quiet. I've been talking all day."

"Sounds alright to me."

Back at the hotel room, a brief nap led to a credible sexual encounter which they repeated for surety shortly after. After a little rest, Tomas made a quick phone call, letting out a victory howl when he replaced the phone in its cradle.

"Get dressed," he said, prodding Alex. "But don't shower."

"Where are we going?"

"Come on, get up," Tomas said, his pants already up around his knees.

"Tell me you're not taking me to a sauna out in the woods," Alex deadpanned, putting on his suit trousers.

"No, but, it's somewhere quiet. Don't you have anything more casual to wear?"

"I have a hat. And I have sneakers, but that is about it. I don't get any more casual than this outside the house."

"Here," Tomas said, rummaging through his own bag and pulling out a pair of black sweats. "Put these on. And your sneakers."

They crisscrossed the city streets until they reached an imposing building with a dark brick veneer. Tomas weaselled his way through to a side door and tapped gently on the glass panel. As Alex heard a door open, Tomas and another male had a friendly discussion complete with sound effects.

"Alex!" Tomas called. "This way. Come on."

Alex followed him through and closed the door behind him.

"Alex, this is Eetu, he is an old friend of mine. He does the security here."

"Hi Eetu. Where are we?"

"Oh, you'll see," Tomas chuckled.

"One hour maximum," Eetu warned. "I have put the lamps on for you, but not the lights because they can be seen outside."

"I promise, one hour!" Tomas agreed.

Tomas took Alex around the waist and led him through the corridors. At a certain point Alex could detect the smell of chlorine, but when Tomas finally led him into the main hall, Alex's jaw dropped. He was standing on the mosaic tiles in what he soon learned was the Yrjönkatu Swimming Pool, a palatial, neo–classicist indoor pool built in the 1920s.

"Take off your clothes," Tomas said, stripping. "It's actually forbidden to swim with a costume. And, besides, I want to see what you've got in the light."

The lamps added a touch of drama to what was already an extraordinarily beautiful and layered setting.

"This is a public pool?" Alex asked, undressing but distracted by the surroundings.

"Yes. But we have to keep an eye on the clock. Eetu is my friend, but he is strict about these kinds of things."

They dived in and proceeded to immediately make out in the pool before Alex laughed, took a deep breath and began a lap. He'd swum naked in the ocean plenty of times, but this was the first time in his life he was swimming naked in a pool of this size. He swam a half a dozen or so laps without stopping to let the day's nervous energy pass through his body before he stopped and watched Tomas, who was alternating between freestyle and backstroke.

Stopping for air, Alex looked around, noticing that the place needed some restoration, even if it was remarkable. Tomas' naked bobbing body eventually pulled Alex's thoughts away from the building work.

After more laps and some romantic leanings, the two finally crawled out of the pool in time for Eetu's deadline, but realised they had no towels.

"Eetu!" Tomas cried. "Pyyhe! Pyyhe!"

A few moments later Eetu threw a towel into the entrance which Alex collected and proceeded to dry himself and Tomas off with. They turned off the lamps one by one and thanked Eetu, Tomas slipping him a banknote, before making their way through the chilly weather back to the hotel. The rain came crashing down just as they turned into the street where the hotel was located, so they ran the last few hundred meters and made their way up to the suite, dripping wet.

"That was awesome," Alex shrieked in the elevator. "So much fun!"

Tomas smiled. "Yeah. Shall we order some food? I'm so hungry."

***

The press conference announcing Alex's new album and show dates was a long and protracted affair, with portions given over to the corporate sponsors who explained why they were partnering with Alex despite recent controversies. The spin was that, as progressive organisations, they were delighted to work with an artist who was prepared to go against the grain. Alex's ego enjoyed the positive spin, but sitting with his management team, Alex wondered if the press would see it all as corporate art wank.

Aside from in Japan, Alex had never used his name for celebrity endorsements, despite all the offers that'd come his way since the eighties. He wasn't averse to the idea, but he'd always figured it was cynical of stars of his stature to do so. That said, touring was expensive and money tight. Truth was, he was quite late to the party, sponsorship already long a part of the pop landscape. This was just another area he needed to catch up to his peers on.

He was back on comfortable ground when talking about the themes of his upcoming show and his new music, whose release was imminent. The press had been invited to a listening preview of the album that morning and Dylan opened the floor for a forty minute Q & A session. Afterwards, Alex sat five, back-to-back, one-on-one interviews with MTV and other handpicked media. It would be the only conventional promotion he'd do for the album (and tour).

At the end of the media engagements, Kōji, Celia and Dylan headed straight to the airport for their flight to London. Alex himself had been rescheduled onto a flight for the following day. He'd explained to Celia that he wanted to spend another day in Helsinki, she responding with a raised eyebrow, a kiss on the cheek and a knowing glance.

"He's smoking hot! Half your luck!" she said as they made their goodbyes.

Back at the hotel, Alex organised for a driver to be waiting for him and Tomas that evening. It'd been another exhausting day of talking, which Tomas had taken in and observed from the press gallery. Tomas' observations suggested the media contingent had been decidedly split on the album and the slickness of the PR event. But the music industry was changing and far-flung junkets like this one were becoming the norm.

Alex had asked Dylan to make reservations at the old school Russian restaurant after Dylan, Celia and Kōji had spent the entire morning raving about it.

On their arrival, the two were ushered in through a private entry and taken directly up to a room that was ornately, if not entirely tastefully decorated with heavy trimmings and dark wallpaper.

"People seem to always be fascinated by Russia. Are you?" Tomas asked absently, as he let the waiter set his napkin on his lap.

"Yes, I guess so. But not because of the usual reasons, I suspect," Alex said, nodding in appreciation as the waiter poured him a glass of water.

"So, not for the Soviet empire or the handsome men or the amazing scenery?" Tomas chuckled, flipping through the menu.

"No."

"Well then?"

"There are people in my family that insist we have ancestors from Khabarovsk. I don't really know anything about them or about the place. No one in my family really does. My grandpa once told me that his father had simply fled when the opportunity presented and made his way to Europe. I don't know how true it was or if it was just a myth. I think it was news to my father, but my grandfather used to insist on telling me about him. Always. Just me and no one else because he thought I resembled the guy."

Tomas looked at him, astonished. "*You* are part *Russian?*"

"Well, no. It's probably all fantasy. I guess mine was never really a typical Australian family though. My parents were born in Italy."

"I never imagined life could be so complicated for an Australian person."

"It's all quite silly when you think about it," Alex said, dismissively. "Anyway, Russia does kind of fascinate me. I really would love to be able to explore that part of the world. Dylan told me about this place. They all came here last night and basically demanded we come here tonight. I assume it's okay with you."

"Yes, it is a well–known place," Tomas demurred. "But I'm still trying to understand how you can be Russian, Italian and Australian at the same time, especially when everyone thinks you're British."

"And wait for it," Alex said, sarcastically. "I also have an American passport."

"Does the rest of your family look like you?"

"No. I don't look like any of them. Unless I have family in Khabarovsk that I don't know about," Alex said. "I'm the black sheep. Maybe the postman's son."

"Well lucky you. I always wanted to look different to everyone else," Tomas said, putting down his menu. "Instead I looked like everyone else until I got to Stockholm. I think we need a drink Alex. Let's leave the conversation about genealogy for another time."

***

By the time tickets went on sale the following fortnight, Alex's new single, *Holy Word*, and *Mantra* were scaling the charts despite the lukewarm reviews they received. Finland was among a handful of territories where the single and album took up a long residence at No.1. On the pan–European chart Alex topped the albums and singles charts for a solitary week, but across the Atlantic he had to content himself with the album debuting and peaking at No.8 on the charts. In the US, *Holy Word* made it into MTV's high rotation, but struggled at radio. It was through sales alone that it mustered up a lowly peak in the top twenty.

Despite the prevailing obsession of the time to strike a *Jesus Christ pose*, Alex filled the video with Asian motifs that played out like a Mariko Mori photo in motion. The wholescale adoption of Asian imagery also underscored much of the tour's visuals. By heavily mining Eastern references, his new material correctly predicted the wave of pan Asian influence in Western pop that soon followed.

The press went to great pains to note the new material signalled the arrival of a more guarded Alekzandr.

Was there one underlying message to the album? If so, the press felt it was hard for any objective listener to hear, even if one of the main themes was the idea of freedom.

The lyrics from one track, *From The Shores,* spoke of a desire to abandon everything for a bit of peace and quiet; whereas on *Freak Show,* one of the album's singles - and a minor hit to boot (US No.15) - Alex likened himself to a court jester, banished from the kingdom for refusing to *'draw the line, and never saying no'.* On *Deeper,* the closest thing to a house number, and the album's one unqualified smash (No.1 in sixteen countries, No.8 in the US), the lyrics suggest a wish to be reborn; *'I rediscovered my-*

self one day as I plunged into the bay/ hues of blue and marine/ so clear now, so clear I can see'.

Reviewers observed that the lyrics seemed to scream '*You've all put me through hell but I've moved on*', yet, for the first time in his career, they felt Alex's music was a little passé and predictable. The album's sound, a hybrid of dance pop, house and some lightweight R&B, was unified by the south Asian instrumentation on many of the songs. Some tracks even incorporated the sound of *bhangra* that had swept the UK a couple of years earlier and inspired the likes of Siouxsie and the Banshees. But critics overwhelmingly felt *Mantra* was a product of an artist in flux, labelling it 'competent' but something of a disappointment from someone who always strived for innovation.

After Tomas and Alex put themselves through a fair bit of to and fro between London and Stockholm during the last phase of tour rehearsals, the time arrived for Alex to return to Helsinki to officially open his *Holy World Tour*.

"I've been having nightmares about this show since I announced it," Alex told MTV news at the final sound check. "But I've had so many ideas in recent years that I've become quite impatient… I can't wait to perform for my fans again."

"Why has it taken you so long to get back on the stage?" the VJ asked.

"Things just seemed to fall through every time I wanted to tour. There was a movie or something else to focus on. And then I hate the concept of being on the road for so long. It's not like I can just do lots of mini tours like the last one. Bringing this show to life and taking it across the world is very exciting for me. I know people are going to love it. Hopefully, they'll forgive me for not having toured in such a long time."

The night before the first show he was his usual bundle of nerves, taking a light sedative before bed, roused awake in the morning by Tomas' misplaced excitement about the first show.

Over breakfast, Alex tolerated Tomas' hyperbole about how the show was going to be spectacular, but he just wanted to keep his breakfast down. *How is it possible that these nerves are still here?*

Tomas attempted a few pep talks here and there before Celia and Kōji came by to discuss the plan for the day.

Alex meditated a little after everybody left and then met Stefan in the gym for a quick work out. After lunch, momentum carried Alex through the rest of his day; before he knew it he was being fitted into his costume and was in a circle with his band and dancers. He collected his thoughts and ushered in a silence.

"The moment has finally come. Everything we've been working so hard for has been for this moment. I bet that each of you is feeling as nervous and excited as I am. Be there for one another tonight, push each other to do your best and remember that you're here because you're the best at what you do. This is a moment for us all to share, to create something together. Let's get this show going! Let's blow the roof off this place and give these people *more* than what they came for! Amen!"

He exchanged long hugs with his dancers before being led behind the stage and onto a metallic staircase, which shook as he made his way up. Waiting for him at the top was Laurence, his stagehand, who sat on the suspended catwalk with a smile.

"Don't worry mate," Laurence smiled, "you'll be safe," he promised in his thick Australian accent, as he snapped the supporting harnesses around Alex's waist.

Far below Alex could hear and feel the crowd erupt as the house lights went down sending a combination of adrenalin and dread coursing through his body. The obligation to please and entertain a stadium full of people was again on his shoulders. He positioned himself on the prop, a regal throne, as he'd practiced countless times before, and secure that he was in position, gave Laurence the thumbs up. It was a routine which would play out night in night out, and one that signalled for the opening strains of *Holy Word* to be played by the band.

Shaking somewhat, Alex breathed as Stefan had taught him to, adjusting his earpiece before he began to chant into the microphone, the entire band and backing vocalists chiming in on the refrain of his comeback hit. Slowly, the platform lowered, and even through his closed eyes Alex could sense the heat of the stage lights on his face, indicating he was just about in view of the audience. As the light shifted to the upper periphery of his vision, he opened his eyes and belted his greeting to the now visible audience: *"Helsinki! Are you ready to make me sacred? To give me your holy word?"*

The audience erupted at the sight of him: perched on the throne, dressed in a skin tight blue body suit, a headdress sitting above his now short, dyed blonde hair, blue garlands, a bindi and the kohl around his eyes. Alex felt larger than life seeing his face amplified on the huge adjacent screens. He smiled, setting off a roaring wave across the audience.

As he rose from his throne and went through the choreography's paces, the nerves lightened. His new breathing technique was helping immensely. He was determined to have some fun and not let his insecurity swallow him the way it always tended to.

Holy Word's dazzling choreography, complete with complicated Indian hand gestures called *mudras*, gradually gave way to a freestyle interpretation of *Paean*, in its club remix form. An updated version of *Tightrope* followed, it also more faithful to the remix than the original, bringing out another enthusiastic reception from the fans. Closing the first act, one of the new tracks, *From The Shores,* slowed down the pace, paving the way for a musical interlude of *Velvet,* for which only the dancers remained on stage. *Velvet's* inclusion represented a compromise, in that no matter how many times they'd rehearsed and altered the original number, a full, live version just didn't seem to work.

As Alex changed into the next of the costumes and caught his breath, his attendees plied him with compliments. He'd learnt to take these kinds of moments with a grain of salt; people were being paid to be supportive but they too were caught up in the euphoria of the live experience. The line between sycophant and supporter was sometimes very thin.

An elaborate introduction to one of his older hits, *Dangerous,* introduced the second act, one dedicated to a more light hearted segment where Alex focused on the more dance oriented hits from his catalogue.

"Moi moi Helsinki! Hello Helsinki!" he shouted, "Are you ready to dance?"

As the old hits played out in their new forms, the choreography became slicker, and Alex focused, compartmentalising the frustration of his microphone cutting in and out, and chastising himself for forgetting some of the words for *Feel*. He threw dirty looks at his stage manager and began making mental notes of who'd receive a bollocking for all the technical faults that were occurring in the show.

"We're having some technical difficulties Helsinki," Alex sang at one point as the screens also started to cut in and out, "forgive me!" When he went off stage for the second of the costume changes his staff gave him a wide berth as he cussed and shouted. The irony of finally feeling like he knew what he was doing, only to be let down by technical issues brought him crashing down to earth. Tomas smiled at him and winked, which normally would have pissed Alex off even further, but Tomas' forced nonchalance helped Alex shake it off. *They're technical problems: so they're out of my hands. Not like forgetting my own damn lyrics.*

The third act of the show was its darkest, plumbing the tracks from *Androgynous* and *Mantra* in a mini theatrical sequence that the tour director and choreographer had worked on together. This was the most challenging part of the show. Not only for Alex but for the dancers who had individualised choreography to carry out while also dealing with stage props and hydraulics. Different areas of the stage were used, with some mini stages suspended in mid-air to help shift the eye's attention around. An additional challenge for Alex was that by this stage of the show, his voice began to demonstrate wear, yet it was where he had to do his most rigorous singing. His dancers had to variously chase him down, lift and propel him, tango with him and simulate sexual positions while he sang throughout. After the first few shows, where he attempted to sing live through it all, the decision was made to adapt his choreography to give him a chance to belt the numbers out better. Though arduous, this act of the show, devoid of actual *hits*, was singled out for its ingenuity and compelling staging.

At the end of the act his dancers lowered Alex onto a make shift bed which sat in the middle of the stage, as they moved to another mostly instrumental interlude, this time a section of *Thinking About You*, his monster hit from the eighties which he had no intention of singing. As each dancer left the stage, it grew darker, a singular spotlight positioned onto Alex, who slowly rose from the bed and sang an interpolation of *Decision Never Made* and *Without You I'm Nothing*. He never once made it through the number without missing a few notes, but it was the emotional highpoint of the show for him.

A six-minute break for Alex followed the performance of those songs. It was designed to give him time to regain his breath while the dancers enjoyed the spotlight.

The final act, a kaleidoscope of old and new songs, switched the focus from the dancers to the band. Eighties hits like *All My Love* and *Respect* were coupled with the newer songs *Past Caring* and *Warmth of Your Touch* which showcased the talents of Alex's band and backing vocalists. This was also the segment of the show in which Alex interacted with the audience if they'd impressed him enough.

When the final encores rolled around, Alex was almost always on a high. The show felt cathartic, like real theatre for him, and technical issues aside, he enjoyed the experience, his audience a tonic to the chronic press criticism that had plagued him.

Surprisingly, it was a hit with the critics. One in particular referred to the show as "a pop opera that will remind you Alekzandr isn't technically brilliant at any one thing, but he's amongst the best there is when he throws everything into the mix."

Given only a handful of shows on the tour had failed to sell out, his management team shielded Alex from the press, adamant they needed to manage Alex's media exposure. In any case, the reviews were more than favourable with most of the European critics playing nice.

Alex only felt relief that, for the first time in nearly two years, he wasn't being vilified. The same couldn't be said for the other members of pop royalty. Each and every one of them were trying to quash their own revolts. *A prince who had taken to scrawling 'Slave' on his cheek. A king whose many failings were being gleefully documented and in tawdry detail. The Brit who ruled white boy soul losing his lawsuit and on the brink of a public sex scandal all his own. And pop's reigning queen unravelled by her own spiral bound book of sexual fantasies and a string of expletives.* One by one they were being taken down like villains in a comic book. But in front of his own fans each night, who numbered anywhere between ten and sixty thousand, depending on the venue, Alex felt that perhaps all wasn't lost. Perhaps there was more beyond what the headlines seemed to be obsessing about.

Looking out into the audiences each night during the final act, Alex saw his fans were now predominantly women and teenagers, with a pinch of his trusty club kids. There were times he didn't see a single adult male for rows at a time. The *gays* had abandoned him. Perhaps they thought him unfashionable or kitschy now, or simply someone they no longer wanted to identify with publicly. *Gay men will support a fallen diva,* Alex thought, *but only if she is a biological one.* Having one of their own made to crawl back up to the top just doesn't engender the same kind of devotion, he surmised.

After each show Alex was much too spent to socialise or party like his assembled cast and crew did in his name. Occasionally he ventured out for a drink, but mostly, he returned to his hotel room, where he spent hours reading, meditating and adjusting from having had thousands of people eating out of the palm of his hand to ending up alone in his room.

"Why the sour puss?" Celia said, the morning after his show in Frankfurt and another night in which Alex put himself to bed while his crew partied. "Why can't you be like a normal rock star?"

"What do you mean?" he said, pouring himself a coffee.

"You know, you should be out on the scene, enjoying this time. Socialising. Hanging out with the rest of us. Have the odd one night stand. It's going to be a long five months if all you do is work out with Stefan, read and rack up huge phone bills with Tomas. Get out a bit. Enjoy the experience."

"I'm just not in the mood."

"Well get into one," Celia said. "We're about to hit Italy and Spain. Make me a wish list of what you'd like to see and do. Kōji and I will see to it."

"I can't be bothered," Alex said, getting up and walking back into his room to get ready for his workout.

"Suit yourself," Celia hollered.

In the car on the way to the stadium that afternoon, Alex turned to Kōji.

"Did you have fun last night?"

"We did," Kōji replied. "What time did you end up reading until?"

"Four," Alex said, looking out the window.

"We were all in bed by then," Kōji replied.

"Is it true? What Celia is saying?"

"What?"

"That I'm a bore?"

"I wouldn't go that far," Kōji said diplomatically. "But I know some of the dancers would like to spend some time with you. Even if you don't want to do something late night, maybe we could organise some excursions during the day."

"Like?"

"Museums? Art galleries? Maybe some matinee performances?"

"I'll think about it," Alex said.

Alex finally relented as the tour reached Spain. He instructed Kōji to make arrangements for a private tour of the Reina Sofia collection in Madrid, asking him to extend an invitation to the band and the dancers.

A few of them took up the invite, among them the bassist Arden, a tall, strapping thirty something from Atlanta, and the only loner in the band. When the band was out partying, Arden was more likely to be holed up in his hotel room reading, plotting how he was going to use his earnings from the tour to put down a deposit on a house in Miami. He was a good looking guy with aquiline features, a spiky afro, dimples and three rings on each hand, along with a silver cross which sat above his dark brown chest. He was a competent musician who had come up the hard way, working as a session player whenever there was a gig in the offing, and steadily working away on his own compositions which he tried to sell to music publishers.

Alex recognised Arden's aloofness; moving to take the shy musician under his wing when he saw Arden was having trouble penetrating the cliquey dancers' circle at the museum. Alex took Arden by the arm, and together they strolled through the galleries, the only two in the group who listened reverently to the curator.

***

After Madrid, Alex and Arden began to spend more and more time together. Their huddling teased curiosity and jealousy out of the dancers. And as the tour made its way through Portugal, France and the UK, gossip among the crew suggested theirs was more than just a friendship.

Arriving in London in time for the last of the UK shows, Tomas was quick to notice the dynamic.

After the last of the four shows, Alex had Kōji book a venue for a wrap up party to celebrate the end of the European leg of the tour. As the night progressed and the cocktails flowed, Tomas sidled up to Arden who was watching Alex and the dancers tearing up the dancefloor.

"You know," Tomas said. "I see the way you look at him."

"At Alex?" Arden asked, turning his attention away from the dancefloor. "No it's nothing like that. We're just friends."

"He talks to me about you all the time," Tomas said.

"It's not what you think," Arden said, his heart hastening its pace a little. "We just clicked. It's tough being on the road with all these young kids."

"I just want to be clear," Tomas said, looking Arden in the eye. "I don't respond well to people stepping on my toes. To people that would want to take advantage of someone like Alex."

"You don't have anything to worry about," Arden said. "Excuse me, I'm going to get another drink," he said, shaking the beer bottle to demonstrate he was now empty.

Meeting Tomas had an effect on Arden. It had caused Arden to recalibrate his behaviour with Alex. He reminded himself that he was on Alex's payroll. And as innuendo about their relationship swirled around the crew as the show snaked through Asia and the Pacific, Arden withdrew a bit, returning to his solitary habits, taking up Alex's invitations only regularly enough to avoid any suspicion on Alex's part.

***

In any case, by the time the tour reached the Americas, Alex's interest in organising excursions for his dancers and band had waned. His thoughts had shifted to the filming of the Miami dates for cable TV. And with more than six million sales of *Mantra* and projections that ticket and merchandising sales would top $100million, the frequency of his business meetings increased as his management team began to think about the next project.

That said, Alex insisted Arden attend a dinner he'd organised with Ian and Michael in Miami. Alex wanted Michael to consider contracting Arden as a songwriter for a couple of the pop/

soul bands Michael was developing at Kēvala and also wanted Ian to meet Arden.

Long after the tour, Alex and Arden's friendship endured. At one point when Arden found himself in financial difficulty, behind in payments for his house in Miami, Alex gave him a sizeable "loan" to get him back on his feet.

Passing through Miami many years later, the connection between the two was still evident. He and Arden locked themselves in at Arden's for two days, watching videos and having frantic, no holds barred sex together before Alex had to leave for South America for a film shoot. Had their timing been better, there perhaps could have been a chance for the two of them.

| 9 |

THE MINISTRY OF (UN)FUN

One of the main reasons to practice meditation is to release yourself from the endless cycle of pointless thoughts. The premise is a relatively simple one. You consciously make the effort to liberate yourself from the notions and fears that skewer your perceptions. If you can manage to concentrate, open your mind, and cross your eyes without nodding off, then there's a reasonable chance you'll experience something.

Most people describe the accompanying visions of their meditations in colours, or of seeing nature and wildlife. Few report visualising episodes of persecution. But that seemed to be standard for Alekzandr's early attempts. More often than not, they started with the best of intentions; green hills, so thickly forested they gave the impression that the sky too was fertile and textured. He'd trample under lush canopies, the sound of water cascading nearby. But each and every time, everything would fade to a bleak grey and his tormentors would catch up to him.

Although his meditative experiences were patchy, he found them constructive. And as he began to take meditating more seriously, honing his ability during the world tour, he gradually felt he was benefitting from the practice. He'd eagerly recount his journeys to those around him, unfazed when they dismissed them the way they also dismissed his dreams. Celia, beyond even humouring him by the time they'd reached South America, would simply roll her eyes the minute Alex started recalling his latest "trip", desperate for an escape of her own.

Celia, the closest thing Alex had to a legal guardian, wasn't entirely convinced that meditation alone could address all of Alex's anxieties. Though he was determined to work through his difficulties and his scepticism of new age thinking, Celia ensured he maintained his telephone appointments with his shrink, and that when March rolled around, his schedule was always free for his annual in person visit. This was a non–negotiable, that Celia had put into place shortly after the recording of *Without You I'm Nothing*. While Celia was more than happy to field phone calls from Alex at any time, she wasn't prepared to be his one stop shop when it came to his mental health.

Alex's shrink was a well–respected professional whose stiff upper lip drove Alex crazy. Alex began each annual visit in the same way, trying to engage the doctor in small talk before posing a decoy question to test the waters. Alex would then try to take the conversation out onto a tangent before the psychiatrist steered it back into more meaningful territory. For years, Alex was loathe to speak about his personal life. His friendships, lovers and family were topics he only ever reluctantly shared. He only saw the psychiatrist in the hope of gleaning some insight into the peaks and valleys his stardom seemed to put him through. But after *Androgynous* and the accompanying media circus stripped Alex of much of his self belief, he began to warm to the psychiatrist's insistence that Alex's personal and professional lives were one and the same thing. That their ups and downs were something he could manage better.

"So," the psychiatrist asked. "How are you feeling now that the tour is well and truly over? That you're not working every day?" emphasising *working* with air quotes.

"It feels like I've come out of another bubble," Alex admitted. "I'm not always sure what to do with myself."

"Would you prefer to be back on the road?"

"No!" Alex said, shaking his head emphatically.

"Then what's going on?"

"I'm living in London now."

"And?" the psychiatrist asked, clicking his pen.

"It feels weird," Alex confessed.

"How so?"

"Because, okay, I have a couple of friends there. And I'm doing my best to meet new people like you said I should. But it feels really weird to pick up the phone and say, 'hey, I'm Alex. I want to get to know you. Will you have lunch with me?'"

"There are millions of ways you could meet people more easily if you wanted to."

"I know. But I want to cut to the chase a bit. I feel like I've taken ten steps back leaving New York the way I did," Alex admitted.

"That's normal," the psychiatrist assured him. "How are things with your new beau?"

"Good. I think. But he's a bit like London."

"What do you mean?"

"I don't know. He just keeps pushing me out of my comfort zone."

"Ah," the psychiatrist said, "you mean he's still got you on the program? How did you put it? Yes, he's always 'pushing you to be a little braver and a lot more foolish'. Do I have that right?"

"Yes," Alex replied. "And it's getting worse."

***

Tomas had, very quickly, altered Alex's life in unimaginable ways. He'd bought Alex his first electric guitar and a violin, an instrument that Alex had always dreamt of playing, but never even attempted, for fear he'd be no good at it. Tomas also bought lessons to go with the instruments, in the hope that it would engage Alex even more with his song writing.

He'd also encouraged Alex to resume drawing in his free time. Tomas was convinced Alex needed to be stimulated, and that he needed more leisure choices than simply clubbing or dining out.

Tomas also dragged Alex along to all kinds of sporting events like soccer matches, sailing regattas and fencing tournaments, keen to introduce Alex to the world of professional sport. They would spend their nights speaking at length in London and Stockholm about all sorts of things; literature, art, athletes, politics... the works.

Tomas worked hard to convince Alex that life in Europe was his for the taking if he wanted it; reminding him that commuting between London and Stockholm was far less taxing than flying between the East and West coasts.

It was a relief being out of the States. Spending a week there had been enough to remind Alex of how drastically things had changed. The top ten there was now almost completely made up of R&B hits, radio dripping with its smooth beats and harmonies. For so long, Alex had prided himself on his ability to weave in and out of musical genres and to bend them to his own creative needs. Ever since he'd emerged from the Holocene of the *New Wave* and *No Wave* scenes, he'd shaped his own unorthodox path. His instincts had usually paid off, earning him a place among an exclusive club of artists who could move effortlessly in and out of pop and dance music, and all of their iterations. But Alex's music was no longer welcome on US radio.

Worse, now that he was approaching 37, his management were encouraging him to play it safe. They had pitched two projects which they believed would help him return to solid ground: two *greatest hits* collections; one full of his dance hits, the other his ballads. He was even free to curate the track listings and to choose collaborators for the new songs needed to entice buyers. But Alex rejected their proposal. Though he couldn't relate to the sounds shaping the US charts, he still had ideas. He wanted to work with a range of collaborators; something he'd never done before on a single album. Doing so would allow him to co–opt some of the emerging sounds he did like; the electronica emerging out of Europe; trip hop and drum n bass out of the UK... even Northern Soul.

His approach to writing music had changed. He was determined to form his own ideas rather than rely on producers to realise them for him as he always had. And his lyrics were now less linear than ever. He found himself constantly writing, ensuring he always had a notebook on hand, especially now that he was traveling so often. Years later, Alex realised that Tomas had influenced these changes. In hindsight, Alex also saw that the desire to impress Tomas had seeped into his creative process. But, back in London in 1995, on the lookout for new collaborators, Alex baulked at Tomas' suggestion of working with the Swedish pop producers who were having huge success in the European market. Back then, Alex felt Tomas had overstepped by merely making the suggestion.

In any case, the prospect of working in Stockholm held no appeal. Stockholm was already tough enough for Alex. He found it oddly middle class and conservative, and was often nostalgic for London when he was there. With Tomas working, the only thing that made Stockholm tolerable was when an old Swedish friend from his squatting days, and an actor friend of Tomas' would drive by, kidnapping him and insisting he be part of their Ministry of Fun. At times he would find them downstairs, warning him to bring his passport for quick runs into Denmark or Finland.

Thick as thieves, Marin and Jakob understood Alex's frustration with Stockholm. And though he couldn't always rely on their distractions, Alex knew he always had London to fall back on, which proved especially convenient when the complexities of Tomas' life made things sticky for everyone. Including Tomas' ex–wife, Lena.

Alex felt that he'd understood Lena from the beginning. Though Tomas liked to paint her as a *woman scorned,* Alex felt Lena was simply suffering from seller's remorse. She had once been Tomas' everything. And despite their problems, she'd always figured their marriage would overcome its difficulties. But when Alex first met Tomas back in Helsinki, Tomas and Lena had already been divorced for six months and were still struggling to reach a compromise about Victoria, who was already turning one back then.

Much of Alex's discomfort in Stockholm centred around Tomas' irritation with Lena. Tomas was convinced Lena was using Victoria to try and make him accountable. Not just as a father, but as a "husband", despite their legal separation. He was exasperated by her refusal to see him as her ex. And when Lena began refusing Tomas access to Victoria after a series of miscommunications and arguments, the tension became unbearable.

Frustrated by the effect the stalemate was having on his own life, Alex made the radical decision of intervening in a way he would never have done before. He decided he owed it to Tomas. After everything Tomas had done for him, Alex figured he should at least try to broker a truce between the warring parties. Anything to help relieve Tomas' growing anger and frustration.

Soon Alex began to think of his time in Stockholm as a chance to resolve the impasse between the separated couple. Deciding to campaign for Lena's approval, Alex felt it was his responsibility to help Lena see Tomas as an ally and not an adversary. He took it upon himself to contact Lena daily, offering to help out in any way he could. It took weeks to eke out her trust, but he spent a full month in Stockholm, careful to be available to her. Checking in with her morning and night, he offered to run errands, to babysit or simply hear her out. At home, he went to equal effort to mediate Tomas' views of Lena. Though he felt sullied by being so deeply involved in their business, he persevered because he knew he was besotted by Tomas. And standing by watching as Tomas suffered was simply not an option for him.

Alex suspected Lena's eventual warming to him was merely a by product of his fame. But he was surprised when Lena began calling of her own accord. Initially it was only with half truths about Tomas. Alex saw the calls as tests; attempts on her part to see if he would report back to Tomas. When it was clear that he wasn't taking the bait, Lena began to truly let down her guard. She began calling to recount Victoria's latest milestone, or to confide in Alex about her desire to date again. As their bond strengthened, she began to backtrack on many of her other positions and granted Tomas and his family regular access to Victoria. As Tomas and Lena resumed their own communication, both began to consider the possibility of experimenting with an informal shared custody arrangement.

After the breakthrough, Alex kept in contact with Lena. In London every other week recording for the new album, he regularly checked in with her, happy to talk about whatever she wanted to. When in Stockholm, their phone calls became lunch appointments, and their conversations broadened beyond Tomas and Victoria to incorporate music, Alex's new record and Lena's desire to introduce him to some of her friends in Stockholm's creative crowd.

Though Tomas maintained his end of the peace that Alex had brokered, Tomas also made it clear he didn't want to cultivate the relationship with Lena any further. He promised Alex that he'd be courteous and diplomatic, but also asked Alex to consider pulling back from his daily interactions with her.

"I appreciate everything you've done," Tomas said over dinner. "But I don't know how healthy this arrangement is. For us or for her."

"What do you mean?" Alex asked, his mouth full of salmon.

"I just don't think it's a good idea for you to be so connected to her. It's not good for anybody. She needs to find her own path now."

"You know, there's a million ways to go forward," Alex said, chewing faster so that he could swallow. "There's no reason to abandon her."

"If we are so available to her," Tomas countered, "she'll never take the initiative for herself."

"I don't think that's really fair," Alex said, surprised by Tomas' conviction. "Besides, I would think it's better for all three of you that we're all friends. That we make it work."

"I'm not sure about that," Tomas said, pouring himself a glass of wine. "I know her better than you. I know what she's like."

Alex contemplated whether to go on. He was afraid that if he did, the other uncomfortable topic would rear its head. The one about him wanting a child of his own. He knew now it had been absurd to confess to wanting one. Not because he lacked the means. He'd just mistimed it, having expressed his desire right when things with Lena had been at their worst. Tomas had ridiculed him, reminding Alex that there was already a child in the mix, and that they were already struggling to play a significant role in her life.

And Alex knew it wasn't just Tomas' typical bluster. Tomas' patience may have been short in recent months, but he never failed to think things through. Alex admired how resolute Tomas was about practically everything, even if there were times when he wished Tomas simply didn't have an opinion.

The next day at lunch, Alex could've sworn Lena was reading his thoughts.

"You know I have to admit I was wrong about you," she said as she dished out lunch. "I had two ideas in mind. One, that you wouldn't be able to stand up to Tomas for long. And the other was that I thought you were the kind of person that didn't respect people's commitments to one another."

"What, like a home wrecker?" Alex asked.

"Is that what they're called? It's similar in Swedish I guess. *Familjesplittrare.* Anyway, I have to admit, and I am embarrassed to say it now, but when I first met you, I did think of you in that way."

"I get that a lot," Alex said, mostly for his own amusement.

"Yes, but I started to think a little differently. I think talking to you was necessary for me. To help me be more honest. And the truth is a strange thing, because it sounds different in the heart."

"And what did it tell you?" Alex asked, adding some mustard to his plate.

"I thought the truth was that I wanted to fix things with Tomas, especially now with Victoria. But in my heart, I knew the time to do that was long gone." Lena paused for a moment and Alex smiled sympathetically, because it seemed like the kind thing to do.

"I never took the signs seriously back then," she said, shaking her head. "I'm glad that he met you, because it really could've been anybody else," she said, chuckling. "The way he started looking at other men, the looks they had in their eyes. It was terrifying… so alien. Nothing like the way he used to look at me. Wherever we were I would see it – at dinner, or the supermarket or the park – he was expressing things through his eyes and his body language that I just couldn't understand. And the men would do it back to him in return."

"Was that when you first realised?" Alex asked.

"No. I suspected it many years before. But it was like it took control of him in the last year we were together. Like he couldn't fight it any longer," she said, nodding her head and closing her eyes for a moment. "He wasn't always aware of it, but his real nature really was *coming out*."

Alex smiled, pouring her a glass of water.

"So, when you started calling me, I was horrified. Who wants to speak to their husband's boyfriend? Sorry. *Ex–husband!* But in the middle of all the visits to the counsellors and the mediators and everything it was strange."

Alex watched as Lena relaxed, taking a bite of bread.

"My family thought I was crazy when I told them I was going to see you. They couldn't understand why I was curious. But I was. I wanted to know what Tomas had found for himself. And so quickly. Especially because Tomas was keeping everything about you a secret."

"You know it was an accident that we met? Like a bad Hollywood cliché."

"Yes," Lena said. "I read about it," she said sharply. "Your calls made me curious but also nervous. I don't know of anyone that has done that, you know? A new partner calling the old one like that. People just don't do that. It was like an uncomfortable gift. But I'm glad for it. It made us grow up a bit."

"I know it isn't easy," Alex said, a little tired of the conversation.

"It wasn't easy. He's different you know. He's not like you. You get soft when you're with Victoria. He doesn't. He's a pragmatic man, Alex. He takes a long time to get comfortable with things."

She looked at him conspiratorially.

"Ah, so he has told you?" Alex said. "That I want to be a dad?"

"Yes," she replied, nodding.

"You think it's crazy too?"

"A bit," Lena said. "He's still getting used to Victoria, Alex. And she's almost two already. I don't know how he would cope with another child in his life right now."

| 10 |

BRAVE AND FOOLISH

After the tour Alex kept a low profile, during which time, he authorised the use of some unreleased songs onto benefit albums. The home video of his tour sold well, and Kēvala was riding high on the success of three of Michael's artists in the charts.

Alex though, was well and truly focused on his new project, obsessed with his new, emerging sound. It wasn't so much *his,* as it was other people's music he was trying to make his own.

With Alex's cheque book in hand and generous royalty scales to offer, Alex's team had no trouble procuring the services of some new collaborators. After meeting with Alex's management, a handful of producers and DJs on Alex's wish list eagerly signed up to put their stamp on his new record.

Though Alex loved their textures and grooves, he didn't intend to merely jump onto their bandwagons. To that end, he pushed himself with his lyrics and melodies. Tapping into his more commanding vocal range, his verses incorporated ad–libbing, poetry and spoken word. It was all a bid to inject something new into his work and come up with something unexpected.

Treating the project like a mixtape gave Alex the freedom to colour outside the lines. But with his producers scattered around the UK, he was reduced to shuttling between London, Edinburgh and Bristol to fit into their schedules. Though Alex resented accommodating their timetables, in time he relished the constant change of scenery.

On his first working trip for the album, Alex spent a fortnight in London where he worked with the Step Brothers, two unrelated DJs who'd remixed singles from his recent albums. Irreverent, competent and more or less both his age, Alex enjoyed the unexpected nature of working with them. In the studio, they constantly added new layers to the songs, shaping the tracks into woozy mixes of electronica and ambient music.

For Alex's second round in the UK, he spent his first week working with a young American producer, Corey, in Bristol. Corey's trademark sound was a mix of triphop and Atlanta R&B. More straightforward and predictable by nature, Corey's approach to work was more methodical than Alex had expected. In that first week the two workhorses buckled down and completed basic demos for four songs.

The Edinburgh sessions were the most eventful of the second trip. Flying up from Bristol, Alex finally met Declan, the youngest of the collaborators. Alex had stumbled across his existence by accident. Declan had submitted a demo tape to Kēvala's newly opened London offices. It eventually wound up on Alex's home office desk, where it sat untouched for months. It was only on a cloudy afternoon, when Alex was winding up his research for the new album that he discovered it. Listening to the three songs on it, he was charmed by their mix of acoustic instruments and chopped up programming. He instructed his staff to contact Declan, and after negotiations with Declan's manager – his father – Declan was invited to work on Alex's new album.

The first few days in Edinburgh proved chaotic. Declan's father initially blocked Alex and Kōji from entering the tiny studio, informing them work couldn't begin until Declan's royalties were renegotiated. Alex stepped back and let Kōji do the talking, silently taking in their heated exchange as he watched Declan watching on. It was only when Declan's father began shouting that Declan stepped in, dispatching his father back to his native Glasgow in no uncertain terms, apologising profusely to Alex and Kōji once his father sped off.

Declan arrived on day two to find Alex and Kōji waiting outside the studio. Unlocking the door he soon realised the studio was partially flooded. He spent a good hour mopping up, apologising for the draught as Alex and Kōji looked on, rugged up in their jackets, bemoaning the cold air as it swept in from the open windows. The misfortune repeated itself the next day, but this time, the rain made it into the circuitry, short circuiting the lights and some of Declan's equipment. With an impatient pop superstar and an equally terse manager to deal with, Declan maintained his cool. Despite being faced with a ruined studio and the possibility he was about to be booted from the project, he came up with a plan. As Alex wandered into one of the backrooms, Declan handed Kōji the keys to his apartment, giving him the address and telling Kōji the two of them could wait there while he cleaned up. As soon as he was done, they could get to work at his home studio. Kōji's heart broke for the kid but he knew Alex had reached his limit. He wished he could simply send Alex off somewhere while he helped Declan with the clean up. But Alex had made things clear the night before. *The kid's not getting any more chances.*

"We're not going anywhere," Alex finally said, emerging from the backroom, with a mop in one hand and a bucket in the other. "We're going to clean up. Then I'm going back to the hotel and this afternoon we'll get to work. While Kōji and I see to this, call a plumber and an electrician for god's sake."

Declan smiled at Koji.

With significant repairs needed at the studio, the three decamped in the afternoon to Declan's house, where Alex and Declan attempted to make up for lost time.

Having wasted almost half of the working week, Alex was reluctant to fly back to Stockholm when Friday afternoon rolled around. But he had to abide by Tomas' rule. *No more than two weeks apart from each other for work.*

Back in Stockholm for the week, as Tomas filled in as a sports anchor on the news bulletin, Alex pored over faxes and responded to phone messages in the mornings, worked out at the gym in the afternoons and descended into panic in the early evenings as he desperately tried to make dinner for Tomas. This was another of Tomas' conditions. Their time together had to be as "normal" as possible. No more restaurants, no more reliance on domestic staff or social engagements during the week.

Marin, Alex's old friend often made an appearance in the now sprawling apartment in the early evenings. She'd helped

Alex furnish the extra space he'd acquired when he'd bought the neighbouring apartment. She'd also taken to dropping in to help him with his nightly meal preparation, but for the most part she was only there to keep him company. Still a willowy, blue eyed, blonde who insisted on dyeing her hair black, she'd changed with the years. She was now a furniture and textile designer, but referred to herself as 'a divorcee' at every possible moment, her mouth still curling at any mention of her ex–husband, even after all these years. Alex loved her company but often wondered how she could afford to be so available when he was in town. She'd routinely swing by, suggesting a new restaurant to have lunch at, or, even insist on joining him at the gym so that she could *check out the talent* while Alex went through his paces.

Their conversations regularly turned to babies and to how they both wanted a kid, even if they weren't convinced they were prepared for the commitment it entailed. More often than not, their chats descended into cackling about how terrible they'd both be as parents.

And though Alex did his best to remain present when in Stockholm, much to Tomas' irritation, Alex's mind was often elsewhere. Even on the sunny afternoons he spent on Tomas' yacht as Tomas navigated around Gamla Stan. Only the bitter splashes of cold water brought Alex's thoughts back from Bristol or Edinburgh, reminding him of the trouble that Tomas had gone to in arranging the day out on the water. Alex envied Tomas' passion and expertise at steering his tiny yacht around the historical centre.

He knew things were going well with Corey in Bristol, where he was realising some deeply personal songs with Corey's help.

There was *My Pathway*, a mid–tempo number about love that Alex was having trouble coming up with a great chorus for. He was also struggling with *Human/nature*, a song Corey was certain could become an anthem, but one which Alex felt wasn't quite *there* yet. And then there was *Lullaby*, a love song for Victoria. Though it was charming and sweet, Alex feared it was also too sentimental.

Then there were the Edinburgh songs, quite unlike anything he'd ever made before. He loved the groove of *Brave and Foolish*, but Alex was anxious his lyrics were just a rip off of Bono's. With Declan he'd also come up with another innovative song, *Gypsy's Heart*. It had flourishes of Berber percussion, and he and Declan had even improvised with kitchen pots and pans to add something special to its mix. But Alex worried people would find it corny, or that it was too much like a Paul Simon moment from *Graceland*. Declan had pushed him even further out of his comfort zone, with a glam rock styled number called *Personal Mirror*. Alex loved its lyrics and melodies, but he had reservations about whether sonically, he was just trying too hard.

In any case, as the summer of 1995 rolled in, Alex made his peace with the songs after a final raft of changes, signing off on the album in mid July.

Despite his doubts, his management decided on *Gypsy's Heart* as the lead single for North America and *Renaissance,* a Step Brothers collaboration, as the first single elsewhere.

Arrangements were made for two wildly different videos. *Renaissance* was filmed in a London studio, while *Gypsy's Heart* was done on location in Morocco.

With filming of the videos behind him, in August, he and Tomas set off on a three-week sailing trip around the Greek islands. Coming into port intermittently to pick up or drop off friends, they were only occasionally snapped by the paparazzi.

Tanned and rested, Alex was back in launch mode by September, racking up the miles with promotional duties across four continents.

Renaissance hit the charts running, but while *Gypsy's Heart* quickly became a top ten hit in Canada, the lack of radio airplay hampered its progress in the US.

In October, as album reviews and interviews began to appear in the press, two of the interviews created a stir.

In the cover story for UK's *The Face,* Alex was asked about his "ban" at American radio. "I'm tired of a handful of people making decisions for me. Radio programmers are not elected officials. They're modern day fascists. I think they should let audiences decide what it is they want to hear. Not the other way around."

After lengthy negotiations, Alex also landed the cover of *Rolling Stone.* In his interview he was asked to comment on whether censorship had improved after his last run in with the conservative press.

"Honestly, I thought I had overcome some of that with my last album. I'm not interested in pressing people's buttons just for the hell of it. The themes my work addresses are about people's freedoms. Dignity. Honesty. Encouraging people to be more open about things. It's strange that my record hasn't come out yet and there are already people talking about censoring it. They're adamant my music shouldn't be on the radio. That it shouldn't be stocked at places like Walmart. Why not? It seems odd to me that the same people who are waging a war against me, are the same people that turn a blind eye to the culture of violence that is ravaging the States. You can watch someone being shot or cut up into pieces on TV in the US, but not two people of the same sex showing affection for one another. It's ridiculous."

As the mini media storm echoed, Alex's album, *Brave and Foolish,* hit the stores. As reviews for the album came in, they gave mixed interpretations of the record. While lauding its experimentalism and its textures, some reviewers also condemned the use of multi producers, and the lack of a cohesive sound. "Alekzandr," one reviewer crowed, "has still not found his way back to dry land."

The lack of discernible singles was also an issue for many reviewers. One writer lamented how Alekzandr, once the consummate singles artist, now seemed to have trouble coming up with even one clear standout.

In his New York apartment, Alex waited patiently for Celia and Kōji to arrive with the latest chart and sales reports. Letting them in, he led them to his kitchen table, poring over the reported sales figures and chart placings they laid out before him.

"It's not good, is it?" he said.

"We were hoping for better," Celia admitted.

"It's not going to reach number one anywhere," Alex said. "This is a disaster."

"Alex, I think we need to start pushing *Gypsy's Heart,*" Kōji said. "It's still climbing the chart."

"It's not even in the top thirty," Alex said. "It's dead already."

"You're looking at it the wrong way," Kōji said, making eye contact with Celia. "You've made a record that your fans weren't expecting. You have to help them get used to it. I want to book you on some TV shows. Get you performing it like the old days."

"Can you imagine how desperate that is going to look?" Alex said.

"No, Kōji's right Alex. It'll be a coup. *Top of the Pops. Wetten Das...*"

"And we can talk to VH1," Kōji said, interrupting. "They want you at the fashion awards. We'll ask them to give you a performing slot. You're up for an award anyway."

"I am? How did that happen?"

"A lot of phone calls and some persuading," Kōji replied, Alex unsure whether he was being sarcastic or not.

Over the following two months, Alex did as he was ordered, performing *Gypsy's Heart* and *Renaissance* in a two–for–one deal for a few TV shows in Europe and Japan, before flying back to New York to perform at the awards night. He found the premise of the show a little flimsy, but, surrounded by some of his most famous peers, he realised he'd completely underestimated their pull.

As usual, he walked away from the awards show empty handed, but with the help of a seven piece percussion ensemble, pulled off a stirring performance of *Gypsy's Heart* which was lauded by the press as the night's best. In the weeks that followed, he was surprised to see the song enter the US top twenty, some three months after its initial release. Back in Europe for Christmas and the filming of two more music videos in London, *Brave And Foolish* began to finally find its feet, proving the season's sleeper hit.

Done with his promotional duties, in late January 1996, he flew Tomas and a group of their friends out to Australia, bunkering down at his coastal house for a late summer holiday. With his album now approaching platinum status in many markets, Alex did his best to switch off, making arrangements for his family to join them at the property.

Marin's attendance made things a little tricky at times. Though Alex and Marin bounced off each other as always, resuming their conversation about becoming imaginary parents, the triviality of their conversation irritated Tomas. He found their constant fantasizing about having a child together frivolous and would tell them outright.

But Marin enjoyed the tension. Even in front of Victoria, Marin grilled Tomas on his opinions about her and Alex's conversations. Marin pricked and prodded Tomas, whether at the beach, walking in the dry surrounding hills or when sitting down for meals on the patio. Anywhere he had a comment ready, she had a follow up question prepared.

"Tomas," she said, positioning her seat closer to his as he busied himself with chopping up the salad.

"What now Marin?"

"I want to talk to you. While Alex is busy. Before his family get here."

"I'm a bit busy. There's enough salad here for an army," he said, wiping the sweat off his forehead with the back of his hand.

"We have time now," Marin said. "All you have to do is hear me out."

"It sounds serious," Tomas said, turning to look at her. She seemed to be coping even more poorly with the dry heat than he was. "Perhaps we should speak in Swedish?" he said, motioning towards Alex who was just metres away at the grill with another guest.

"No," Marin said, "I don't want Victoria getting confused."

"Has something happened?" Tomas asked.

"No. I want to talk to you about Alex."

"Oh," he said, sighing. "Not this again."

"No really," Marin said, knowing she had to lower her voice. "I'm not talking on Alex's behalf. I'm talking to you as a friend."

"Go on," he said, dicing the tomatoes and being disappointed by how dry they were.

"I know that you think the two of us have been acting like teenagers. Talking about things the way we do. I also know that you've had a couple of difficult years. That you hadn't planned on becoming a father."

"Yes, but I am one now. A good one I think."

"Yes. I know," Marin affirmed. "And you're doing a great job. Even if the decision was made for you about becoming a father."

"Yes. But what's your point?" he said, using the knife to send the tomatoes plummeting into the two salad bowls.

"Think of how you felt when Lena made that decision for you. To go ahead with the pregnancy even if it was against your judgement."

"I don't think about that anymore," Tomas said, lining the lettuce up on the chopping board.

"No, you don't," Marin said, "because you've come to terms with it and it turned out to be the right decision in the end. I know you think Alex and I are being stupid, talking about having a baby together. It's been almost a year now. I want to become a mother. He wants to become a father. And in our own way, we've got our ideas about how we can do it. How we can bring up the child."

"But?" Tomas asked.

"But right now, even if you don't know it, you are taking the decision out of his hands."

"I don't understand what you're saying," Tomas replied.

"Every time we talk about it, you dismiss the idea in front of him. You tell him it's not the right thing. And maybe it's not, for you. But, it shouldn't be your decision to make. It should be his, don't you think?"

"But it's not so black and white," Tomas said. "Let's say you did have a child together. If you did, in a way, I would also have another child. I live with Alex. Well, sometimes, you know."

"Yes, but are you really the right person to decide for Alex and I? The person that stops us from doing something that is so important to us because it would be, what, inconvenient for you?"

"That's not very fair to me," Tomas said, solemnly. "I should have a say in things too. It's not only Alex's life or your life that we are talking about."

"I agree Tomas. And you should have a say. But it shouldn't be you that makes the decision. It's not yours to make."

"But Alex has always been free to make his own decision."

"Has he?" Marin asked. "I've known him for more than fifteen years. I have never seen him so prepared to compromise for somebody before. That to me is a sign of how much he loves you Tomas. How much he listens to you. Look at him. He's cooking for goodness sake. That's you in him."

"So?"

"So perhaps you need to compromise for him. On something that is more important than you permit it to be. Give him the sign that he can make a decision like this for himself. Give him your blessing."

"I don't know if I can. Not on something so big," Tomas said, putting down the knife.

"Alex and I both want a child. We are both in a position to help each other. Your role in this is critical. Your opinion is necessary. Your approval is necessary. Without your *yes*, we don't have a road to go down."

"Victoria already turns our lives upside down Marin. I don't know what effect another child will have on us."

"Yes, no doubt it will make things more complicated sometimes," Marin said. "The times Alex will look after the baby will be busier. But have you thought about what always saying no could do to a relationship?"

"Are you saying, he will leave me if I don't?"

"No. But I'm saying you risk him resenting you for it."

Tomas looked over at Alex who seemed to be having the time of his life learning how to grill fish on the barbeque. Alex *was* making strides with everyday things he'd probably taken for granted for years. And he *was* a natural with Victoria. But it had already taken all of Tomas' effort just to get Alex to stay put in the same place for more than a week at a time. How on earth Alex would manage to do that with a kid, without saddling Tomas with the responsibility, remained a mystery to him.

"Marin, you do me a favour and I will do you one," Tomas finally said.

"Shoot."

"Go easy on the baby talk. At least for this holiday. His family is arriving today and I don't want that to become the topic of the day. In return, I promise to think about what you've said."

"Deal," Marin said, offering out her hand.

| 11 |

STOCKHOLM

With the dimmed cabin humming to the sound of restless sleep, Tomas opened his window shade. He desperately hoped they'd already crossed a time zone and that he'd finally see some daylight. But everything was still pitch–black outside. Worse still, he was certain they were still flying over the Indian Ocean. That Endless Ocean. He had something that he was desperate to say, but Alex had already been sleeping for half an hour, and Tomas wasn't sure how to wake him. By whispering something into his ear? By gently prodding him? Or trying a romantic gesture like a kiss? In the end he decided on a quick nudge with his elbow.

"What?" Alex grumbled.

"I wanted to talk to you. Before things get hectic for me," Tomas said.

Alex opened his eyes and looked around.

"Hectic? What do you mean?" Alex asked, stretching his legs and tucking his blanket around them.

"Before we get distracted by everything else."

"What's on your mind?" Alex groaned, Tomas recognizing the mix of sleep and irritation in Alex's voice.

"I've been thinking," Tomas said.

"About what?" Alex asked, sitting up.

"About Marin," Tomas said.

"Oh," Alex said. "You know what she's like when she's got an idea in her mind."

"But it's your idea too," Tomas said.

"I know. But I'm making my peace with it. I'll adjust," Alex said quietly.

"But that's the thing," Tomas said, lifting the shade again to check if anything had changed. "Maybe it's not something that people should have to adjust to."

"What do you mean?" Alex asked, squinting.

"I mean, I don't think it's the kind of thing that I can stand in the way of," Tomas said, slowly. "I can't just ignore it and pretend it will go away."

"I see," Alex said, straightening himself, his voice thickening. "So that's it? We're ending things over this?"

"Ending things?" Tomas asked, the hair on the back of his neck bristling.

"I get it," Alex said. "We end it now so we don't end up hating each other later."

"Are you mad?" Tomas said, unsure if Alex was on one of his dangerous tangents or was deadly serious. "No, I'm not ending things. I'm telling you that I can't stop you and Marin having a child together."

"Oh?" Alex replied.

"I'm not crazy about the idea, but I'm not about to end things over it. What's gotten into you?"

Alex closed his eyes, shaking a little.

Tomas resumed his questioning. "Why would you think walking away is even an option?"

"I just… I don't know," Alex said.

"You know," Tomas said, "you and me. It's real. We can't just end things when we disagree about something. We owe each other more than that."

"I'm trying," Alex replied.

"I've always thought you'd prefer me to be honest with you. To not always agree with you."

"Yeah, I don't want that," Alex said.

Tomas rested his head on Alex's shoulder.

"You know, I have time to prepare myself for it. For you and Marin and the chaos it's going to bring! I don't know how the two of you will cope, to be honest. But I guess you'll work it out."

"And you're okay with it? I mean, honestly?" Alex asked quietly.

"I am. I will be. I worry you haven't thought about it completely. But I have to trust you."

"Tomas, I don't want you being pressured into the decision. If you want more time to think about it, we can pretend we didn't have this conversation."

"No, I'm clear," Tomas said. "It's a decision you have to make and that I have to support. Anyway, it will be nice for Victoria to have a little brother or a sister."

***

Soon after touching down in Stockholm and receiving Tomas' blessing, Alex and Marin began visiting the country's most exclusive fertility clinic.

Marin's friends had warned her about how draining and emotional the process could be, but Marin proved one of the lucky ones, the staff delighted to report that she'd fallen pregnant on the second try.

Though Alex was overjoyed at the news, he received it in Tuscany, where he was already working on a new film. His production company had secured the rights for a gothic novella and he'd taken the starring role.

With Marin working from home and Tomas swamped with work commitments, Alex was miserable in Tuscany. The damp of the early spring crept into his clothes and seeped into his bones during the long days on set.

He would've preferred being in Tomas and Marin's company rather than working on his own, without even Celia or Kōji to keep him company. With only a landline and a fax machine at the hotel to keep in touch with friends, he did his best to overcome the Tuscan bubble he found himself in.

Between scenes Alex found himself obsessing over how different his life was going to be by year's end. His daily phone calls with Marin in the mornings and nightly chats with Tomas seemed to be dominated by the idea. But each time he hung up the phone he wondered whether he was doing the right thing being away, alone with the thoughts that consumed him right until he closed his eyes in the evening.

***

By the time he returned to Stockholm, Marin was only barely showing, her tiny baby bump nonetheless offering Alex his first visual proof that their horizons were soon to be expanded.

While Alex had plodded away in Tuscany, Celia and Kōji had been busy coordinating new recording sessions. Declan, the young Scottish producer with whom Alex had worked on *Brave and Foolish,* was invited to work on new material, while two up and coming Swedish producers – Andreas and Edvin – were also brought on board for the new project.

Declan had tasted more success since working with Alex, but it was the two young Swedes whose music was now exploding on the European dance scene.

Celia had rented them a cottage on the outskirts of Stockholm from a Swedish singer–songwriter who'd enjoyed success in the late 1970s and 1980s in his own right. The cottage's recording studio was up to date and in an idyllic setting. Declan was its only resident for the time being, having arrived in July. He'd been set the task of sorting through Alex's cloth bag of demo tapes and those of the Swedes to try and fashion a working track list.

Once Declan had finished cataloguing the demos, Alex began a spate of daily visits where the two would sit in the living room, making notes and discussing possible directions to take each song into. Without the pressure of a looming deadline, it was the most languid development phase Alex could remember ever participating in. The organic nature of their discussions also gave him the opportunity to look over his newly filled note-book of lyrics. He'd written nearly all of them in Tuscany, their tone dominated by introspection and self reflection.

Once the track list and schedule were drawn up, the cottage was overrun by technicians who converted the guest bedroom into a makeshift studio for the Swedes and the tiny attic into a live room for the musicians and Alex's vocals. The cottage floors were swallowed by a maze of cords and cables which often got the better of the boys as they rushed between the rooms and up the attic staircase which the techies had also buried; in sequencers, laptops and other equipment.

When the studio sessions finally began at the cottage, they quickly established themselves as marathons. They'd begin precisely at 10am when Alex would arrive armed with coffee and pastries to cajole his younger cohorts into action. Though Alex struggled to get the boys into work mode, he couldn't fault their work ethic once they got started, the boys typically working long after Alex returned to Stockholm in the evenings.

After six weeks of solid work, there were already a number of nearly completed songs for Alex to take with him on vacation. With Marin's baby bump growing, and Tomas finally due back from the Atlanta Olympics and Paralympics, Alex organised a ten-day break for he and Tomas in Greece.

Though Declan and the boys were happy to be working on the new album, they were overjoyed at the prospect of Alex getting out of their hair, albeit briefly. As the three farewelled Alex who drove back to Stockholm, Edvin turned to the boys in the driveway.

"Finally, some peace and quiet."

"Yeah, but imagine how many more notes he's going to come back with. And how much more work that's going to mean," Andreas replied, ruefully.

"I need a beer. Anyone else want one?" Edvin asked.

***

The time on the islands was something of a renaissance for Tomas and Alex, the two quickly falling into a routine of morning lovemaking, lazy lunchtimes in the village, and afternoons beach hopping. After dinner and drinks, they'd return home for more lovemaking and quiet nights on the terrace.

Alex's new demos provided part of their holiday soundtrack even if he'd never been particularly comfortable playing his own music in Tomas' company. Though Tomas seemed comfortable withholding his own comments about the new music, Alex studied the new songs intently, committed to shining a light on even their most superficial flaws. Alex was anxious his new songs sounded pristine and perfect this time around.

To that end, when he returned to work, he did so with a comprehensive list of changes and corrections that he wanted made to the songs, much to the surprise of no one at the cottage.

On his return to the cottage Alex handed out gifts but Declan too had a surprise waiting for him. In Alex's absence, Declan had fished out one of the demos they had originally dismissed for the project.

"You have something here," Declan said, handing Alex a tape. "But I think you need to develop it yourself. I have a bit too much on my plate."

Develop it myself? Are you nuts?

"Don't look at me like that," Declan said. "You can do it. Frankly, there's not much you need to do to it. Just give it a listen and you'll see how well it fits in with everything else."

Weeks went by before Alex listened to the demo. He spent his days hopping between the cottage's two bedrooms to help steer the latest batch of songs being conjured up, and nights surveying the renovations to his and Tomas' apartment.

It was only during a second time out from the recording sessions that he felt prepared to listen to the demo. Marin's bag was already packed even though the baby wasn't due until around Christmas. Nevertheless, Alex decided to spend his week off with her, doing his best to coach her through her growing anxiety, and trying to resist the temptation to play with the *protools* software on his computer. But as the week and Marin's nerves wore on, Alex increasingly shifted his attention to the software, much to Marin's annoyance.

After finally listening to the demo, he agreed with Declan that there was potential in the song. But its lyrics no longer suited him, so, with Marin asleep one afternoon in the guest bedroom, he quietly set about rewriting them, ignoring the sound of his recorded voice as he listened to the demo on repeat, singing the new words over himself.

I have a secret that can be shared/but never betrayed

Feel my heart filling with hope/I know I'm going to be saved

So now I'm just longing for you.

I hate to think of who I am or what I might become/If it wasn't for you

I want to be straight up/and get to know everything about you

I didn't think I could ever change/ What I'd carved all over my
heart
But I am finally shedding the past/ And I'll be brave
As you forge our new path.
Because I've been longing for you.
I can't wait to feel and see life/ With a fresh set of eyes
Tired of all the wrongs, the tears, the lies
The things that I hide.
I hate to think of who I was or could have become/ If it wasn't for
you
Thank god time has a way of restarting
And erasing the pain we put ourselves through
But that is a secret that we can share/ yet never betray
We can live off hope alone/ even in the darkest of days.
I can stop giving up on everything/ now I have changed my mind
Walking out of the fog/ moving back into the light
Because I've been longing for you.

That week, as Marin slept or fretted, Alex worked away at
the demo in *protools*. He had little else to do to distract himself,
given that Tomas was away for a string of correspondent jobs;
in Berlin for the Speed Skating World Cup, Lillehammer for a
Ski Jumping Cup and Zurich for a Track Cycling event which
somehow had an audience in Sweden.

And while Tomas was busy relaying the sports news, Alex
played host to a visiting MTV crew who spent two days at the
cottage filming interviews with him for an upcoming special.

***

The line from Switzerland was terrible. But Alex intimately knew the voice on it.

"Tomas?"

"Where are you? I've been trying the apartment and your cell all day," Tomas said, his frustration evident despite the crackling line.

"I haven't been at home. I'm at the hospital."

"In the hospital did you say? Goddam it, I can barely hear you Alex. Why are you at the hospital? What's happened?"

"I've just become a dad," Alex shouted, much to the amusement of those in the waiting room. "So that means you're a dad again too," he said, lowering his voice.

Alex had arrived at the hospital after a tense night rushing back from Gothenburg. He'd flown to Gothenburg on a whim after Andreas and Edvin had invited him down to one of their nightclub appearances. They were planning on playing some instrumentals of the new tracks and wanted him there to gauge the crowd's reaction. With Marin not due for another week he'd barely given it a second thought and had been in the process of getting dressed for the night out when his cell rang.

"It's happening," Marin had said, calmer than she'd been in weeks. "You need to come back to Stockholm."

"What do you mean it's happening? Do you mean now?" he'd asked, tucking his shirt into his jeans.

"My waters broke ten minutes ago," Marin said, matter of factly. "The ambulance will arrive any minute now."

"Jesus," Alex said, leaning on his hotel room wall. "It's one in the morning. There won't be any flights at this hour. I don't think I can even organise a charter at this notice."

"You're going to have to drive, Alex I have to go, I don't feel good and I can see the ambulance lights outside."

"I'll be there as soon as I can," he promised, ending the call and swearing in continuation as he threw his belongings back into his bag.

After a long night on the highway in a rental, terrorised by the idea of driving in snow, on ice and at the prospect of errant wildlife, he sighed in relief when he reached Stockholm. Parking, he meandered through the wards at the hospital using his minimal Swedish to get answers and directions and eventually an explanation from the attending physician, who explained the situation to him. He had a premature, yet seemingly healthy son waiting for him in the nursery, but Marin hadn't had an easy birth. From what he'd understood, the baby had been delivered by C–section more as a precaution for the new mother.

The doctor carefully explained the situation, and as best as Alex could follow it, he understood that due to her Trichomoniasis and the significant blood loss during the C–section, Marin needed rest. The doctor assured Alex that Marin was receiving the best possible care, and that as her blood levels had been relatively normal in the weeks leading up to the birth, the child was statistically unlikely to contract the virus. The newborn, the doctor reiterated, was premature but doing well.

Alex went into Marin's room and sat by her bed, looking her over. It was distressing for him to see her looking so small, pale and fragile. She even seemed tiny in comparison to the plush toys and flowers that flanked her bedside. All those doubts and concerns brought on by Marin not letting him in on her condition until well into the pregnancy evaporated. He was happy they were doing well, even if the baby had arrived early and she looked like a tired Barbie doll in a kingdom of ogres.

Alex was exhausted, and although he wanted to see his boy, he felt he needed to stay with Marin. He quickly fell asleep, and was only woken by a buzzing sound. Marin was sounding the bell by her bedside to get someone's attention. She was thirsty.

"I'm sorry," she said as he came to.

"For what?" he asked, spying the clock in the room and realising he'd slept for hours.

"I thought things would go to plan."

"Don't be silly," Alex said.

"Have you seen him yet?"

"No. I came straight in here," Alex replied.

"Oh, he's beautiful Katz!" She sipped at the water and then mumbled to the nurse in Swedish, who turned around and congratulated Alex in crisp English.

"Come on, I'll show you through to the nursery," the nurse said, not waiting for him to follow.

Alex put on the hospital issue gown and was shown into the incubation area. His son had arrived a few weeks early but in Alex's eyes he resembled the full term babies. Alex figured now was the time to well up, but his tears denied him, even as he saw the baby in front of him. It seemed so strange that after months of speculation, fear and wonderment, his son had arrived and was here with him. The emotion all the new parenting books had promised didn't seem to coincide with the moment. Something in his brain was telling him it was just another newborn.

He scanned the child's face, not seeking recognition, but merely to drink in its foreignness. He could well have been green, blue or purple and still he wouldn't have seemed as strange as he did to Alex in that moment.

"You can hold him," the nurse said. "It's good for him to have some physical contact."

And so he did. His first contact with his baby, permitted by the woman in the starched uniform.

After years of believing he was no longer capable of being surprised, that nothing seemed to shock him anymore after all the things he'd seen and experienced, this simple moment with his newborn son shook everything. For a moment at least, his cynicism and sadness seemed to evaporate. In minutes he was lost in the baby's tiny sounds and its smell.

Fascination filled Alex as he took in the baby's tiny hands and feet and the dark head of hair that seemed knitted onto the newborn's skull. Alex couldn't do anything other than take in the sight. *His own child. Flesh and blood and all that.*

When the child scrunched his face Alex was taken aback, afraid he'd awaken. But he didn't. He continued sleeping, watched by a now astonished man who sat transfixed on the armchair, holding the child until the woman in the starched uniform said that it was enough for now.

By the time he returned to the hospital room he realised that he'd been away for over an hour, sitting in silent awe. And shock. In Marin's room the bubble evaporated.

Weeks passed with a new routine. A morning trip to the gym to burn off the love handles, followed by a few hours at the hospital, and afternoons spent fine tuning the album with Declan before the nightly run back to the hospital and a taxi back home once visiting hours were over.

Marin's condition improved but mother and baby spent Christmas day in hospital visited by Alex, Tomas and Victoria and surprise guests, Celia and Kōji, who with Marin and Tomas' help, had flown in for an unconventional white Christmas.

| 12 |

GLASS CEILING

When Marin and the baby were finally discharged from hospital, Tomas felt the nerves more than anyone else.

Marin and Søren, named after Marin's grandfather, had effectively ushered in a new era for everyone in their orbit, including Amila, the Bosnian born nanny with whom Tomas was waiting nervously in the front room.

If Amila was nervous, she was playing it cool. She'd only met Marin and Søren a few times at the hospital, but Marin had liked her immediately. Tomas was more worried about Alex than he was about Amila.

In the years Tomas had been with Alex, he'd always been wary of Alex's chameleonic nature. Since Søren's arrival he'd noted changes in Alex but they didn't seem premeditated in the way that Tomas had grown accustomed to. Something in Alex had rightly shifted, but Tomas wondered how far Alex was prepared to take the changes.

The day Alex, Marin and Søren returned to the apartments, Tomas was overcome with conflicting emotions. He experienced a euphoria similar to the one he'd felt when Victoria came into his life, but this time, it was tempered by a voice in his head warning him not to overstep.

The next morning after initiating sex with Alex, Tomas headed into the kitchen to make breakfast and to check in on Marin in the adjoining apartment.

"He's sleeping," she whispered.

"Come over for some breakfast then," he said quietly.

When Alex eventually joined them at the table, Tomas watched as the new parents interacted with each other, noting that they seemed to be communicating in their normal way.

As the days passed, Tomas' apprehension lessened as it became clear that Marin was making every effort to involve, but not overwhelm him with the new reality. Alex however, seemed to be having trouble doing the same, trying instead to play separate roles of lover and parent. It was early days, Tomas reminded himself. Alex would need time to bridge his two worlds.

Within weeks, their new lives began to resemble their old ones a little more. Amila had grown into her role, allowing Marin the chance to spend a few hours in her studio each morning.

Back to presenting the nightly sports bulletin, Tomas spent his mornings with Søren and Amila in the adjoining apartment. Bonding with Amila and Søren made him feel less a third or fourth wheel. At the very least, he figured he could be on hand to speak fluent Swedish in the baby's presence, given that Amila and Alex were hardly going to be language role models.

Alex, whose musical commitments had reared their head again, was now spending the evenings with Søren to give Marin and Amila a breather. He'd typically have Søren down by the time Tomas returned from the studios after the late, late bulletin.

In short, they were the sum of three parents wearing all the physical signs of newborn elation and exhaustion, rarely leaving the house unless it was work related, and doing their best to entertain their own parents; Marin's who dropped by twice a week to spend time with their grandchild and both Alex and Tomas' who were capable of calling at all hours.

When a conference call was scrapped at the last minute, freeing Alex up, Alex rode his bike to Tomas' offices and had the surprised receptionist call the news desk to advise Tomas he was downstairs waiting.

"Hej," Alex said, hugging Tomas.

"Hej yourself. What are you doing here? How is everything at home?"

"It's under control. Marin's mum is there, so I thought I'd come down and have a coffee with my man."

"Well, it's a nice surprise."

They walked towards their regular café and took a seat in the courtyard with its rough approximation of greenery.

"I wanted to see you. I missed you," Alex gushed, "I couldn't wait for tonight." Alex ordered for them both.

"I had a moment to myself this morning and I was thinking how lucky I am. I just think you're amazing and I think sometimes I forget to tell you even if I am thinking it all the time."

Tomas mentally blushed as he lit a cigarette.

"I mean, really, these can't have been the easiest of months for you… you're just… a good man Tomas."

Tomas knew not to interrupt. For all his passion, Alex only ever had a tendency to be emotional if he was overtired; otherwise he pretty much verged on being a *WASP* most of the time. Tomas allowed him a moment to recover without acknowledging the tears as the waiter returned with the drinks.

As Tomas sat there watching him try and regain his composure, Alex helped himself to one of Tomas' cigarettes.

"That's really nice of you to acknowledge. I think we're all doing okay."

Alex smiled his lopsided smile.

"And I think you're pretty special too," Tomas continued, leaning over the table and placing his hand on Alex's.

"I didn't come here for compliments," Alex laughed as he wiped a tear from his right eye. "I came to ask you what I could get for your parents. I want to get them something special."

"Oh God," Tomas replied. "They're the kind of people that already have everything."

"So? Do I go expensive or expensive but borderline modest?"

"Expensive," Tomas smiled. "You don't want them thinking you're rich and cheap."

Tomas, Alex, Victoria and Søren headed up to the north of Sweden that Friday to spend the weekend with Tomas's family.

It could've been the long drive, or the stress of having two kids to look after on a cross country journey, but whatever it was, Alex felt the tension in the car.

As he drove, Alex's playlist ebbed effortlessly backwards and forwards between Everything But The Girl and Grant McLennan, even if his and Tomas' conversation stuttered.

"Is this the first time we're doing something since Greece?" Alex asked as he took a curve a little tightly, causing Tomas to instinctively reach back towards the children who were fast asleep.

"Yes. And to think we're going to my parents' house of all places!" Tomas replied.

"Oh well. I thought it was a good idea," Alex said. "To give the ladies a break."

"And my family get to see the kids too," Tomas said. "It's just that since Søren has been sleeping at our place lately, we haven't had much alone time. And we're not likely to get any this weekend either."

At the halfway mark, they switched roles as was customary for them, Alex checking on the kids before getting into the passenger seat.

"Tomas is it just me or is there some distance between us?"

Tomas looked at Alex and then out the window, beyond the trees that the car whizzed by.

"Well, no. I don't know. I think we just have a lot on our plates right now."

"Yeah. I think I read somewhere that we mustn't neglect each other even if we have a lot on," Alex said.

"You know, you're doing a good job Alex, but I think you should stop reading all those new parenting books. They're messing with you."

"I don't think I can. I think I've got too much to learn," Alex confessed.

"I don't think you can learn it from a book. You just have to work it out for yourself."

"Mmm, I'd prefer someone tell me what I need to do in this case," Alex said.

The conversation had ended long before they reached Umeå, but just being in the area was starting to have a relaxing effect on the Swede.

Tomas's parents were waiting out front as they arrived, Tomas having tipped them off on his mobile phone once they'd reached the outskirts of town. As Alex carried Søren, and Tomas Victoria, up the driveway, Tomas's dad, Karl, snapped a few shots on his little pocket camera. Alex felt mildly threatened, after having avoided the paparazzi for months. But when he saw the elder gush and coo and offer to take the carrier after kissing Alex on the cheek, Alex came to his senses.

Karl and Karin, Tomas' mother, doted over the kids while keeping up the pretence of speaking to the couple, feigning interest or digitally maintaining conversation without any real interaction. The kids were just too much of a distraction for them, even though Søren was sleeping and Victoria was little more than a zombie.

"You must be tired after the drive," Karl said. "Why don't you both go have a lie down. We'll put the kids down."

Tomas looked at Alex expectantly.

"Okay, great, thank you," Alex said, seeing Tomas mouth *thank you.*

***

That night over dinner, the conversation was heated, but the pace and vocabulary were way beyond Alex's ability to follow, he only catching expressions like '*it's hard*' or '*can't compromise*' and even something about '*lawyers*'. Alex hadn't seen Tomas that agitated (or tipsy) for a long time. He seemed to be the only person at the table concerned by Tomas' shouting and his repeated thumping of the table. At one point Karl patted Alex reassuringly and Tomas's sister, Greta, also threw Alex a reassuring glance. *Perhaps they were just letting him vent.*

In any case, the debate at the table proved lengthy and the four of them took turns in stating their case and wiping the odd tear from their eyes. With the meal long over, Alex began to clear the plates from the table despite everyone's protests. He relished the opportunity to disappear from that room; the tension, frustration and all the Swedish irritating him.

After checking that Søren and Victoria were sleeping peacefully, he returned to the kitchen, popped an apron over his Prada shirt and proceeded to wash the dishes, doing his best to tune out the discussion in the dining room, even though he was sure he'd heard his name. Once he was done with the dishes, he fished out the bottle warmer and the sterilizer and set up a makeshift baby corner on the kitchen counter, methodically placing everything he needed next to the microwave. He toyed with the idea of stepping out into the cold for a cigarette, but Søren announced his presence with a piercing hunger growl. Alex made a beeline to him, bringing him into the kitchen and setting about warming up his formula. Victoria may have slept through all the fuss Søren made, but his clarion call brought all the players from the living room into the kitchen.

"Look at you," Karin beamed. "You are like a machine," she said to Alex, caressing Søren who was mercilessly drooling all over that sacred Prada shirt.

"Alex can you come with me for a walk? I need some air," Tomas said abruptly.

"Can it wait? I gotta feed Søren and then put him back down."

Greta stepped forward, gently stroking the back of the baby's head. "I can do that, I don't mind. Go on, some air will be good for you both. It's been a long day for you. Besides, we want to take advantage of Søren being here."

Alex reluctantly passed his son over to Greta while Karin took over at the baby station.

"Come on," Tomas said, "let them have a turn. He'll be fine."

Embarrassed, Alex smiled and took the parka and gloves that Tomas handed him. With one last look at Søren he followed Tomas out the back door.

"I needed some air," Tomas said.

"I figured you might have been able to wait for me to feed the baby."

"Oh, don't worry. They were looking forward to doing it. You can get up during the night and feed him if it makes you feel better," Tomas joked, nudging Alex along the pathway out back.

It seemed strange that after such a loud and lengthy argument that Tomas was somehow lighter. Though he was calmer, Alex knew Tomas well enough to know that some silence was in order. They traversed the city's little inclines, the sound of snow crunching the only thing Alex could hear from the cocoon of his hoodie. Alex looked around at the architecture. It was so different here to Stockholm. It felt... *anonymous*. Everything seemed clad, well maintained. Practical, economical. When they finally veered around a colourful corner the dreariness lifted slightly.

"Doesn't the monotony of this place make you angry?" Alex finally asked.

"Why do you think I live in Stockholm?"

They sat in front of the city church, some way back from the river. The air was cold, but not bitterly so. There was still a smattering of snow on the church's roof tiles but it must have been from days before.

"Tomorrow I want to take you and the little ones into the countryside. There's a beautiful little beach called Bettnesand that we can try and visit tomorrow if it's a calm day." Tomas said, sighing.

Alex waited for him to continue his thoughts.

"I think I need to resolve things with Lena and Victoria," Tomas explained. "I think the little guy has really made me think about Victoria. I don't think it is fair that I can only see her occasionally. For holidays. I want her to be equal to Søren."

"So what are you suggesting?"

"I have to negotiate with Lena. Maybe you could come too? I want Victoria to be with us on the weekends. And I think we need to think about the little guy and Marin too. We should formalise something with her."

Alex was worried about where Tomas' thoughts were headed. He collected his own before responding.

"If you don't like the way things are with Victoria, you should speak with Lena. Before doing anything official."

"I know. It's easier said than done."

Alex leaned into Tomas's chest. "I know. But everything is fixable."

***

Back in Stockholm it was time to try again.

"Edvin and I will be at The Spy Bar on Friday night," Andreas said. "We want to play some of the new songs. But with your vocals this time. Will you come?"

"Okay, but I think I'll have to bring some of the people from the label."

"Really? Why?" Andreas asked.

"I've already been putting it off long enough."

That week, Stockholm's club scene was buzzing. Thanks to a few well placed calls, news had been circulating that Alex was going to be making his first public appearance in over a year and that it was happening at one of the clubs in Stureplan.

For his first night out in who knows when, Alex dressed in black from head to toe, garnishing the look with a red belt, a side part and more than just a hint of kohl.

He'd had no trouble convening record execs and some influential music journalists to Stockholm for the event, which was already being heralded as an exclusive sneak peek.

Knocking back Negronis in The Spy Bar's office, the excitement was palpable. Alex and Tomas chatted nervously with Andreas and Edvin, who planned to play three full album cuts and six other new songs in partial form. Sars, the venue manager, informed them that there was a full house and that the VIP area was heaving with industry, press and local celebrities.

The group stayed back in the office as the opening DJ did her thing, mixing current dance songs with some of Alex's more recent dance hits. Tomas and the boys occasionally popped out to gauge the mood of the crowd, Edvin re–entering the room after disappearing for fifteen minutes.

"It's wall to wall out there and the minute she plays one of your songs they just erupt," he said, smiling. "Let us go out first. Give us some time to warm up and then come out. But when you do, don't come to the stage. Just head to the VIP area."

"Okay," Alex said, looking at Tomas who was uncharacteristically excited.

As Andreas and Edvin, now stars in their own right, made their way up to the DJ booth, the crowd erupted. They high fived the DJ and set about playing their opening songs.

Alex waited nervously for his cue, Tomas standing by the door.

After a tense ten minutes or so, Sars arrived with two of the club's bouncers.

"It's time, the song is winding down. They'll make the announcement the minute they see us. Are you ready?"

Alex shivered and nodded, then took Tomas' hand, following them out towards the pulsating lights and sounds.

Walking through the heavy black curtains that separated the back rooms from the main dance floor, Alex caught his first glimpse of the crowd. He estimated that there were five or six hundred people crowded below the DJ podium, but by the time he'd processed the thought he'd been spotted and the crowd began to cheer, some screaming out his name.

Climbing up the stairs with heavy legs, he heard Andreas excitedly introduce him in Swedish over the microphone, sending a rippling applause through the audience. Alex turned to the crowd, smiling and waving for a moment before Sars prodded him up the staircase.

There were some familiar faces in the VIP area, but it was mostly Tomas' and Marin's friends that he recognised. Tomas wasted no time to schmooze with friends while Alex headed straight to Marin and Jakob.

"You're shaking," Marin said, concerned.

"I'm fine, I'm just a bit nervous," Alex said, smiling goofily.

"It's great," Jakob said, reassuringly. "Drink it in."

"I think I need another drink," Alex said, waving a waiter over.

A couple of journalists approached Alex and politely asked him some questions about the new album which he answered. Marin and Jakob stepped back to allow him to do his thing, but when a photographer nudged his way in, uncomfortably close as he snapped photos of Alex, Alex was left with no room to move. It was then that another actor friend of Tomas's stepped in, shielding Alex and dispensing with the photographer in a terse exchange of Swedish.

"Thanks Markus," Alex said, giving him a peck on the cheek once he ended things with the journalists.

"He seemed like a pest. You're baby free tonight?" Markus noted, tilting his head towards Tomas and Marin who were chatting. "By the way, when does everybody get the chance to see him?"

"We're keeping him under lock and key for now," said Alex. A combination of the time the family spent indoors and Sweden's general indifference to celebrities had so far worked in their favour.

"I've never seen Stureplan so full of paparazzi like tonight. How is it at home?"

"They rarely bother with us. We are really careful, so they just move on," Alex explained.

"The time will come I'm sure. They will get more insistent. Especially when you put this record out."

"I know. Half of me feels like doing a deal just to get it over and done with. Maybe just give the money to charity or something, I don't know. I've been out of this world for a while, you know?" Alex said.

Markus studied him. "I haven't seen you properly for what, two years now?" Markus asked. "I've been waiting so patiently since then."

Alex glanced towards Tomas who was completely absorbed in his own conversations.

"I had a great time with you too Markus, but, it was a long time ago, you know. Things are different now. I've got a kid."

"I know, I just... I still think about it," Markus said.

Alex let out a laugh. "If things were different, who knows, you know?"

"Yes, I know," Markus said, wryly. "Tomas doesn't like to share his toys. Maybe that's why he doesn't really talk to me much anymore."

"I don't think he knows," Alex said. "And it was a long time ago. Anyway, can I get you a drink?"

"No, let me get you one. Still a Vodka martini?"

"Always," Alex cooed.

***

As Markus called over a bus boy, Alex thought about that night. He'd remembered it as being particularly frosty, and that he'd wanted to stay in London, but Tomas insisted he be in Sweden for his brother in law's birthday party. The week leading up to the party, they'd had heated discussions on the phone about how it would be important for Alex to be there, even if the party had been hastily organised, and Alex already had plans for the weekend in London. With each phone call, the testosterone level inched up a notch, until each begun slinging accusations at the other regarding their lack of commitment and their selfishness.

By the time Alex had reached the apartment it was clear that Tomas had been drinking, fresh from another marathon argument with Lena. Tomas had unplugged the phones and his mobile was switched off. In the midst of his fury, he'd forgotten that he'd promised to pick Alex up from the airport. Alex had had to make his own way and to let himself in. Tomas, shocked by having forgotten his own promise, couldn't think of any other way to react other than angrily at the sight of Alex on his doorstep. Tomas then began to rant in Swedish.

"Before you start, I've had it up to here today; Lena, work, the negotiations for the apartment across the hall. I can't take it anymore. I don't even understand why you came. You said you didn't want to come to Matteus' party. You turn my world upside down. You come and go as you please, and you leave me to deal with everything. Yes, I was supposed to pick you up from the airport. But I forgot. I got caught up in something else. It happens. Like it always happens with you and your damn commitments."

Alex stood there. He was tired and unprepared for this version of Tomas.

"I don't think it's a good idea for you to stay here. Maybe not anymore. I think you should stay in London. Go back to your life there. It seems too hard to do all of this with all the distance."

Alex was numb, but Tomas still had more to say.

"You know, I've never been more miserable than I am now. Every time I think about it, it comes back to you. You. You're the centre of my problems. You're only here when it suits you."

Adrenaline coursed through Alex's veins.

"Okay," Alex said, "I get it. I'm going. Don't waste your breath on me one minute longer Tomas," he said.

As someone who liked a drink himself, Tomas' drunkenness wasn't bothering Alex. If he himself had also been drinking, he would've just thrown down. But as he had no patience for drunks when he was sober, he resisted the temptation to engage. Instead, he knew he could drive Tomas crazy by reasoning.

"I'll call you tomorrow," Alex said. "When I'm on my way back to Heathrow. Just to check that you're still breathing. See you around."

Tomas began screaming at Alex in unintelligible Swedish, but Alex simply pulled his trolley noisily down the stairs, knocking a picture frame down onto the cement steps, not caring as its glass shattered everywhere.

In the cab on his way to a hotel, Alex's cell began to ring insistently, but the third time it rang he simply switched it off.

At least he wouldn't have to go to the boring birthday party.

Alex made his way to Östermalm and checked into the boutique hotel he usually used for business meetings. Tomas would never think to come look for him there. The hotel was one of Sweden's top establishments, and its bar was strictly for the A list and the diplomatic set.

Alex wheeled his suitcase into his room, freshened up and went to the bar for a martini. Sipping on his drink he turned on the phone and felt it hum as its alerts vibrated. *1 Message Received, 2 Messages Received, 3 Messages Received, 4 Messages Received...* it continued on to 9.

He opened the inbox and began to read and delete each message. They were all from Tomas. The first few messages demanded he answer the phone. The later messages approximations of *"we should end it"* in Swedish and English.

He wasn't really sure what to make of it, whether to pass it off as a bad day, or think of it perhaps as Tomas' true position on things. But it seemed coming back to Stockholm had been a mistake.

At the bar he looked around and saw a reasonable mishmash of people, almost all in chatty mini groups hunched over beverages, cigars and cigarettes. A waifish woman tinkered away on the baby grand. As he watched her, he felt a warm hand on his back. He turned to see that it was Markus.

"What are you doing here?" he asked, kissing Alex on the cheek.

"I just flew in and I was desperate for a martini."

"And Tom?"

"At home," Alex said, before smiling half–heartedly.

Markus understood.

Practically everyone in Stockholm knew that Tomas had been in a foul mood of late. The papers had it that the network was reluctant to send Tomas to Atlanta because of his growing profile as boyfriend of a superstar. They were allegedly worried it might discourage some advertisers.

"Listen, I'm sure it is just a phase. Don't worry about it. When did you arrive?"

"I literally just got here," Alex said.

They spoke a bit at the bar, and then Markus saw a table free up in the corner. The two sat together on a tiny, green velvet couch and continued to speak in their mix of Swedish and English.

Alex liked Markus: he was a little show pony at times, but he was a good conversationalist, and the friction of their thighs rubbing together was sending Alex into overdrive. Markus had a rocking, good body and a chiselled face that just invited attention. After another round of martinis, Markus whispered.

"Why don't you get your jacket from your room and come to mine tonight?"

"I don't know if that's such a good idea," Alex said.

"Come on. It doesn't have to mean anything. We can just have some fun together."

They made the short trek to Markus' on foot. The moment they got into the elevator Markus pounced. "I've been dying to do that since I saw you," he said when the elevator doors re-opened.

The apartment had a reasonable view of the bay, even if it was partly obscured by neighbouring buildings.

"A drink?" Markus asked, kicking off his shoes.

"Vodka would be great. Vodka anything," Alex said taking off his boots. He ambled around the apartment, slightly curious as to what was lying around and, seeing Markus' cigarettes and an ashtray, asked if he could smoke.

"Sure, help yourself," Markus replied, dropping ice into some glasses.

Alex walked over to the sliding door and lit up a cigarette. He stepped out onto the balcony to feel the weak sun on his face. Markus joined him, casually handing the glass over, his fingers inside its rim.

"Thanks," Alex said.

Markus stood next to Alex and took in the view. He then un-ceremoniously wedged his hand into the back of Alex's jeans.

"Give me a drag," Markus said coarsely in Swedish, to which Alex obliged. Alex prised back the cigarette and took some last puffs before extinguishing it in the ashtray.

"Come on," Markus said, taking Alex by the hand and leading him down the corridor. The room at the end of the corridor came to life as Markus turned on a floor lamp. Attached were a walk–in closet and a small en suite, which Markus walked di-rectly into. After availing himself of the bathroom, he staggered out without any elegance, but on seeing Alex, righted himself and regained his composure, proudly tugging his pants down to reveal a pair of Y fronts.

'Ever the showman', Alex thought to himself, walking straight up to the Swede and kissing him, first on the mouth, before moving his mouth over the rest of Markus' pinkish body.

Later that afternoon they retreated to Markus' living room.

"You're so beautiful," Alex said, watching as the last of the day's light spotlighted Markus' blond mane.

"You–are–fucking–gorgeous," Markus replied. "And a real animal in bed. Or on the floor perhaps. God, I could marry you."

Alex laughed. "Where did you learn to do things like that? I've never done it that way," Alex said.

"A gentleman never tells. But seriously, I could eat you up," Markus said.

"I bet you say that to all the boys."

Markus winked in agreement.

The next morning, after having slept soundly with Markus, Alex made his walk of shame back to the hotel, stopping en route for a steaming hot coffee for which he had just enough Kronor left in his pocket. He had to remember to get some cash out. He turned on his phone as he drank his coffee and watched the escalating number of *Messages Received* appear on the screen. Seven of them. First message: *Which hotel are you at? I will come and get you at 11.* Second message: *Sorry about last night. I was a complete fucking asshole. Forgive me.* Third message: *Marry me. Seriously. Last night was amazing. I already miss you.* It annoyed him that he would have to delete the latter message in case Tomas ever scrolled through his message bank.

***

Back at the Spy Bar, Markus had briefly disappeared, coming back with the vodka martini, after greeting a number of people including Tomas. He was determined not to be disrespectful even if he thought Tomas wasn't a good match for Alex. Tomas made eye contact with a friend of his and as soon as he went off to join him, Markus leant in towards Alex.

"Sorry I took so long. I had this huge hard on that I had to get rid of. Can't imagine how I got hard in the first place."

Alex laughed and did his best not to let his eyes snake down beyond waist level. "I'm feeling nervous."

"About us?" Markus asked, and then shook his head as he understood. "Oh, about your music. No, these people will love it. Have you been paying attention to the crap they listen to? Besides, you drink like a fish; you shouldn't be feeling anything at this stage."

Alex smiled. "Thanks."

"By the way, is Tomas planning on spending any time with you tonight?"

"I think it's a bit tough on him to play the first lady. He's with his friends. It's nice to see him having a good time."

Sars apologised for interrupting.

"Alekzandr, the boys are ready for you. They're going to make an announcement. When they invite you up, just follow the catwalk along there and it will take you to the booth," he said, pointing.

"OK, thanks."

"No, but seriously. They're going to love it," Markus said, "Just remember to smile. You have the most beautiful smile, especially when you are naked and you have me in your mouth. Happy to give you the opportunity again, any time you say."

Alex blurted out a laugh. "It's not going to happen. I adore you, but…"

"No, you're right, I'm sorry. If I marry you though?"

"You don't need to marry me. Besides, I don't know which one of you I'd prefer to marry," Alex said, looking down at Markus' groin.

As Andreas announced Alex's presence in both Swedish and English, Alex tried to walk across the catwalk with confidence. Through the metal mesh he could see the people below, their excitement filling him with belief.

In the glass booth he high fived the boys and graciously accepted the microphone they handed him.

Summoning his best Swedish, he congratulated the boys on all their hard work, noting that their reward seemed to be that they were surrounded by beautiful people. It was a corny line, but as he motioned to the people below them, the crowd erupted.

"Listen, everyone's been waiting for too long. Edvin don't waste anymore of our time. Just put my damn record on for everyone. It's time to dance!"

As the electronica kicked in, Alex danced, using the microphone to occasionally sing over himself. With some silly chitchat with the boys and two more full tracks, Alex teased out yet more reactions from the audience before he earnestly thanked everybody in Swedish and crossed the catwalk back into the VIP enclosure.

In the VIP area he posed for a few photos with some of the staff and management, signed some autographs and pondered whether or not his fortunes were going to change this time around. Hearing his music on that kind of sound system had mostly pleased him. He figured it was as close to perfect as he was capable of.

"Do you want to stay babe or do you want to come with me?" Tomas asked, slurring a few of the words.

"Where are you going?" Alex asked.

"We are going to stop by Max's for a couple of joints and then after that I'll walk home."

"Why don't you just stay there tonight?" Alex said, patting him on the shoulder.

"I don't want to completely ruin tomorrow," Tomas said, his head wobbling.

"Tomas just relax and go enjoy your night. Whatever happens tomorrow, happens tomorrow."

"Ok, well if you're sure. You were great tonight. You had them in the palm of your hand."

Alex gave Tomas a peck on the cheek and slowly worked his way through the room, engaging in brief conversations with the record execs, and some press before squeezing himself into Marin and Jakob's booth, their friends getting up and letting Alex take the inner spot close to the wall.

"You alright?" Marin asked.

"I'm good, it's just, I've forgotten what it's like to have to be *on.*"

"You did good kid," Jakob said. "They're clearly loving the music."

"God, I hope it's a good sign," Alex said, taking a sip of Jakob's drink.

"We're going to head off. Jakob is off to Gothenburg tomorrow morning and I, well, you know," Marin said.

"Thank you for coming. Both of you. It meant the world," Alex said.

"You kidding?" Marin asked, kissing him on the cheek.

"I was hoping you'd stick around," Alex whispered to Jakob. "To stop me from doing anything foolish."

Jakob looked over at Markus who was lurking nearby.

"Oh," he said sighing, caressing Alex's cheek. "You don't need me for that."

"See you when you get back? From Gothenburg?" Alex asked.

"You bet," Jakob said. "Come on Marin, your chariot awaits."

"Are they going?" Markus asked, pulling Alex out of the booth.

"Yeah. You?" Alex asked, straightening himself up.

"One last drink?" Markus suggested.

"Why not?" Alex replied.

An hour later, Alex and Markus were ushered out to an awaiting car. Markus gave the instructions to the driver and closed the partition.

Alex rested his head on Markus' shoulder. "That was more fun than I expected."

"They loved your stuff."

"Yeah," Alex said trailing off.

Markus lit a cigarette that the two of them shared.

"Do you think you might like to have lunch or dinner this week Alex?"

"I'd like that very much. We could have a lunch. And a dinner."

"We could," Markus replied, kissing Alex on the lips. Alex opened his mouth and Markus slipped his tongue inside. Minutes later the car pulled up.

"Stockholm is not a very big town. So, I think we're here," Markus said. "You have given me another burning hard on, so I'm going to thank the driver, and just let myself out."

"I bet that this is just a normal Friday night for you," Alex noted.

"It is," Markus said, sarcastically. "So, lunch?"

"Monday?" Alex suggested.

"Perfect. I'll come by and get you. Pointless asking you to come up again, I suppose."

"No, I'm just going to go home," Alex said. "It's been a big night."

"Alex, I can't tell you how happy I am to have seen you tonight. I've really missed you."

"It's been swell. Good night Markus," Alex said, kissing him on the cheek.

"Godnatt Alex," he said, alighting from the car.

A few moments later, Markus stuck his torso back into the door.

"We'll talk about the wedding on Monday," he promised, slamming the door shut before Alex could reply.

A week later Alex was pulled back into a hurricane of commitments. He flew to New York to meet with his management who were planning the album's promotional campaign. The singles had been decided on, the title track, *Glass Ceiling* having been chosen as the lead.

Celia and Kōji worked furiously over the months, securing one of the year's hottest music video directors. Alex was spotted all over New York in Kōji's company, visiting designers, his record label offices, and MTV headquarters where Celia had brokered an exclusive deal for the first six months of the album's promotional campaign. In a first, she'd offered MTV and VH1 exclusive premieres of the videos in North America and more behind the scenes access.

After New York, Alex flew on to London to rehearse with a choreographer before filming began that week. A mostly black and white set with flourishes of red was constructed for the video, a colour combination which would carry over to the album's overall look. Alex had his hair dyed a blue–black and then cut short but plans for a *Caesar* cut were scuttled when they realised that it would be too similar to George Michael's new look which was already all over the media.

On set, Alex was literally pulled in all numbers of directions by assistants, compressed between large plastic glass sheets and filmed dancing on a spectacular, custom made dance floor which lit up in a sequence of white, red and blue squares. Powered by hydraulics which could shift the stage vertically and horizontally, the director had a number of cameras trained on Alex from a variety of angles.

The video director got along well with Alex, but the video shoot had to be condensed into three days to accommodate both of their schedules. An MTV camera crew and Alex's preferred journalist at the network had flown in and were filming behind the scenes footage for a *Making of the Glass Ceiling* special. A shortened version would air in the premiere month of the video single in March, and the extended version in April, in the lead up to the album's release. Additional footage from the second planned single, *Longing For You* would be added to the extended version.

On camera Alex and the journalist spoke mostly about the video and the meaning of the songs on the album, but due to the ferocious pace of the video shoot, he never managed more than twenty minutes of chat before being called away.

Back in Sweden, at the cottage, a few days later, things were much less hectic. Although the recording equipment was now long gone, the MTV crew set up once again in the sitting room, which had a view on to the garden and the abutting canopy of trees that marked the edge of the surrounding forest.

"You're a bit unlucky that it's not snowing, it's gorgeous here in winter," Alex said. "It snowed just a couple of days ago, but I missed it too."

"So why are you here? Why Stockholm? Or the outskirts of Stockholm to be precise?" the journalist asked.

"Well, my son was born here so I live here now. Plus, I wanted to work with Andreas and Edvin who are *Stockholmarna*. It's a cute little city. I think since I moved to Europe my thinking and my expectations have changed a bit. It's beautiful here too so I guess that also plays a part."

"Things have completely changed for you since we last spoke, haven't they?"

"That's an understatement," Alex quipped.

"The music sounds pretty extraordinary. It's really unlike anything you've done before. Maybe unlike anything anyone has done before."

"Thank you. Well, it's definitely new territory for me. On the one hand it's dance music which I've always made, but while I was in London the music I was often drawn to was this techno sound. I liked it but there was something missing in it for me. I thought I could add something interesting and more personal to it. I think techno and electronica can be cold, but if you do it right it can be incredibly moving. Andreas and Edvin, and Declan especially have helped me do that. But we approached it really unconventionally. I started by composing things on instruments before bringing out the toy box. So I think that we created something quite fresh because techno music isn't usually composed on an acoustic guitar or in a kitchen with a crying baby in the next room. But that's my version of it."

"Listening to it, and people already associate you with being a bit of a chameleon, but it really is a new, new you, isn't it?"

"Yeah. It's a new me but also a new sound that I don't think many people have recorded before me. I mean change has always been an important part of my music. But if I look at my life today compared to two years ago, it's never been more different than now. My priorities always change, but more than anything, I think my thinking has changed now."

"What do you think the main themes of the album are?"

"Well it's a dance record, and, um, a really good late night album. You know, you're out at night and you're thinking about what happened that day. But, because you've got the stimulation and the inspiration of the music, you don't dwell on things. You prefer to think about what's coming around the corner, you know? Like, 'how long can I keep going tonight?' 'Is the next song just going to give me more life?' And I think that's how I approached this album. The idea that it was an experience and a chance to look back but look forward at the same time. Not to limit myself. And if you can do that, you can overcome a lot of limitations. You know the purpose of breaking a glass ceiling isn't just for yourself, but it's to let other people come through too."

"There's a lot of buzz around this album. More than we've seen for many years in your career. Do you feel like perhaps your time in the sin bin is over? That people are ready to give you a proper chance now?"

Alex looked out of the window for a few moments and tried to gather his thoughts. He wasn't interested in being negative or defensive, and in searching the garden and the trees he was searching for the words as if they might be hanging there, waiting for him.

"This is another album that comes from my heart. The four of us in the studio had a great relationship and something great has emerged from that and I think people can see that this time."

"In anticipation for the new album it looks like people have been rethinking the last few that you've made. Saying maybe they weren't properly appreciated," the journalist said, tapping his clipboard.

Alex felt a sadness for the acknowledgement he'd just received.

"I think I haven't been fairly treated in the last few years, but I stand by the fact I did actually have something useful to say. I think we are starting to make some progress socially and I think it could've been about the timing. If I'd been saying those things today they would have been interpreted differently. Someone had to say and do it, you know, to get the ball really rolling."

"So was it worth it?" the journalist asked.

"I think I've always been prepared to fall on my sword and not for marketing or silly reasons. I look around today and see a glimpse of hope. It feels like a world away from where we were just three or four years ago. And I'm *still here.* I've still got things to say."

"Would you change anything?"

"No! Not at all. In a way when you're under attack from everybody, it helps you get real clear about what you want to say. I've been dragged more than anybody but the flipside is I got through it. You know, in my case it sent me on a bit of a journey and helped me find some more balance between my personal life and my artistic one. And in both I've got much more freedom than I've ever had because I can be true to myself in both of those worlds now."

"Did you think that while you were going through it?"

"No of course not. It was a really painful time in my life. But I'm a fighter and I always have been and I think it was something that I had to go through. That I had to learn from and ultimately it's made my work better and probably helped me in my thinking."

"Talk me through the process of this album. A lot of artists at the moment are collaborating more and more with different writers and different producers and people from different genres. I know you kind of play some instruments and you write your lyrics but Declan tells me you've taken a bigger role this time around. How involved have you been here?"

Alex and the Swedish producers all laughed in unison.

"What? Did I say something wrong?" the journalist asked.

"They're laughing nervously. They think I'm a draconian, a slave driver."

"Any truth there?"

Alex thought for a few moments. "The thing is as with all of my projects I've been really heavily involved. I need to be with people who can help me realise my ideas. But this time a lot of the musical ideas were mine and the boys helped me reshape them more than anything. I can strum out my song and make it hum but their talents are such that they can make it bang, you know? They can completely breathe it into life whereas I can probably just give it a heartbeat."

"Have you enjoyed making this album?"

"I have actually. This album has been a little different for me in the sense that it's had a starting point and a finishing point. Usually I'm flying in and out of places and there's a whole logistical complexity to making an album for me. This time we just sat in one spot and did it. And it came about in a very organic manner, which is kind of strange for an electronic album."

"But were you writing music and producing with the guys or just waiting to see what they came up with?"

There were more sniggers from the boys.

"You can't turn a knob in this place without him deciding how it needs to be done. If you so much as change a note without telling him, he will discover it and make you pay for it," Andreas said, sending the others into a fit of laughter.

Alex gleamed. "It's true. I'm a nightmare. We've had a really good working relationship, even if there's a bit of treason going on right now. They're incredibly talented. They're so young but so polished and they know their stuff inside out so I had to be extra sharp this time around."

"Declan told me you worked on a track by yourself. Is that song going to make it on to the album?"

"Yeah, I think it is going to be the second single. It's called *Longing for you* at the moment."

After a break and an off–camera discussion, the crew shifted their cameras into the attic. While Andreas and Edvin prepared for their turn with the camera crew, the journalist interviewed Declan.

"You've worked with Alekzandr before on his albums, how do you see this one?"

"I think this one is great. He's been brimming with ideas, and they seem to have translated really well."

"What's your role here been? Tell us about a typical day here in the studio."

"Well I'm a producer of some of the tracks, and I guess I was also the Executive Producer. My role was to make sure that the album was cohesive. I think when we sat down to discuss the music, Alekzandr made the point that he wanted to make something powerful. And the more we thought about it the more we thought it was important to be consistent and not play with genres like he often does."

"And a studio day?"

"Well, we usually got an early start because he got to the studio after Søren had his morning feed and then we'd work pretty much through the day. Alekzandr would head home around 7 or 8 and we'd keep working to finish things off. The days were pretty long in the studio, but we had incredible creative freedom. It was the first time we worked on a project and didn't have a record company breathing down our necks every five minutes."

"You've already worked with a lot of rock bands and singer songwriters. How does it compare to working with, you know, this popstar, an icon who's not your typical kind of musician?"

"I think when you work in pop you have to remember that a good pop act is someone who can tap into ideas and make them their own. Most rock bands get years and years of development from their labels and they work as a group. When you work with a pop artist, it's do or die. A lot of them just want someone that can give them a good hook or a chorus. But someone like Alekzandr, working at the level that he does, it's quite different."

"In what way?"

"He has to rely on himself to spin what *we* do into gold, not the other way around. I think when you work with a band, it's a bit of a democracy, but someone like him needs a great instinct to survive. People want him to sound great, but they also expect him to push things forward at the same time. And once he's done that on one album, he has to do it all over again with another sound on the next one. A lot of bands and a lot of popstars don't have that pressure on them. They can just do more of the same."

"Has he succeeded this time around?"

"Of course he has. He doesn't get nearly enough credit for what he does in the studio. I've worked with a lot of people and more technically sound musicians you know, but they don't have the instincts that he does. And I don't think he gets enough respect for that. He's almost like the consummate pop artist even if no one is prepared to admit it."

"OK we're ready," Andreas announced through the intercom.

Moving up into the attic, Andreas and Edvin were in a playful mood.

"When we were last here, Alex was recording some backing vocals with you both. It seems that this is the first album that Alex has basically decided not to use backing vocalists on. What's that been like?"

"He's been taking vocal lessons for the last few years," Andreas said. "I think we used some vocalists only on one of our songs and Declan maybe two? His voice doesn't really sound much like it did on his last album. It has definitely changed. When he would get here in the morning he would do his ridiculous warm ups that had us in stitches. Edvin was always threatening to record him and send the tapes to the tabloids."

"How did you both get involved with him, with this album?"

"Well, as a bit of a joke we sent a version of *My Pathway* to his label in London, which we'd sped up and turned into a dance version," Edvin explained. "It was too late because the single was already out by the time they discovered our tape, but a couple of months later we heard back and they said that Alex had listened to it and liked it."

"They asked us to go and meet with him, which we did in Stockholm, probably back in January or February, I can't remember when. We played him some things we had in mind for him, and we all got along very well, and at the end he asked if we wanted to work on the album that he was going to record here, so of course we said yes," Andreas explained, adding, "No lawyers, no suits, nothing like that. He gave us a basic idea of the things he was listening to and what he was planning to do, and he gave us a bunch of demos to listen to. Like, songs that he had recorded for himself."

Edvin smiled and laughed.

"He is really thorough. Sometimes when we thought something was finished he just looked at us with *that look*. It's terrifying. It's like a controlled monster. You know like when your dad looks like he is going to explode? We often changed things to suit him, but if we believed enough in something, he respected our opinions. When he'd hear the playback he'd smile if he liked it and if he didn't you knew you were going to spend the rest of the day working on it."

"At the beginning we were really nervous about working with him, because you know, we mostly work with new artists, and he is just like Zeus. You know, it's like Mt. Olympus arrives in the studio and you have to act like it is the most normal thing in the world. One time we wanted to have him record his vocals bit by bit, and we would ask him to re–record them again and again, so that we could have some choices, you know, but he hated that!" Edvin added.

"Yes, at one point he just got very angry and said to us 'this is not the way to treat a singer. Let me sing the damn lyrics all the way through.' I thought he was going to fire us that day, but he didn't. I think sometimes when you want to do a good job and make things perfect you get too technical. It was a good lesson to learn. Don't get Zeus angry!" Andreas explained.

"Yeah, and don't ever ask Zeus to go to the shop for you either," Edvin snickered.

As the sun began to set, the MTV journalist sat for one last time with Alex, who'd been pottering around the cottage making phone calls and making notes in the downtime.

"Does your son come out here to see what you're doing?"

"No. He's a bit young for that right now. But I'm sure at a certain point he's going to be a fixture in the studio. But I feel like he's been here in spirit. The album came along roughly when he did."

"How does it feel going back home to him after a day in the studio?"

"I don't have the words for it. But it's not sappy. It's a mix of guilt and relief most of the time. It depends on what I think I missed on the day. It does feel a little weird though that I was making a club record and tucking him in at night."

"There seems to be a bit of a spiritual theme to a couple of the songs if I understood them well when I heard them today."

"Mmm, not intentionally. I mean, I'm sure it's the same for any first time parent in that it's an awakening. You're searching for the meaning of things and you're full of the best intentions, no matter how tired you are. When you have a kid for the first time you start thinking differently about things. You think about how you're going to explain things to them, but every day is full of surprises that you can't prepare yourself for. It's life changing I guess. Some people travel and other people get high or whatever, but for me this last year was a pretty inspiring time."

"Is it true that you meditate these days? That you're studying Buddhism?"

"Not really. I mean, sometimes I went to Buddhism classes in London and in New York, but here in Stockholm I've... I don't know life has been really different for me here."

"Are you going to tour with this album? It seems like it would be a good one to take out on the road."

"Oh I think it would be great to do these songs live, there's so much energy. But I have a four month old at home right now, so I don't think that I'm going to be getting out on the road anytime soon."

"There's a lot of controversy flying around in the media about your new family arrangement. Do you want to say anything about it?"

"Not really," Alex said, smiling icily.

"Not at all?"

"You mean other than my personal life is my business."

"There's an idea out there that you embarked on having a child to make a point to the world about diversity."

"Must've been a slow news day that day."

"I mean you've also gotten a lot of people in the GLBT community talking too…"

"Yes, but that's all opinion. I don't pay attention to it. I'm human and so are the other people involved in my child's life. Anybody who's stupid enough to think that I would bring a child into the world just to make a statement deserves to be ignored. Let them say what they want, I will just get on with my life in the meantime."

"Do you think it's going to create an obstacle, you being a gay dad and all?"

"An obstacle to what? To selling records? That's a silly idea. Again, nothing that is worth our time discussing."

"Is being No.1 important to you anymore?"

Alex thought about it for a moment. It was a fair question. The hope that he could return to his glory days had almost completely been trampled out of him after recent years. But the faint heartbeat of that desire still flowed through him.

"All I will say is that I don't define myself by that like I once did. I've been in this game for a really long time. That said, if it happens, great, I know I will be ecstatic, but if it doesn't, it won't stop me from keeping at it and trying to make the best music I can."

By the time the journalist flew to London to meet Alex again, on the set for *Longing*, the *Glass Ceiling* single had become an unqualified smash. In four weeks, the single had raced up to the No.1 position in more than thirty countries, including the US.

In their enthusiasm for the new album, which was receiving rave advanced reviews, the press recrowned Alex as the *King of Cool*. *Rolling Stone* referred to the album as "an electronic masterpiece", Q contending it was "a game changer".

Between takes Alex engaged with the journalist on some light banter about the success of *Glass Ceiling*. But if the reaction to *Glass Ceiling* had been positive, the reaction to *Longing* completely eclipsed it. In the US, the song entered the charts at No.9, his highest ever debuting track, and two weeks later was lodged into the No.1 position for what would be a five week run, his longest ever at the top of the US charts.

The album outsold its competitors 2:1 in most markets in its opening week. Hearing the news by phone, Alex broke down and cried in his home office, Søren gurgling away in his arms.

Three more singles followed throughout 1997, each acclaimed for its sophisticated, adult take on electronica, and for bridging the gap between mainstream and underground sounds. This album was his first in almost a decade to maintain its sales over time, buoyed by the singles, the ever more technological videos and the word of mouth that kept the album's profile high. With the first of the year's awards arriving in September, he picked up multiple trophies at the MTV awards, sending the album sales back up again.

And though he cherry picked his public appearances and interviews throughout the year, preferring to spend as much time as he could with Søren, his profile was once again at a high.

All told, the album sold almost 11 million copies in its first year of release, eventually clicking over the 14 million mark with time. Awarded two Grammy awards, the first ever in his career, as well as a Brit, the album was unanimously lauded as one of the albums of the year, the *King of Cool* praised for playing his cards so well.

And deciding Søren was finally old enough, he flew over to Australia with Tomas and Marin, for a month long break with his family in December 1997. It was time to begin planning his next move.

| 13 |

THE KANSAI

It started out with a series of emails that went back and forth. They hadn't spoken in a long time even if they'd never really fallen out. As Alekzandr amassed his huge personal fortune and the accoutrements of global success, so too did Ian. They'd both come from nothing and proven instrumental to each other's success.

But after a decade of being near inseparable, they'd both felt the need to step away from each other to move in different directions.

As such, the last time they'd seen each other was when Alex was a witness at Ian and Jessica's wedding, where he'd even sung at the ceremony, as requested.

It was no secret Alex's fans missed their collaborations. Ian had a way of bringing a sophistication to Alex's simple, heart-on-his-sleeve creativity.

Though their mutual friends lamented how Alex and Ian went from all to nothing, Jessica never truly understood the friendship. She hadn't been there to witness it first hand, and only experienced it through Ian's nostalgia. Occasionally, she'd flick through Ian's photo albums, but all she could see in them was proof of the awful fashions and hairstyles of the period. But even in their new social circles, their friends still gushed over how Ian and Alex had once been inseparable; two peas in a pod who'd also been an invincible music making force.

Jessica had come into Ian's world at the end of his fruitful decade with Alex. Alex's collaborations with others had increasingly left Ian free to manage life in Miami on his own terms. Though Ian continued working for others, he was selective when it came to accepting new projects. He and Jessica had a full social calendar by then, even if Ian occasionally kept tabs on his old best friend.

But hearing that Alex had become a father had reawakened Ian's need to reconnect with him. The news had shifted something in Jessica too, and she began to actively encourage Ian to reach out to Alex from that point on.

Though the boys had rarely kept in touch, their worlds still overlapped, especially through Michael, who remained Ian's manager. Though Ian felt uncomfortable talking about Alex with Michael, or simply picking up the phone and calling Alex directly, he was desperate to get in touch.

It was Jessica who suggested asking Michael for Alex's email address.

"Send him an email. That way you can be in each other's worlds again at anytime," she'd said, helpfully.

Ian used email so rarely that he'd never considered it an option. And though he felt like a dork for not having thought of it himself, he also felt a bit stupid asking Michael to help reconnect him with his main muse.

When he finally mustered the courage to ask Michael for the email address, Michael scrunched up his face.

"Why don't you just call him? He's family to you."

"I don't know. I've got this thing that I want to write to him."

Michael shook his head in disbelief but pulled out one of his business cards, scribbling the address on the back, calling Kōji on his cell to check the address was still current. Michael wasn't a fan of email. Yes, he knew it was efficient, but it made his job harder. Convincing people to do something over the phone was always easier.

After Ian tucked Michael's business card into his pocket, it took him days to decide what to write. Eventually he decided something short and succinct was in order.

Hey Katz.

This is my email address.

Write me. I want to hear from you.

It's been too long.

He checked his inbox daily, hoping the whirring and beeping of the dial up connection would deliver for him. After a week of emails from Jessica's family and some business related items, Ian finally saw what he'd been hoping to see. A message from 'A'.

You dick.

Why didn't you just call me?

I'm still in Stockholm, but I'm suffering from Stockholm syndrome.

I don't think I can manage it anymore.

In a nutshell I'm thinking of moving back to New York or London as we speak. The novelty has worn off.

I've got to think about my kid's welfare and I've just been told I need to get cracking on another record.

How are you? Still married?

Ian sent off his reply and then headed off to Cabo San Lucas for the week with Jessica and a couple with whom they often travelled. On his return he checked his email and found another reply.

I chose London in the end.

I still have the same number here.

I don't know anything else at the moment.

Are you planning on being in Europe any time soon?

I'd like to see you but I can't travel much. It's hard on the kid.

Ian gave it a couple of days and then called the number he still had.

There were loads of silences. Not because they had nothing to say to each other, but because it was clear that Alex wasn't in a good head space. It had been a long time since Ian felt like he needed to pull Alex out of an abyss.

During one of the silences, in which Ian was sure there was some muffled sobbing coming down the line, Ian ventured whether it was "a good time to visit."

"Yes. Whenever you want," Alex replied. "But seriously, come if you want to, not because you feel you need to. I'm just stuck in a moment. I'm a bit shocked by how quickly things are changing. And I hate this house. I'm not used to it anymore. I want to completely change it. Tear it down and remake it from scratch. Jesus, what was I thinking when I bought this hole?"

"You were in the middle of your *London; the place to be* phase. Don't you remember?" Ian said.

"Mmm," Alex replied. "I think I said the same thing about Stockholm once."

***

Nobody could quite place when they'd first been introduced, but the memory of when Alex had first really spoken to Musashi was clear. It was during one of his umpteenth visits to Japan, there to promote *Glass Ceiling* and film a whisky commercial. While there, Alex had been invited to a dinner party by one of his oldest friends, an avant-garde fashion designer named Tadao. It wasn't so much a dinner party as a festive sit-in at one of Kansai's top luxury hotels. Alex and Kōji were among the special guests of the evening.

"I'm not going to translate for you all night," Kōji warned him in the car on the way up the steep slope.

"I'm pretty sure I didn't ask you to," Alex snapped.

The driver was taking them high above Hyogo Ken, a snail trail of tour buses and coaches up and down the mountain, all but guaranteeing a hot spring was in the vicinity. The automated voice warning the driver about his speed was the only other contribution to the conversation.

Just as they preferred, Alex and Kōji were the last guests to arrive, shown directly to their rooms under explicit instructions to head back to the foyer as soon as they were ready.

As they freshened up in Alex's larger, brighter room, the phone rang.

"Yes?" Alex answered.

A high pitched voice pierced Alex's eardrums before it transformed into a cackle.

"*A–re–san!*" the voice croaked. "We are waiting for you! Come now! And bring your beautiful assistant. He has a fan waiting for him!"

Alex laughed and promised they'd be right down.

"Tadao said you should brush your teeth," Alex said, as he replaced the receiver with a chuckle, deciding not to say anything to Kōji about how Tadao had referred to him as being an assistant.

Their personal resort staffer ushered them through the foyer and into a private, concealed wing of the hotel. He slid open a rice paper door known as a *shoji*, to reveal a scene of pure bedlam. Inside were groups of boisterous characters, the room well and truly lubricated, the tables littered with empty bottles of the whisky Alex had sent over in advance.

Alex and Kōji were greeted with a disproportionate amount of *oohs* and *aahs*, and immediately separated, Kōji quickly accounted for by Tadao's manager while Alex was taken by the elbow by Tadao himself to a seated group. A lightning round of toasts, immediately followed by adamant choruses of '*kampai!* left Alex clear about where the night was headed.

Immaculate waiting staff in Tadao–designed suits and kimonos entered the room with hors d'oeuvres which the guests descended upon, no doubt relieved to have something to help soak up the alcohol.

Tadao, designer and party ringleader, joked Alex should appear in his next ad campaign or that, at the very least, invite him into the studio for a duet. Pressing Alex's shirt, dryly noting it was Italian made, he admonished Alex for not having already duetted with him.

"A travesty! With my fantastic voice it would be a number one!"

"You're right, Tadao san, everything you touch turns to gold!" Alex said.

Alex loved Tadao's mind games, so he wasted no time feigning insult that Tadao had chosen the latest Hollywood sensation for his new advertising campaign.

"You paid that kid so much when I, *a much bigger star and a friend of yours,* would've done it practically for free."

"Mmm, you're too exotic Alex. And too gay for America!"

Alex chuckled and playfully slapped Tadao on the shoulder.

Tadao looked at Alex approvingly and then turned to one of the more silent types in the room who'd gravitated over to them.

"Oh, Are–san, this is Musashi San," he said. "Very important musical genius!"

"Yes I know," Alex smiled. "I have all of his records," Alex said, bowing slightly.

Turning to Musashi, Alex then tried, in Japanese, to express that he'd seen him "perform in Yokohama with the Philharmonic. I still *forget* it."

Tadao and Musashi looked at each other and burst out laughing.

"Oh *A–re,* your Japanese is terrible!" Tadao said, laughing so much he had tears in his eyes. "But you're right," he continued with deadly seriousness. "He is a real genius."

Nervously laughing off the compliment, Musashi quietly reminded Alex they'd met at one of Tadao's shows in Tokyo years' earlier.

"And I think we also met in Nagoya for Tadao's fortieth birthday," Musashi added.

Tadao's eyes went a little wild.

"*Daijobu*? Are you alright?" Alex asked, putting his hand on Tadao's shoulder. But Tadao was too busy panting and making a show of clutching his heart.

"Forty!" Tadao yelled. "I'd forgotten about that. You know that actor in my campaign just turned 27 this year? So depressing!"

"That is fucking depressing!" Alex replied, relieved that Tadao was just playing around. He could smell the booze pouring out of Tadao's skin as if it was a fragrant aura.

A moment of awkwardness descended upon them, but Alex didn't miss a beat.

"That party was the bomb!" Alex said, topping up their drinks.

"Mmm, Musashi had a party for his fortieth birthday last year. *Disgusting!* So much fun! Much better than mine."

"Well, it's my turn next. You must help me organise it!" Alex said.

"I am busy! I have collections. Contracts," Tadao said, feigning exhaustion.

"Oh bullshit! We could do it in Hawaii. It could be more *disgusting* than Musashi's!"

"Yes!" Tadao said, his eyes lighting up. "Musashi, you don't have to be so formal with Alex. He is *dirtier* than you are. He is my disgusting little brother," Tadao said, nudging Alex and planting a sloppy kiss on his forehead before walking off in the direction of the bathroom, but detouring at the last minute towards some other guests.

"I think he *destroyed* his brain in the eighties," Musashi said in Japanese.

Alex smiled, understanding the inference.

"Yes, but he's still a treasure. He's not like other people who've done what he's done to himself. Neurotic but as lovely as ever. By God, I just love him!"

"Did you really see me in Yokohama?" Musashi asked.

"Yes. And in Osaka too when you did that puppet theatre project."

"Really? Oh. I don't think I've ever seen you. On TV sometimes. But I don't really follow pop, sorry."

Alex flashed his patented smile for the situation.

"Oh well, it's not for everyone," Alex said, helping himself to something on a passing tray before somebody in the room announced it was time for the first course.

Alex ventured over to Kōji who was at the centre of Tadao's manager's attention. After checking in with each other, they re–joined their respective troupes.

Musashi had quietly saved Alex a spot between him and Tadao. Alex figured he was about to be subjected to cannon fire in one ear and awkward silence in the other. But as course after course was delivered, Musashi monopolised his attention, interrupted only by Tadao's outlandish double entendres and announcements.

Despite the obvious diplomacy and the copious alcohol, it was clear to both that they were sussing each other out. The occasional blips caused by a mutual lack of language only gave them more to ponder. Musashi couldn't always understand him, so when he remembered to, Alex simplified his English. But more often than not, he reverted to his trickster's version of the language; running the gamut of American and British twang with some unpredictable Australian sounds thrown in at times, transforming words into noises that Musashi couldn't decipher.

Alex contemplated Musashi's greying hair, parted in the middle of the composer's head and falling in front of his wispy eyebrows and moist, glistening eyes. He seemed almost a caricature to Alex. And though Musashi was being careful, his body language occasionally betrayed him. His wiry fingers nervously wrapped themselves around his *hashi* (chopsticks) when lost for words, or, more agonizingly, would run up and down his forearms when he struggled to express himself. But when Musashi hit his stride, his face and hands would relax and Alex found the transformation fascinating.

When Kōji eventually stole Alex away after the fifth course, Musashi's body language changed again, Kōji feeling the force of Musashi's stare when he rested his hand on Alex's shoulder.

"I need some air," Kōji said, looking at Musashi apologetically.

Once the bathroom door closed behind them, Kōji unzipped and began speaking.

"Things looked like they were getting a bit intimate between you two. Are you hitting on him?"

Alex sat on the toilet bowl as he watched Kōji piss into the urinal.

"No. I don't think it's like that. I mean, I like him. I guess he's alright if you like that pent up kind of thing. But no, there's nothing romantic or sexy on my part."

"Are you shitting me? I've seen that look on your face a million times. I know what it means," Kōji said, zipping up.

"I'm not even in the mood," Alex said. "I've had so much to drink tonight that I wouldn't even be able to get it up."

He got up and washed his hands and face. "I think it *is* true. I *am* getting older."

"God you're a whining bitch sometimes. You know Musashi's room is two doors down from yours, right?"

"Oh yeah? Who did you hear that from?" Alex asked, wiping his hands dry and watching Kōji in the mirror.

"The singer at my table. She's a country girl. She has to pretend that she's from Tokyo in public. She's lovely. Maybe a little rural once she gets talking."

"I think you have been living in London for too long Kōji. Too much talk of class."

"You're probably right," Kōji said, retouching his hair with a bit of water. "Let's go. Lover boy must be dying knowing I'm in here with you."

"Why do you say that?" Alex asked.

"Oh, no reason. Come on, you look fine."

Back in the banquet room, the number of guests had swollen dramatically. Apparently, a few town cars had made the journey from Kobe and Osaka. The room was swarming with Japanese television talent and some invited press members who'd arrived alongside them. With the party now in full swing and the loom-ing threat of photo calls, Tadao sobered up a little.

Alex was called on to make a few appearances in the photos, but he and Musashi made a pact around 1am to slip out of the party long after Kōji had already disappeared with his admirer.

"You know, there is a VIP area of the *onsen* open all night," Musashi had said as they left the banquet room.

"Really?" Alex replied, quickly trying to consider the implica-tions of an invite to the spa.

"Yes, it's very peaceful. And it has a spectacular view, even at night, down the hills. You can see all the lights of Kobe. Let's go!"

Musashi led him down a corridor where they passed by the exhausted shells of the foyer staff, who had to remain available while the party kicked on behind the *shoji*. Walking past them, Alex felt pity for them, knowing they were at the edge of a world they didn't have entry to, but were expected to service nonethe-less.

The walkway was dimly lit, the only light coming from the illuminated, green exit signs. In their light, Alex saw the metic-ulously arranged hard hats and torches that hung on the walls beneath. It was then he realised he wasn't in some stealth VIP passage, but rather an emergency corridor in an area prone to earthquakes.

Once outside, Musashi expertly led him through a shadowy garden towards what Alex imagined was a sheltered grotto, it announcing itself with the sound of gushing water.

Musashi fumbled around as Alex waited, unable to see the lights of Kobe and at the mercy of the bitterly cold air which made him shiver. With Musashi's flick of the switch, the grotto finally revealed itself. It was a pool, dappled in soft light.

"See? The water is really warm," Musashi said. "Look at the steam!"

"Yes," Alex replied, wondering where the appeal was in taking communal baths.

Musashi had clearly been there before. He robotically pulled out dressing gowns, towels and even nifty change bags from the storage areas next to the outdoor showers. Content he had what he needed, he stripped off, folding his clothes and methodically putting them into the cloth bags, impervious to the cold. Alex followed his lead and undressed, rolling his belongings up and leaving them on a wooden bench. He didn't care to give his host the impression he needed instruction.

Naked and shivering, he caught Musashi taking a cursory glance at him before Musashi got the shower running, stepping under it and immediately soaping himself up. Alex mimicked him under the adjoining shower, and as Alex was busy washing the soap off, he watched Musashi gently ease himself into the pool, which Alex now noticed was artificial but artfully natural in its appearance.

When Alex joined him in the water, he found it uncomfortably warm and was desperate to get out.

"Your body will adjust," Musashi said. "Give it time."

"It's been a long time since I was in an *onsen*," Alex said.

"You know," Musashi said, "when I was a child, my parents used to send me to school in shorts. Even in winter. There could have been a blizzard but I still had to wear those shorts."

Alex listened. From his position in the pool, he could finally see the lights of Kobe in the valley below.

"I hated it," Musashi said. "For years it marked me. I don't think I've ever worn a pair of shorts away from the beach. Maybe just on holidays. But obviously, my parents had a plan. And it worked. The cold doesn't bother me as much as it bothers others. But for years, I hated them for making me do it," he admitted, grunting as he wiped his brow.

Alex smiled in sympathy. "I think parenting is the worst job on earth. You have to make it up as you go. The only way you can get better at it is to have more. Like, if you have a second kid, then you can treat the first one like it was a rehearsal."

"Yes. To a degree. My parents were very traditional. They loved rules."

"Well rules or no rules I don't think any kid can win. I mean, there was a time when I absolutely hated my parents, and they were so easy going and open minded."

"Why did you hate them then?" Musashi asked.

"Because I was strange looking. My brother and my sister were like Barbie and Ken. You know? Blonde haired, blue eyed… I was the complete opposite, and I got picked on for it. Somehow I found a way to blame my parents for it."

"Isn't it funny that being different to everyone else is a problem when you're a kid?" Musashi noted.

"Yeah. Character building. Like having big ears or a big nose," Alex said.

"Just part of life," Musashi added.

"Yep," Alex agreed.

"It's so lovely here," Musashi said after a few moments of silence.

"It really is," Alex said, now luxuriating in the pool's warmth. "Thanks for bringing me here."

***

Back in London when he next checked his email, Alex saw there was a post from Ian explaining that he, Jessica and a couple of friends were thinking of heading to the north of Italy on vacation. There was an invitation for him and Søren (and Tomas) to join them. There was also an email from Musashi, but it was simply a brief message with a hyperlink attached. Alex clicked on the link and was taken to a non–descript site. A *geocity*. He was greeted with a few kanji and hiragana characters that he surmised were a welcome of some kind. Beneath them was an embedded file that Alex double clicked. Just as he clicked, music filtered out of the link. He recognised it immediately. He still remembered writing those chords almost two decades earlier. Listening to it, keywords flooded his brain; *New York, record execs, squabbling. B–side.* After a minute, the music morphed into something inspired by his original song, but that dwarfed it in every respect. It was an electronic piece, dripping in synths that Musashi had cleverly used to mimic the classical instruments he was famous for working with.

A wry smile crept across Alex's face as he recognised further references Musashi had made to Alex's second album. He listened intently with his headphones to try and pick up all the quirks that Musashi had wedged into the four and half minutes. That in itself was a surprise. Alex had always imagined Musashi as the long, lost Glass brother who undoubtedly preferred epic, elaborate pieces.

Throughout the day he found himself thinking about Musashi's clip. How it had ignited a nostalgia that he normally forbid himself from indulging in. Aside from when he toured, Alex almost never listened to his old songs. If he was honest with himself, he'd have to admit to having forgotten the lyrics for most of them. Maybe Musashi's little party trick was more than just a showcase of the composer's talent. Maybe it could be fun to push forward with a new project that made references to his back catalogue. For days Alex stewed over the idea. Musashi's genius turn might have proved the inspiration, but the idea of revisiting his past was something Alex unexpectedly found himself open to. Perhaps it was because he was approaching the big 4–0, and that soon enough, he'd have to admit to having worked at his career for almost half his life. He quickly availed himself of a pen and paper and began writing.

Could be the pull of the moon

Or just the pull of the tide

But something got me thinking

And you're back on my mind.

Distracted by commitments, Alex only remembered to respond to Musashi a few days later.

Why don't we hang out together in the studio and see what happens?

We could do it in Osaka. When's good for you?

As he did his best to entertain the past and the present, Alex came to regard his email account as a portal to his old life and to the new one he was reshaping.

Between quips about Jessica's *cruise ship mentality*, Ian suggested Alex join him in Como. He'd rented a villa and had some material he wanted to work on with Alex there.

There were also emails coming in from his lawyer in Sweden, who was busy negotiating with Marin. Marin had made a sudden and life changing decision. She'd decided that she wanted some time out to pursue an opportunity that had arisen in Copenhagen. She wanted Alex to look after Søren for the foreseeable future despite the disapproval of her parents. Her decision had led them to apply for temporary guardianship of Søren. In their petition to the courts, they'd had outlined Marin and Alex's deficiencies as parents to make their case.

Marin wanted out; out of Stockholm and her parents' orbit. Since Alex had returned to London, she'd moved out of the adjoining apartment and back into her own. Her newly reasserted independence had coincided with her rekindling her relationship with an old beau now based in Copenhagen. Marin had made it clear she expected Alex to hold up his end of their bargain and ensure Søren not get trapped in a traditional environment, like the one her parents wanted to put him in.

Although Alex had taken Søren (and Amila) with him to London, he hoped beyond hope that Marin could resolve things with her parents amicably in the meantime. The last thing he wanted was everybody being dragged into the courts. But since he'd arrived in London, Marin had begun suggesting a more permanent custody arrangement, where she would sign her legal rights over to Alex. She reasoned doing so would enshrine his ability to legally protect Søren, yet also leave them free to informally resume their coparenting once she was settled.

Alex couldn't fault her logic. He agreed their unconventional arrangement needn't preclude Marin's happiness or the chance to pursue it. But the legal manoeuvring required was creating headaches for everyone involved, and playing out by email.

Tomas too it seemed had moved over to email, reconnecting for the first time in weeks, skirting around an event that neither of them seemed prepare to talk about yet.

So by the time Alex arrived in Japan with Søren and Amila, he was desperate for the distraction of the creative process. Really, anything that could take his mind off all the simultaneous drama taking place in his inbox.

Shuttling between Kyoto and Osaka, Alex felt a world away. The time on the motorways reminded him of those early days back in Tokyo when he thought he had some potential as a model. Once again he was here for work, but it wasn't a simple fly in, fly out commitment like it was when he was in town for promotion. Even Musashi's Osaka studio felt like a workplace. Its soft lighting and non—existent decoration screamed 'functionality' to Alex. Beyond the recording and control rooms, Alex even spied the polystyrene tiles he thought only existed in office spaces. For a week they struggled as they sat and listened to each other's demos, trying their best to discuss their ideas in depth even if the technical concepts sometimes proved impossible due to their mutual lack of language.

After a second week of confused discussions, the two decided to throw caution to the wind and begin working on a track where their ideas seemed to have more or less converged.

A mid–tempo ballad, it proved equally slow to come to life, as each step in its development was help up by lengthy talks and justifications.

"I've been in the studio with him for a month already," Alex told Jasper over the phone. "We don't have anything to show for it. We're still working on the one song and even then it's just couple of bars and a loop. It's doing my head in," Alex said, spinning the mobile that hovered over Søren's cot.

"I mean, do you like the song at least?" Jasper asked, biting into an apple as he looked at his computer screen.

"It's not even a song yet. It's just, he's great. He's got magical ideas, but at this stage I'll be 50 by the time this record is ready."

"He's probably used to working in his own little world. See if he can get an assistant in to help him. Make him feel like it was his idea all along, not yours. And make sure the assistant is perfectly bilingual. Anyway, I've gotta go, I've got, erm, something to do."

"You do not," Alex snapped, closing Søren's door as he crept out of the room.

"You're right, I don't," Jasper said, "but I'm kind of done with this conversation. Just find an engineer who speaks both languages and it'll all work out. And next time you call, maybe ask how I'm doing before you offload. Anyway, laters."

"Sorry. Later," Alex replied.

After a few more protracted working days in the studio, in which Alex began to feel like a studio technician working for Musashi, Kōji came through. He'd found a bilingual studio assistant, bashful and respectful enough to not make Musashi uncomfortable. Musashi knew the assistant from a previous project so responded better than anyone had anticipated, relishing having someone else on side in his studio.

The combination of Musashi's slow pace and the arrival of the engineer gave Alex more free time and, as such, he used it to explore Kyoto with Søren. Together they discovered the city, plodding along its bike tracks and discovering its historic sites and contemporary centre.

Through his local assistant, Alex organised lessons with a Japanese teacher and a yoga instructor, building his schedules with them around his studio commitments.

The house he was renting was grand and had a guest house within the walled gardens, where two elderly caretakers lived. They were there to attend to the garden and be at Alex's disposal should he need them. But he decided it was best to make his local assistant run his errands, and instead found great comfort in befriending the couple, practicing his childish Japanese with them, and watching them play with Søren.

The woman of the couple often insisted on teaching Alex how to cook local dishes, and though he feigned interest, Alex enjoyed the domesticity the living arrangements offered. He grew to love the couple: even if they frequently gave him the impression they were surprised he wanted to get to know them. With time, the work in the studio began to demand more of his time, and on nights he'd return late from Osaka, he'd find one or both waiting for him in the living room, concerned that he might not have eaten or that he was working too much.

As the weeks passed, signalled by the arrival of spring and the blossoming of the cherry trees, Alex rearranged his schedule to keep his mornings mostly free for Søren. At times they were joined for *sakura* (cherry blossom) viewings by the couple, otherwise his only other constant were the increasingly belligerent Japanese lessons he did daily with his professor, who the couple admitted was a noted alcoholic with a hint of scandal still hanging over him.

As spring progressed, Musashi and Alex found their stride, working on a triptych of songs that perfected the sound they'd been aiming for; a kind of classical sound thrown into a computer and spat out again, coming out a little wonky on the other side.

Glass Ceiling may have come from the heart, but for Alex, there was nothing like the end of a decade to spur him to stretch his creative wings. While he'd loved recording *Glass Ceiling* because it had felt fresh and been fun to play with beats again, his work with Musashi was forcing him to dig into his emotions more deeply than he had in almost a decade.

But the deadline had well and truly arrived before spring was over. And although there was still work to do on some of the tracks, Alex was due back in Europe to begin work on the other half of his album. Surrounded by moving boxes and aware he needed to give the house a final inspection to check for anything he might've forgotten, he made a call to his business manager in London. The call was brief, but instructed his adviser to make an offer on his behalf to the owners of the Kyoto house, adding that the offer should include provisions to keep the couple on as caretakers.

| 14 |

PULL OF THE MOON

Before Alex could go on to Como to reunite with Ian, there was business to attend to in Stockholm.

He made the familiar journey from the airport to his favoured hotel, unwilling to stay with Tomas at the apartment. From there, he went straight to the family law studio where he was secretly meeting with Marin and their legal representatives before they were due in court later that week.

"I've missed you," he whispered, as he embraced her with all his might.

She cooed over her delighted son who was ecstatic to see her, taking him in her arms. "I've soothed things out a little and tried to make everybody see reason," she said. "But they still want to go ahead and try. I'm flying to Copenhagen this week and I've set up a room for him in my place there. When I feel settled, you can bring him over."

"We're heading to Italy on Friday. My parents are going to fly over too and spend some time with us while I'm in the studio," Alex said.

"Oh, that'll be nice. How was he in Japan?"

"Honestly, I got to spend a lot of time with him; it wasn't as bad as I had feared workwise. He did great. Cost me a sweet fortune bringing all his toys back. I mean there were boxes and boxes. Couldn't bring myself to leave any of it behind."

"I've missed him," Marin said, Søren quietly investigating her nostrils and mouth.

"Any improvement? Have you been getting some rest?"

"Yeah," she said, acknowledging his concern. "Really, I was just overwhelmed. I'm on some light medication just to help me sleep from time to time, but other than that, Garett is great, and Copenhagen just feels… I don't know… it just feels right. I feel lightened. Not so tired anymore."

"And the hotel project?"

"It's become three hotels, one in Norway too. It's a big job, but it's going well."

"Are you sure you want to do this love? It seems so final, we don't have to sign anything, we can just keep the arrangement as flexible as we like," he said.

"No, it's better for everyone this way. You'll do the right thing, I know, and we should protect ourselves and him. It's important my parents feel like they have been heard, but they'll come around eventually. Bring him back every now and then, and I'll come find you when I can. I don't know, it's been a big couple of years, and I lost myself in them. But when I'm back to feeling 100% again I'll step up again, I promise," she said, Alex rubbing her upper arm in support.

"How is Garett?" Alex asked.

"Great. He's working for some tech start–up thing… he's always busy, but he's great."

Alex bit his tongue for a few moments, and then, as gently as he could, he spoke. "Doesn't it seem like you're going to be cutting yourself off from everything and everyone to be with him again? I mean it's happened before, right?" He paused. "Garrett is always more complicated than he lets on."

"I know," Marin said. "It's different now. Honestly, it has never been this good between us, and it's been months now. But I feel like a prisoner here. If I didn't have Søren to worry about, I wouldn't think twice. I can't stop living Alex, I have to keep trying. And you know better than anyone that things with Garrett weren't really finished. I deserve to give myself a chance with him."

"I'm happy for Søren to come with me, it's not about that. I'm even getting the hang of things with him. And you deserve the world babe, you really do. I just don't know if Garrett is the right way to go about it."

"I know. But, we can't exactly keep playing happy little families forever, you and I. We need to do our own things. And you are in the position to manage it better than I am right now. And I know you don't begrudge me it. You'll bring him to visit me as often as you can, and when I get things under control I'll come and visit or he will. It's the best I can do right now."

"You could do way better than Garrett."

"Can you think of the last guy that knocked at my door? I didn't think so. I can't be that person. But right now, I also can't be that other person, you know? Not a full time mother and also someone with plans."

"I get it. He misses you," Alex said, caressing Søren's head.

"I know. But he has you." Marin said.

"I stuck pictures of you everywhere around the house. I chose the ones with the most embarrassing outfits you ever wore. Lots of eighties ones."

"You're terrible Muriel," Marin replied.

After the meeting, Marin took Søren out while Alex had lunch with Markus, who he learned was now happily partnered.

"So, are you going to tell me about him?" Alex sighed, pouring himself some water.

"No," Markus replied.

"Why not?"

"Because I don't want you getting into my head. Besides, I want to talk about Tomas."

"Oh, I don't want to have that conversation," Alex said.

"Great. Then what are we doing?"

"We could go off and have some mind blowing sex like we used to," Alex joked.

"No, we can't," Markus replied, smiling tenderly at Alex.

"Fine," Alex replied. "Let's just get a little drunk then. Then we can see what happens."

Alex shuddered to think of the last time he'd actually had sex. It had been with a closeted Hollywood actor he'd met at an awards show. The actor had won an award that night but had turned out to be a complete disappointment in bed.

"Just tell me if it's true or not," Markus said, seriously.

"What?" Alex asked.

"You and I both know what happened. Why won't you tell me about it? And why haven't you ended things with Tom yet?"

"I don't know. I don't know how simple it is," Alex said, shaking his head.

"It's never simple," Markus said. "But I'm worried about you."

"I don't know if I want to do all of that again. I don't know if I've got it in me to start over again. I'm almost 40. I don't think I can do it."

"That's hardly a reason to leave everything up in the air. It's an excuse, but it's not a reason," Markus said, sipping his water.

"I know, but he's in the kid's life… I feel like I should probably forgive Tomas. But I'm worried that if I do, I'll have to start making more compromises. I just wish we could both do what we want, you know? Not to have to give up on so many things? I wish Tomas could see that it's what we make of it, not what we think it's supposed to be."

"That's the rub of it all, isn't it?" Markus noted. "But aside from all of that there's the white elephant you're not dealing with. You can't sweep what he did under the rug."

"I'm not trying to," Alex said, defensively.

"Yet you're not prepared to talk to me about it. Alex you're worth your weight in gold. He doesn't deserve you. He never has."

Alex looked at Markus, feeling like he'd chosen the wrong Swede all along.

***

As anticipated, the judge heard arguments from the three parties, Marin's parents represented in their absence by a family lawyer. The cases and petitions were made. The judge ruled in favour of the two biological parents. And as they were in agreement, and because no legal impediments existed, the judged ruled that Alex could take full custody, Marin granted unrestricted access as requested.

Afterwards Marin and Alex went for lunch.

"He's growing fast," she noted. "Who do you think he looks like?"

"I think he's got your eyes… and your nose. Luckily, he's got my brains."

"Hardy ha–ha," she said, shoving Alex playfully. "Anyway, at least it's done now."

"We can undo it at any time, just remember that," Alex said, caressing Marin's cheek.

At the end of the lunch he and Marin decided it was time to visit her parents. Though they were smarting from the newly handed down judgement and greeted Alex and Marin coldly, Alex took it on the chin. He sat silently as Marin argued in Swedish with her parents while Søren slept. When Søren woke, Alex laid him down on the rug in the living room and watched as the boy's chattiness and propensity for noise acted as a siren's call for his grandparents. They gravitated over to the boy and sat and played with him while Alex and Marin squeezed in on a loveseat to watch.

"I feel bad for them," Alex finally whispered.

"Don't. They'll get used to it," Marin said.

"Should I say something? Remind them I'll come for visits?"

"No, just let them be. They'll come around. You'll call them every now and then. They'll adjust," she said.

Marin looked at the child pensively.

"Do you want to come to Como?" Alex asked.

"No," she said. "I have a million things to do, and your parents will be there for him. They can get to know him better. And give them all my love, I can't believe I haven't seen them since Christmas. Barely spoken to them either. Ask them to forgive me."

"Oh, don't worry about them. Do you want me to postpone the flight? Or to have dinner tonight?"

"I can't. I've got to pack," Marin said.

"Really?"

"I think it's best babe. I'm fine, and I'm going to see you both soon anyway. And we'll talk on the phone like we did in Japan, and there's email too. Really, I'm fine. You should see Tomas tonight anyway. You promised you would."

"I'm not sure I want to," Alex said.

"It's a week of biting the bullet for both of us, isn't it?" Marin noted.

Alex called Tomas from the car after the driver dropped Marin off at her apartment.

That night Alex arrived at the restaurant early, asking for a corner table so that he could keep Søren's pram out of the way. When Tomas arrived, Alex stood and Tomas gave Alex a light peck on the cheek and Søren a kiss on his forehead.

The first half hour of their conversation was filled with polite talk and Tomas being absorbed by how much Søren had grown.

"Can I hold him for a bit?" Tomas asked.

"Yeah of course," Alex said, getting up and gently placing the boy in Tomas' lap.

"Just keep an eye on him, he's got a thing for shiny things. Knives in particular," Alex said.

"You look more and more like your daddy, don't you?" Tomas said. "Except daddy is blond again isn't he?"

"Yeah he was a bit surprised when daddy came home that day," Alex said, taking a gulp of his wine.

"Well, daddy still looks good," Tomas said.

Alex looked at Tomas. He looked rested, relaxed. He had a few days worth of stubble, but was wearing a shirt and had even styled his hair for the occasion. He looked better than he had in a long time.

"You been working out?" Alex asked, pouring Tomas a glass of wine.

"Rowing. In the mornings with some of the boys," Tomas said, frowning when he realised Søren had closed his eyes.

"Don't worry, you don't have to put him down right away," Alex said. "He's gotten used to sleeping on everybody. At any time of the day."

"Yes, I'm sure all the flying doesn't help," Tomas replied.

"No, I guess it doesn't," Alex said. "But he's a good sport about it all."

"And Marin?" Tomas asked.

"She had to pack. They're leaving tomorrow morning. I'm worried about her."

"Marin will be fine. She always works things out. But what about me, Alex? Are you worried about me?"

"I don't know. Should I be?" Alex asked.

"You don't miss me? Us?"

Alex looked at Tomas. He wanted to offer to put Søren down and take him off Tomas' hands.

"We have a lot we need to talk about," Alex said.

"Well I'm here. You're here. We should talk. And talk until we've resolved things," Tomas said.

"I can't stay here anymore Tom. I don't want to be in Stockholm anymore. Not in the way we were before I left, that's for sure."

"I know. But I've been thinking. What if I came to London?" Tomas asked.

"I don't know. Is that what you really want?"

"I want to be with you. With Søren," Tomas admitted.

"And what about Victoria? Where's that going to leave you?"

"Lena doesn't want to change things. She says she prefers to keep things the way they are," Tomas said, finally reaching for his wine glass.

"I don't know that coming to London would be a solution to our problems Tomas."

"Maybe. Maybe not. But we're not going to fix things if we are in different countries and not talking to one another."

"No, you're right. I just worry that London could create more problems."

"Why?" Tomas asked.

"Well, knowing that you'd be in London and out of your comfort zone… will that send us into crisis mode again?"

"No," Tomas said, gently rising to put Søren down in his pram. "I won't let that happen."

"I'm not prepared to go down that road again Tom."

"I've been dealing with things better lately. And I've had a lot of time to think as well," Tomas said.

"I mean, your anger towards me lately has been... well, it scares me sometimes I have to say." Alex said.

"I know," Tomas said. "It's frustration. It's mine. I never wanted it to be about you."

"It doesn't come across that way. Not after what happened."

Alex felt Tomas staring at him. In that way that always made Alex panic a little, leaving him unsure whether to say something or hold his ground.

"I'd never do that," Tomas said. "Not again. Ever. Alex, you do know that, right?"

"The physical stuff, Tomas... I don't know if I want to be with someone that makes me feel like I have to defend myself," Alex said.

"It was a once off. I wouldn't ever put you in that position again," Tomas said. "I still go to bed feeling awful about it. It was a horrible, horrible mistake. All of it."

Alex thought about that night. How he'd spent the afternoon trying to deflect Tomas' attacks about the same old issues. *Their schedules. His snobbery towards Tomas' family or anything remotely Swedish. About how Victoria was always coming second to Søren in their lives. About how he never had the energy for sex with Tomas anymore. How he was always criticising Tomas about his drinking.*

Alex remembered how he'd stormed out to get some air. He'd returned hours later to find Tomas in a state, livid and ready for round two. How Tomas was then following up every accusation with a push or a shove. How they so quickly escalated to bitter slaps and punches that knocked the wind out of Alex.

Alex felt the shock of that night still pulsing inside him even now at the restaurant. He looked around the room and saw that people were eating and chatting, and that they were oblivious to what he was feeling.

He remembered being so shocked that night by Tomas' mean streak, that it hadn't occurred to him to fight back. Each time Tomas had struck him, Alex waited for the sign that each blow would be the last and that Tomas would come to his senses. But then one of Alex's eyes clouded up and he couldn't even see Tomas' face clearly. And Alex had crouched down against the wall, the parquetry so cold to sit on. When he'd come to, Tomas was crouched over him with a warm towel which had red spots all over it. And Tomas was crying, begging for forgiveness.

Realising what had happened, and hearing Tomas moping, Alex had pushed him away. He'd straightened himself up and walked a few paces over to the tap, sore. He'd filled a tall glass with water and had drank it, never taking his eyes off Tomas who had taken Alex's spot on the floor. Putting the glass in the sink, Alex summoned what strength was left inside him and walked across the apartment, letting himself into Marin's and bolting the door closed behind him.

He spent days avoiding Tomas until the obligations and schedules had gotten in the way again and given him an even larger buffer to hide behind.

And for weeks, Alex didn't so much as breathe a word in Tomas' direction. Didn't consider him in any of his plans. And soon enough he was in London with Søren, and then Japan, and Tomas had almost been reduced to an afterthought until Alex saw Tomas' name pop up in his inbox again.

Back in the restaurant, Tomas said something. He repeated it, knowing Alex hadn't heard him the first time.

"You know that I won't do that again," Tomas promised.

"At the end of the day, what you did was despicable," Alex said, looking around the room again, keen to avoid any attention. "But it's not that different to what you'd already been doing for a long time Tom. At the end of the day, there's no difference between raising your hand and raising your voice at someone. It's all violence," Alex said, his nerves tingling.

"I know. But like I said, I'm dealing with things better. You being gone helped me get clear about what I was so upset about. What I need to fix in myself. But also what we need to work on as a couple."

"Really? And you think we can do that in London? How would that work for you?"

"Well, it is not the other side of the world. And I can organise work there. I mean, I can come back here whenever I want to," Tomas said.

Alex hadn't really anticipated the conversation getting this far. He wasn't entirely sure what he wanted from Tomas, and he feared Tomas knew him well enough to sense this.

"I just find it a bit strange that I've been gone all this time and we've barely even spoken, but now you're saying that you want to move to London with me."

"Well, first of all, you didn't want to talk to me and you had every right to feel that. Besides, you know that we don't do well on the phone, you and I. We just tune out when we are on the phone together. That's why I was sending you all those emails. Not to pressure you but because I wanted you to understand. I wanted to make sure you were alright. I wanted to apologise. Did you read them? You barely replied to me."

"I read them," Alex said. "I did. But I didn't want to dwell on them."

"You know, that night, that period… my drinking, my frustration… a lot of that is me. It's not just because I think that it's not that easy being with you Alex."

"Whatever it comes down to, you can't just bash your way out of your problems and your frustrations," Alex said. "I'm not a punching bag."

"You're making it seem like I'm constantly aggressive Alex, and it's not true. I understand what you're saying about the words and the hands, I get it. But, you know, you… you just shut me out so much. I'm not talking about you being famous or the shit in the papers that's difficult. It's that you don't want to talk sometimes. You don't want to tell me things. I mean, It's like I don't matter to you."

"Oh don't try that shit with me," Alex said. "That's not a justification."

"I'm not looking for a justification. But you know, sometimes, people need some acknowledgment. Sometimes you have to let them know what you're thinking. You know, I really tried to respect that you had a million things on, yet, you still agreed to come to Stockholm. And how that meant you had to spend time with my family and friends. And now with Søren you've got even more on your plate. But all those things are our life together Alex. That's me tied up in all that. I love you. I know you love me too. And that means we have to find a way to make those shitty things in our life work too. The same way I do for you most of the time."

Their food finally arrived but Alex asked to be excused for a few minutes.

Outside on the street he looked around him. At the end of the street he could see the octagonal building with its faded brass dome. Alex stared at it has he inhaled his cigarette, thinking. Looking inside the restaurant he watched Tomas send the server back to the kitchen. Tomas then checked on Søren, who Alex hoped was still fast asleep. The dinner was turning out to be way more complicated than Alex had hoped. After taking three quick successive drags from his cigarette, Alex butted it out and re-entered the restaurant, going straight to the bathroom to freshen up.

"Feel better?" Tomas asked when Alex finally got back to the table.

"Yeah. Clearer. So how would this London thing work?" Alex asked.

"Wait. You don't intend to say *anything* about what I said to you before?"

"I'd prefer to move on," Alex said. "I hate to dwell on things."

"Well, we need to dwell for a moment," Tomas said, nodding his head at the server who then returned with their meals.

"Really, I insist we dwell," Tomas added.

"OK, I agree... it can be hard to be with me at times," Alex said.

"And?" Tomas asked, sipping his wine.

"But I don't take you and your life for granted. I think if you actually do move to London, you'll see what it's really like to be with someone in another country. You'll see that you'll need some timeouts every now and then. That you have to start drawing the line with things. Otherwise, you feel like you get lost in a world that doesn't entirely belong to you."

"That's how you feel? That our life here, what, swallows yours?"

"No, that's not what I'm saying Tomas. But *my* life, *our* life, doesn't begin and end in Sweden. The same way that it won't in London if you go there. And you're going to have to learn how to juggle all of that without getting overwhelmed by it all. Without getting so angry that you can't think straight. Because if you don't, things will spiral out of control again. And I'm not prepared to put myself through that again for anyone."

Tomas' eyes drooped.

"I have a kid to think about Tom. It's one thing for a kid to be in an environment where there might be some tension sometimes, but willingly putting that kid in harm's way is just not on. You have to really reflect on what clicked in your mind that day Tom, but also what was clicking in the lead up to it."

"You know I will Alex," Tomas said.

"I mean I can only hope so Tom, because really it's a lot of upheaval for nothing if you can't."

"See that's what I mean. For *nothing?* What's that supposed to mean?"

"It's just an expression," Alex said. "I didn't mean it like it sounded."

"Okay, fine. Well, the London thing would be me taking a leave of absence to work in the UK. And if things worked out,

I would resign my position here and stay there, so I think the pressure won't be an issue."

"What would you do there?" Alex asked.

"Work for the satellite sports channel."

"Otherwise?"

"I'd try and get a presenting job in London. That way I don't have to move around, and we can have a normal life together. My agent has already lined up some interviews. We'll see how it goes. And it's close enough for me to come and spend time with Victoria."

"OK. I need to think about it though," Alex said.

"Can *we* think about it together?" Tomas asked.

"OK."

***

True to form, Ian's compositions were sophisticated, fresh and, in Alex's mind, the perfect balance to Musashi's more *out there* productions. By the time Alex arrived in Como, he'd studied Ian's songs so thoroughly that he knew them inside out. He'd already made notes of the changes he wanted to try out with Ian's musicians who had flown in from Miami for the sessions. They were, as Ian had promised, a well oiled machine, rarely requiring more than one or two takes. They too had studied Ian's songs before arriving, having elaborated their own interpretations of the music which they were ready to lay down.

As such, the Como sessions moved along swiftly. There were times when Alex and Ian wondered whether they were spending more time finding their groove again than actually creating new ones for the record.

After a month of solid work, Ian was joined by Jessica and their friends at the villa, while Alex welcomed his parents and Tomas to the villa he'd secured for the rest of the summer. Alex's parents were happy to play babysitters while Alex was in the studio or when he and Tomas wanted some private time.

About three quarters of the way through the Como trip, a furore erupted in the press, initially in Sweden, about Alex having taken his son away from his mother. Alex's management team went straight into damage control. The story had likely originated with Marin's parents who'd communicated their dissatisfaction to family friends, who, in turn, had spoken to the press for financial reward. For a week or two, the scrutiny was so intense and damaging that his management team issued an unprecedented statement:

A mutual decision between the parents was taken and formalised through the appropriate legal channels and subjected to the scrutiny of the Swedish family law system.

Due to the incredibly sensitive and private nature of the matter, we request that the privacy of all involved be respected.

As a result, no public comment on this matter will be made.

The unprecedented nature of the statement became further fodder for the press, who shifted the focus of debate towards one about same sex parenting. Tipped off that Alex was recording in Como, members of the press descended on the town, a small number forming a scrum outside Alex's villa for days, awaiting the chance to capture some valuable footage of Alex, Tomas and Søren.

Alex's security team, usually only in service when Alex was on tour or attending high profile engagements, was called in as a precaution. They'd suggested ferreting Alex and his family off to Milan for a few days to wait out the story, but Alex refused.

Arrangements were made for Mitch, Alex's long time personal bodyguard, and a couple of his staff to move into the villa. Their presence, while comforting, also added some complexity to the experience. At Ian's villa, much was made about the presence of the security agents who patrolled the grounds and policed all comings and goings.

Mitch mused whether Alex would be better off just cutting a deal with the paparazzi. "I heard there's a $500,000 pay day for the photographer that gets a shot of you all. Why don't you just bite the bullet and take the pressure off everyone?"

"And, what, split the money?"

"You could give it to charity. And stop things from escalating."

The bounty on the father(s) and son image and the heavy security presence had town folk talking. But Alex wouldn't be swayed. Although it was a nuisance, the presence of Mitch's crew allowed Alex and Ian to mostly maintain their recording schedule and avoid pandering to the press.

With little recording left to do, other than some final vocals, Alex, a light security detail and an assistant met up pre–dawn one morning with a makeup artist and a photo crew, forming a caravan of vehicles that took the long and winding roads from Como to a tiny town called Verceia, nestled on the edge of a nature reserve.

When they arrived, they saw the awaiting crew had set up on a tiny trestle bridge that someone had scouted some weeks before. The bridge sat rickety but stubbornly against a spectacular and rugged mountain backdrop which seemed to rise out from behind the lake. The crew had covered parts of the bridge with fake grasses and reeds to make it seem like it had been reclaimed by nature, and after Alex had been made up, they stripped him down to a white–grey wife beater and khaki–grey pants, his now wavy blond–brown hair tussled to look windswept.

On the bridge, the latest darling of the fashion photography scene snapped away at Alex, before dawn, at dawn, and later in the morning. It wasn't gruelling, but the ever changing light meant that the crew had to regularly accommodate for variations.

Satisfied there were enough good shots at the location, they moved on to the next, this time a slightly rundown village which also offered mountain and water views. The weather at a certain point turned, and the crew had to quickly prepare for the threat of a storm, again adapting to the light. A series of rapid fire shots in a field and then some others in and around the water were done, harnessing the eerie light, before everybody stopped for lunch. As they ate, the rain finally bucketed down, clearing the humidity, and blocking them on location for over an hour before they could move again.

"It's raining and I'm stuck somewhere with no name, sitting in a car and eating crew food," Alex said.

"It's always such a pleasure speaking to you on the phone," Jasper said. "He's a great photographer, you won't regret it. He's also a great lover. Tomas isn't there is he?"

"No. He went back to Sweden," Alex replied.

"Of course he did. So? What are your impressions?"

"Of Tomas?"

"No, the photographer. I'm feeling ambivalent about Mr Photographer now that he's having all this success. I preferred him when he was hungrier, you know?"

"When was the last time you were with him?" Alex asked.

"I don't know. A couple of weeks ago maybe. Why?"

Alex watched as the photographer flirted with one of his assistants, the assistant barely bothering to put up any resistance. "Just asking," Alex said.

"You know, I'm about to be free soon. Wanna hang for a bit?"

"I'd like that, but you know, I have a kid now," Alex said.

"So does half the damn world, what do you care? Does it mean we can't spend time together?"

"No, not at all. I don't know what it meant. It just came out like a reflex," Alex said.

"Well bring him along. I also meant that maybe you'd like to work on a video or two? We haven't done one in years."

"I thought you told me that you, and I quote, 'would rather a broken bottle up your arse than film another video for one of my shitty songs again.'"

"Did I say that?" Jasper said, laughing. "You know I really outdo myself when it comes to you. But I love you."

"By the way I stopped watching your movies a while back. You do the same shit over and over. Same actors, same scenes. *Sad*," Alex retaliated.

"You know how you've always thought you were funny and that your timing is impeccable?" Jasper asked.

"Yeah?" Alex said.

"You're not. Send me some songs so I can get started, and don't tell the Italian you were talking to me otherwise he'll think I love him or something."

"I don't have time to talk to him, and I don't think he likes me anyway. He, um… he says it's time to go back to Verceia."

"Of course it is."

"Love you," Alex said.

"Hate you," Jasper replied.

Jasper's photographer friend was fast, and managed to get the dusk shots done quickly, before he called a wrap.

The following afternoon Alex was driven to a nearby villa where more photos were taken. In all, it was hoped that the two day shoot would yield everything Alex needed for the new album's cover and promotional campaign.

When Alex left Italy for Stockholm there were a few things he was convinced of: certain Como tracks could do with some extra work, possibly by Musashi. He predicted that a week in Stockholm was going to be more than enough to drive him crazy. And he was also convinced that despite the security and the scandal, and feeling attacked again by the press, Como had also been a wonderful chance to spend time with his parents and his son.

But there were also things that he wasn't convinced of: like that Tomas and he really had a chance to make things work in London. In his gut, Alex wasn't convinced that Tomas would be able to adapt to life there. But, just months from turning 40, Alex was still unsure he had the energy to go through another break up and all that it would bring. He was also unsure he actually wanted the house in Kyoto now that the deal had come through. He'd paid so much more than he'd intended, and worried it had simply been a kneejerk purchase.

But in Stockholm for a week to help Tomas get his things together and to begin attending to the album campaign, he only had Amila to rely on to help him with Søren, who, somewhere under the Italian sun, had finally become one of the *Terrible Twos* everyone had warned him about.

Worse, Amila had just given her notice, preferring to remain in Stockholm close to family and friends.

With so many business emails and phone calls already demanding his attention, Alex didn't know where to start. He figured the priority lay with replacing Amila, with helping Tomas prepare for London, and in finding a temporary way to cope with Søren who, almost overnight, had turned into a handful.

Alex was sure he had the energy to do one or two of those things and to do them well. But he couldn't fathom dealing with all of them in the space of a week. His instincts told him they weren't going to be simple things to resolve. Rather, if he did them poorly, he knew he'd be paying for it long afterwards.

Things with Tomas were reasonably stable, but Alex was being cautious, and there was every possibility that he could find himself a single parent in no time. And not just your average single parent who already has a million things to deal with on their own. A single parent who would also be expected to be available day and night to promote a new blockbuster record.

A record whose reception would determine whether Alex walked away from the nineties with more career prospects intact, or whether his professional life would head into the same murky direction his personal life seemed to be going.

EXPLORE THE MUSIC AND IDEAS OF THE NINETIES FURTHER.

Main artists and cultural references found in *Nineties*:

Janet Jackson, Paula Abdul

Guns N Roses, Def Leppard, The Cure

Bono, U2

Momoe Yamaguchi

Seal

Garth Brooks

George Michael

Michael Jackson

Prince

Madonna

Neil Tennant, Pet Shop Boys

Neneh Cherry

Mariko Mori

Siouxsie and the Banshees

Everything But The Girl

Grant McLennan

Philip Glass, Ryuichi Sakamoto

A NOTE TO THE READER

Thanks for being such an indie icon by reading this novel!

I'm one of the many independent authors who love to connect with their readers.

As an independent author, your feedback and comments are particularly valuable to me.

You can contact me in any of the ways listed below to let me know your thoughts, but one of the most powerful ways to help any independent author – and your fellow readers – is to consider leaving a review for the book you've just read.

Your reviews can make a huge difference in other people discovering the work of independent authors.

In any case, thanks for revisiting the nineties (my favourite musical decade) with me.

I hope I get the chance to hear your thoughts and that you continue Alekzandr's journey into the Noughties!

ABOUT THE AUTHOR

Melbourne born Dave Di Vito has spent much of his adult life on the run, chalking up stints in London, Lecce and Kyoto.

A former gallerist/curator and trained artist, Dave has been teaching and writing in the Eternal City for more than ten years and now considers himself a fake Roman.

A lover of pop and pop culture, Dave writes pop fiction.

Connect with him via:

Facebook at www.facebook.com/vinyltiger

Twitter @ddvinyltiger

Or **subscribe** to his mailing list for (very occasional!) updates at: https://www.paperlesstiger.net/presscontact

ACKNOWLEDGEMENTS

Vinyl Tiger has been haunting me for years. It came into being via scribbled, handwritten notes on Japanese subways, bumpy bus rides in Rome and during downtime in Melbourne art galleries.

It lived on despite the only master copy being stolen in a home break in and its author relocating across three different continents.

With the huge shifts in the way we look at popular culture that have taken place since Vinyl Tiger was first published in 2016, this second edition is the result of revisiting the story with fresh eyes.

I appreciate help I've received, particularly from Lucy and Shane who helped me so much with the first edition, and to my dear Kekks who, more than anybody else, really championed me sitting down and seeing this through.

To my dear, dear family and friends, thanks for putting up with me while I insist on living my bicontinental fantasy.

To the artists of the nineties, opinionated or not, a huge thank you to you for the inspiration.

And to those who of you who have taken the time to read and discover my work, my heartfelt thanks.

Love,

Dave